I0772203

Ridge & Root Publishing
West Rutland, Vermont 2025

ISBN 979-8-9898869-7-5

TWISTED TIES

V. APRILLIANO

THIS BOOK IS DEDICATED TO ERIN HALL MD

AS A SURVIVOR of childhood sexual abuse, I spent decades struggling to heal the broken little girl trapped inside. You kept me from straying into the weeds and gave me permission to feel anger instead of fear and anxiety. While we worked together, I wrote three books. With your help, I led the broken little girl out of the darkness, you helped me feel whole and quiet my mind.

As a child, my passion for writing was discouraged by my parents, which caused me to take a different path in life. Luckily, as I processed my trauma, that journey led me back to writing. You helped me realize I can follow my soul. The ones who failed to protect the littlest version of me had no right to piss in my Cheerios in the first place.

I no longer punish myself for other people's crimes.

-Vanessa

ACKNOWLEDGMENTS

I WOULD LIKE TO THANK my husband and son for supporting the part of me that was meant to be a writer. I am grateful I've finally found the courage to nurture this part of my soul.

John, you have encouraged me to write since you read one of my short stories more than two decades ago.

Angelo, your passion for music, the dedication you have to your craft, and the absolute happiness I witness through your journey, has inspired me to do the same thing with my writing. I am grateful we can serve as inspiration for each other as we bless the world with our creativity.

"If you have a passion, it is your duty to share it with the world." -My son

TWISTED TIES

V. APRILLIANO

PROLOGUE

MY NAME IS AMELIA BIRCH. I'm shorter than average and my weight goes up and down depending on my current cocktail of anxiety medications. I have full lips and magnificent dimples. I have hazel eyes and a chin that kind of looks like a heart. I have crazy brown ringlets, and unless I'm doing something important, they're smashed into an unruly bun. I have a closet that looks like it's shared by three different people, a businesswoman, a hippie, and a broken little girl. What can I say, I like to keep people guessing, or maybe I just like to play dress-up most of the time. That's funny coming from someone who wants nothing more than to burn the costumes and air all of her dirty laundry. My story is dark and raw and unfiltered, because I'm dark and raw and unfiltered.

My story is emotional and witty and deep, because I'm emotional and witty and deep. I'm not someone who puts on airs, I'm not into the theatrics of it all, the false fronts, the absolute bullshit of it all. And I guess more importantly, mine is the story of a broken little girl who finally found what she was looking for. Safety goes a long way to quiet your mind, even when most people would be peering through the blinds watching for the cops, there are different rules in this world.

Sometimes I feel like I'm passing and sometimes I feel like an obvious fraud. Somehow, I'm pulling it off by the skin of my teeth, probably because I'm high most of the time and keep a steady stream of whiskey in my system. Or maybe it's because, over time, I've learned a thing or two. Sometimes when I look in the mirror, I see demons fighting like dragons in the sky. But sometimes I still see a broken little girl who wishes her mother had loved her before it was too late. There is no simple way to sum up who I am or how I got this way, or maybe that's just something people wonder about serial killers. But I know how it goes, I've done it myself a time or two, you hear some horrible story, some tale of one bad decision after another and you make assumptions about the person. Sometimes I wish I could start over, maybe I should have gone somewhere else entirely.

But way back then, I was just a broken little girl in a grown woman's body. I guess you could say nothing has changed, but looking back, nothing has stayed the same. I was innocent, naïve, some sentimental thrift store hippie. I was just a bunch of broken pieces, held together with ratty vintage overalls and dingy white Chuck Taylors. Struggling to find myself and lose myself all at the same time. Looking for love although I had no idea what love was back then. I had this black and white perception of good and evil, this all or nothing opinion of people and I was guilty of judging a book by its cover.

I have a bad attitude and entirely too much emotional baggage, but we'll get to that later. I have a quick wit and the ability to camouflage my fragile mental state with a stellar sense of humor. I have a bachelor's in criminal justice because my mother said a degree in literature would be a waste of money. The summer after I graduated, I got a job at an animal shelter, pressure washing dog shit off cement floors, so I could spend time with stray cats. I also volunteered at an old folk's home so I could share butterscotch candies and instant coffee with old men in the 'Day Room.' One more thing, I love edibles and hate narcissists.

It has been a little over twelve years since I moved to Bunman, Vermont, in some failed attempt at a fresh start. With my life in shambles, I didn't feel like I had much of a choice, but the reality of what I've experienced here is nothing short of a fever dream. Yes, I'm aware it's a mistake to let skeletons out of a closet, it creates the same kind of chaos as opening a can of worms or letting a cat out of a bag. I'm also aware that shoving skeletons back into a closet requires exponentially more talent and dexterity than wrangling cats. It's not so much that my conscience is nagging at me, I've just gotten to the point where I don't give a shit what people think. The whole 'don't judge me until you walk a mile,' and all that.

My thirty-fifth birthday is on Friday and that has me reflecting on life. You know, the successes and failures, the things I should have done differently along the way. One thing I can say without a shadow of a doubt is that nothing about my life today resembles the day I squirted into the world between the knees of my loveless mother. And even though I identify as a broken little girl most of the time, I've figured out how to 'adult' with varying levels of success. My life is what I'd consider normal compared to some of the lives I've seen, but I encounter the occasional 'complication' just like everyone else. I start my day with a latte and end it with a glass of whiskey and a meltdown. Underneath it all, I'm just a broken little girl who wants to feel whole.

All that aside, this might not be the best time to join me since I'm face to face with some dirt bag named Trent who tried to steal my purse. I know the idiot's name because he's wearing the name tag from his shit job at a gas station that sees more shop lifters than paying customers. Listen, I try not to be a disagreeable bitch most of the time, but I've had the day from hell and this guy is getting on my last nerve. I slammed my bag into the side of his head and flipped him off with both hands,

"Go fuck yourself, asshole, you're out of your element."

As Trent stumbled around, clearing the cobwebs, I pressed the panic button hanging from my key chain and held it for three seconds. He punched me in the face, hard, effectively signing his own death warrant. So, here I am wearing a tailored pantsuit and heeled leather boots, blood streaming from my nose, my left eye swelling shut. You might be wondering if my life is flashing before my eyes, but it isn't. After the shit I've been through, this is more of an annoyance than anything, but I'm sick of people taking things that don't belong to them. If I've learned anything over the last twelve years, it's how to handle myself in a sticky situation, so I thrust the pointed toe of my boot into his groin. Trent bent at the waist and coughed several times before righting himself. He hissed, spit flying,

"You BITCH!"

I was in familiar territory and this guy wasn't, I knew we were in the sliver of parking lot that wasn't picked up by the camera. Did I run away whilst this Trent guy was preoccupied with his family jewels? Nope, I thrust my knuckles into his Adam's apple. He released his crotch, grabbed his throat, and gasped for air,

"Geez lady, what's your fucking problem!?"

I ran my sleeve through the blood pouring from my nose and spit a gelatinous glob at his feet, squinting,

"*My* problem!?"

A car skidded to a halt behind us, high beams shedding light on the situation, my reinforcement had arrived, even though I could handle this part myself. Unfazed, I shook the pain from my hand and without so much as a tremor of adrenaline in my voice, I blinked up,

"You're embarrassing yourself, Trent."

He went wide-eyed,

"How did you know my name?"

I pointed at his shirt and noticed he was wearing a wedding band, so I gave him one last chance to reconsider, a get out of jail free card of sorts. Hands on hips, and with a decent amount of confidence, I asked an honest question,

"Do you have any idea who I am?"

Apparently, we were in a figurative dick swinging contest because he replied with,

"I don't give a fuck who you are, if you don't give me that bag, I'm going to slit you from stump to flowers, princess!"

I pinched the bridge of my nose as Trent mumbled under his breath and worked an embarrassingly small pocketknife from his pants, what the fuck was he talking about? Princess? Stump to flowers? Instead of hightailing it out of there, I crossed my arms and rolled my eyes. Trent postured in front of me with a beat-up utility tool, tossing it from one hand to the other like a hot shot, unaware he brought a knife to a gun fight,

"This is your last chance before I gut you like a fish! Give me the fucking bag!"

I wondered what Trent needed the money for. Drugs? Half up-front to have someone whacked? Food for his family? He was barking up the right tree on all accounts, but he didn't know it. As he jabbed in my direction with the two-inch blade, I slid the cute little handgun from its place at the bottom of my vintage leather bag and pointed it at his chest. To push fast-forward for a second here, things went to hell in a hand basket, so I'll spare you the gory details. It's only because of the company I keep that I haven't been killed, locked up in the loony bin, or sent to prison.

Moments later, I was riding shotgun with a warm stiff in the trunk. As we drove through town, I pawed through the tote of body-dumping clothes on the passenger side floor, exchanging the tailored suit and heeled boots for something more appropriate. I worked the silver flask from my bag and swallowed well-aged fire, exhaling loudly as I melted into the seat. The driver, an attractive man a couple years older than me, smelled good and had dark five o'clock shadow. When we stopped at the next light, he offered me a cigarette. I'm not much of a smoker but I partake as part of this particular ritual. I plucked the cigarette from his hand, and he lit it with a fancy gold Zippo. In the light from the flame, I noticed someone sitting in the back seat and went palms up,

"What the fuck is she doing here!?"

The man shook his head and exhaled smoke as he defended, pointing at me repeatedly, liquor on his breath,

"I knew you would bitch about it; I fucking knew it! For Christ's sake, what the fuck was I supposed to do, push her out of a moving car!?"

He nodded his head to the back seat,

"She looks like a goth prostitute in that get-up! Did you want me to leave her in some laundry mat parking lot like chum for some predator!?"

The girl scoffed audibly, and I asked,

"You two were in a laundry mat parking lot when I pushed my panic button?"

He shook his head and gestured at me as he talked,

"You know, Scarface, I thought you were in actual trouble; I didn't know you were just dicking around with some low-rent clown."

I corrected,

"It's not a scar, it's a SCRIMPLE!"

I pressed my middle finger against the stubble on the side of his face and he swatted me away,

"Whatever, you're gonna get us killed, cut the shit, Amelia!

I clenched my jaw and pinched the bridge of my nose, the morbid and hormonal sixteen-year-old girl in the backseat, ecstatic to be included in whatever the hell you call all of this. I glanced over my shoulder at her, she was practically salivating, firing on all cylinders. She was finally sitting with the grown-ups instead of at the plastic folding table covered with drawing paper and shitty markers,

"Absolutely not, I spent a hundred and seventy dollars on that sweater, it's alpaca! You're not traipsing through the woods in that thing, you'll get a snag!"

"Fine!"

She pulled the sweater over her head and tossed it on the seat next to her. She sat there in a black silk camisole with her arms crossed, pouting. I went palms up again and barked,

"And now you're going to be cold!"

The angsty teen rolled her eyes and retrieved the sweater,

"Jesus Christ, what is it with you!? I can't fucking win!"

Nice. I squinted,

"Do you kiss your mother with that mouth?"

She leaned forward and locked eyes with me,

"I can't kiss my mother, she spent the twenty dollars you gave her for food, on tainted heroin."

Whatever. We were both ragging it, and she had just been dumped by her first serious boyfriend. I dug through the tote of body-dumping clothes and tossed a sweatshirt from her father's sandwich shop into the backseat. She pulled the hoodie over her head and proceeded to torch up a cigarette with the hot pink lighter she retrieved from her Doc Marten. On an exhale,

"My dad won't be mad that I'm tagging along, and you know it. He'll probably be happy about it, like I'm popping my cherry on this shit or something. I'm not stupid, I know what goes on."

She was right but I wasn't in the mood to hear it so I moved my eyes to the driver as he nosed the car onto a narrow gravel road,

"You gave her a cigarette!?"

As if they had rehearsed it, in unison they replied,

"Relax!"

Fine, it's not like I wasn't making out with boys and smoking in my bedroom in tenth grade. But I wasn't in the mood to be cool or fun, or pretend I was somehow leading that girl with my derailed example of a weed-addled self-medicator with trauma and multiple mental health disorders. The driver got out to remove a rope with orange flags hanging down. My adrenaline had dumped so I was tired and just wanted to go home. He drove in another tenth of a mile and pulled over,

"Speaking of kissing, you two better kiss and make up, we need to get this done, I have a dinner reservation with the Mrs. at eight-thirty, it's date night."

The man shut his door, leaving me alone with a temperamental teenager who had cramps and a chip on her shoulder, I turned to her,

"Listen, I've had a shitty day, and it seems like your day wasn't much better. Once we're done here, we'll order some food, whatever you want."

I pointed at my eye,

"I'd take you out, but I really need to ice my face."

She nodded and smiled, the tension morphing into concern,

"Does it hurt a lot?

I shrugged,

"I'll be fine. I'm sure it looks worse than it is."

I got out and turned to her with a black eye and dried blood around my nostrils,

"Stay in the car, capiche?"

She rolled her eyes and two minutes later, she was standing next to me. She bumped my hip with hers.

"Many hands and whatever, let me help, it'll be quicker."

I glanced over at her, and she added,

"I want manicotti and garlic bread."

Fair enough.

There we were, three assholes dumping a dead body, and besides the fact that a minor was helping, none of this was out of the ordinary. In an hour or two, I'd be showered and in sweatpants, a pack of freezer peas on my face while my cat makes biscuits on my stomach. We situated the body on one of those blue tarps and dragged his ass to the edge of a marble quarry. My stomach churned, I kept glancing over at her, wondering what was going through her head, wondering if this was contributing to the bullshit she'd have to process in therapy someday. I thought back to my first time and it still gave me chills.

With the tarp at the edge of what was a considerable drop-off into deep green water, we stood there and looked at the guy for a second, she said,

"Should we say something? Like a prayer or something?"

The man scrunched his eyebrows and gestured at my face,

"Seriously, kid?"

She shrugged,

"Yeah, I mean, he had a life."

She knelt on the edge of the tarp,

"I mean he got up this morning and took a shit. Probably ate some leftover Domino's before going to his miserable job at a gas station. I think I remember buying ciga...soda from that guy one time."

The man waved his hands around impatiently, securing weights to the dead guy's waist and ankles. The three of us grabbed the edge of the tarp and as we lifted, the body rolled awkwardly like a rag doll to its watery grave. I gripped the back of the sandwich shop hoodie as the girl peered over the edge, watching in the moonlight as the stiff tumbled and bounced off the wall on its way down. The splash echoed up to us as the final evidence of what I'd done. The driver turned for the car and I put my arm around the girl's waist, pulling her close as we walked,

"You, OK?"

She thought about it for a second,

"I've seen worse, and I didn't even know that guy."

That was the truth, so I changed the subject,

"How's your broken heart?"

She smiled mischievously,

"I broke into his piece of shit car and hid several pairs of my panties for his new girlfriend to find, like under the seats and in the glove box. Oh, and I sprayed my perfume all over the seats."

I opened my mouth to object to her crime of passion, and she turned to me, hands up,

"I don't want to hear it; you've done way worse with less provocation!"

She had a point.

The ride back to town was silent. The headlights illuminated my car and the area we'd hosed off was nothing more than a patch of damp pavement. The man leaned over and kissed me on the cheek before I got out, he squeezed the girl's hand over the seat,

"See ya, kid."

I slung my bag over my shoulder and tucked the tailored suit under my arm, giving the driver a wave before I shut the door. She rounded the car in her black platform boots and bumped my hip with hers, she really did look like a goth prostitute in that get-up. I shook my head, and she asked,

"Can I drive?"

I didn't have the energy to argue so I got in on the passenger side and buckled myself in. She moved the seat back a little and pushed in the clutch. We made our way home with the man following most of the way. They played leapfrog on the highway, and it was nice to see her smile. I tried not to panic that kids grow up too fast. The man flashed his lights as he went the other way, and she honked the horn in reply. As I predicted, exactly two hours after putting a bullet in that guy's chest, I was curled up on my screen porch with damp hair, a joint, and a bag of freezer peas. I replayed the day in my head while my cat made biscuits on my stomach.

The black-haired teen wandered onto the porch and gestured toward the kitchen,

"Come eat."

I knocked the cherry off the end of my spliff and followed her to the table. Something as simple as a clean face and a costume change shifted something dark into something innocent again, her feet in the hot pink wool socks she got at the farmer's market. She was a lot like me at that age, cute on the outside but filled with jagged parts and broken pieces. She nestled in next to me and blew across the top of a steaming cup of tea, I knew she had something on her mind, but it wasn't what I thought,

"Remember the summer I came here and you smashed your face on the door casing?"

I nodded but didn't know why she was asking.

"It looked exactly like this."

I nodded again,

"Yeah."

"Were you lying to protect me?"

I nodded a third time,

"Yes."

She settled in, sipping her tea while I spilled mine,

"I sort of kidnapped some woman who was causing trouble for your uncle, and she kicked my ass a little."

Her eyes went wide but she was more interested than shocked,

"She sounds like a bitch, tell me everything."

I tossed the warm bag of peas on the table and sipped the glass of whiskey that was waiting for me,

"She wrestled my gun away and almost killed me. Your uncle saved my life and then burnt the house to the ground because it had old wood floors and the blood soaked in."

She nodded, unfazed by what I'd told her,

"What did you do with her body?"

"I slashed her tires, that's how I got her. So, your uncle just threw her in the trunk of her own car, had his buddy load it onto one of his flatbeds, and they put it in the crusher at the junkyard."

A man jogged down the stairs, hair damp from a shower. He took a seat and pushed up his sleeves,

"I'm starving, let's eat!"

The three of us sat around our secondhand kitchen table with mismatched plates and silverware, breaking bread together at the end of another day. I have a clear conscience, a busted face, and a warm bag of freezer peas. I'm devouring manicotti and garlic bread, two hours after killing a man named Trent who tried to steal my purse. And I guess if I want you to understand how I became so twisted, I need to take you back to the beginning.

CHAPTER 1
WHAT'S OLD IS NEW AGAIN

TWO MONTHS before my twenty-third birthday, I packed up my twenty-six-year-old Subaru wagon and ran away from Roundelay, Massachusetts. A couple hours in, I stretched my legs at a 'quaint' little general store and side-stepped down a cluttered hallway full of stacked milk crates to a musty little bathroom that was more like a closet. With the flimsy hook-and-eye in place, one hand braced on either side of the ancient pedestal sink, I locked eyes with myself in the grimy mirror. Was I really doing this? Was I *really* running away from home!? I needed to shit or get off the pot and I knew it, figuratively I mean. Fifty miles north and I'd be back in Bunman, it had been forever, and I was feeling sentimental. Well, folks, I decided to shit. I'm no quitter, and I certainly couldn't go back home and admit I was a colossal failure at fresh starts. I snagged a bag of overpriced dark chocolate covered blueberries and a mediocre drip coffee on my way out the door. After one more deep breath, I swallowed my feelings, pushed in the clutch, and headed toward 'home.'

My stomach did somersaults in anticipation as visual reminders led me to my hometown like breadcrumbs in the forest. Bunman, Vermont is situated near ski slopes, hiking trails, and the shores of Clover Lake. While it used to be a thriving community filled with generations of middle-class families, what I found was a bunch of empty storefronts and side-street clusters of condemned apartment buildings. There were addicts begging for change and cigarettes in the shopping plaza, and the Amtrak was delivering a constant flow of drug traffickers, to and from New York City. From the posters I saw around the park, the Chamber of Commerce was trying to revitalize the area, but they were up against a constant battle between growth and destruction. The old mall, family-owned restaurants, and mom-and-pop stores had been abandoned, and empty buildings with plywood-covered windows held their places. I admired the front of a little tea shop and bookstore as I set off to explore modern-day Bunman in the late winter sun. Childhood memories flooded in as I peered through the dusty glass doors of the vacant stationery store, I frequented as a child.

I'm a Vermonter at heart and was born in Bunman. I lived there until my father changed jobs the summer before seventh grade. That July, my parents moved me and my older sister, Opal, three hours south to a suburb in Massachusetts. And besides the occasional overnight trip for a wedding or funeral, that was the first time I'd been back in almost twelve years. I was fed up with my mother's criticism of everything I did, everyone I dated, and every job I had, which was hard to escape when I lived in the same town. My boyfriend broke up with me approximately seven months ago, and any day now, he and his whore would be welcoming their love child. Yes, I can do the math on that one. I needed to get the hell out of Dodge, and my aunt Maggie suggested I seek refuge in Bunman. Maybe I'd be able to find myself and adopt a cat. Spoiler alert, that's not exactly how things went. Buckle up, I have a story to tell.

I meandered along Maple Street window shopping and came to a halt when I spotted the breathtaking three-story brick building that housed my aunt's gift shop, and the cafe next to it. My mouth was watering before I even crossed the threshold of Muddy Waters. The scent of ground coffee beans and pastries swirled in the air. The coffee bar was a long slice of shellacked maple with a row of wooden stools. I admired the dark ship lap walls, Edison lamps, and fairy lights. Trailing plants hung from wrought iron hooks in the windows and tendrils crept along hooks on the ceiling. A realistic electric fireplace added a cozy touch to a semi-circle of secondhand leather sofas. Coffeehouse jazz played over the sound system.

A handsome barista with wavy shoulder-length brown hair and a well-groomed beard, buzzed around with a bar rag over his shoulder. I followed him with my eyes as he ground beans, pulled espresso shots, and worked his magic with steamed milk. He was twenty-five, slender, and right around six feet tall. He was wearing well-loved jeans, Blundstones, and a Muddy Waters t-shirt that revealed the tattoos on his left arm. He caught my eye and winked, I turned and looked over my shoulder to see who he was winking at. When he came to the counter, I saw that his name tag said, 'Kane.' Kane Buchanan had perfect teeth, and his eyes were like dark chocolate. I ordered a maple oat latte and a breakfast sandwich and sat on one of the leather sofas. I was daydreaming about my fresh start when he called my name. When I went to the counter to retrieve my order, Kane made small talk,

"I haven't seen you in here before, are you staying in Bunman or just passing through?"

I sipped the latte and bashfully swiped at the steamed milk on my upper lip with the back of my hand,

"I lived here when I was little and recently decided I need a change of scenery. My aunt's from here and she suggested I move back."

"I know almost everyone around here, who's your aunt?"

"Magnolia Moriarty."

Kane's eyes smiled and his voice went up an octave, which startled me,

"Oh! You're *that* Amelia!"

I looked at him with question marks over my head as he smiled and nodded his head toward her gift shop,

"I know Maggie very well."

Small world. I pointed at the fireplace.

"She's meeting me here in a little while. If you see her before I do, please point her in my direction."

I nestled in, kicked off my Chuck Taylors, and sat cross-legged with the brindle Staffordshire terrier I found curled up on a braided rug in front of the fake fireplace. Her brown eyes followed my hands with each bite as I ate my breakfast sandwich, strings of dog drool pooling on the floor. The biscuit was buttery and flaky, the maple-glazed bacon was sweet and crispy, the egg was sprinkled with spicy salt and was still a little runny. I devoured it in minutes and could have easily ordered another. The maple oat latte was one of the best I'd ever had, and the barista was making me salivate.

My aunt strolled through the door in a swirl of guaiac wood and weed. Kane kissed her on the cheek and pointed in my direction, I gave her an excited wave and unfolded myself from the floor. My father's fifty-three-year-old sister Magnolia, or Maggie as she prefers to be called, is built just like me. She usually wears gauzy skirts and flowy linen tunics with tiny silver bells around her ankles. She wears beaded fringe earrings that brush her shoulders. Her salt and pepper hair was long at the time, and curly just like mine. Some of her hair was twisted into a tidy bun fastened with a beaded hairpin, crazy ringlets cascading over her shoulders. I closed the gap and almost knocked her down as I hugged her with my whole body.

My aunt Maggie was one of the people who kept me afloat on my way up in life. I'll get into all of that in more detail later but my childhood had a good amount of darkness in it. I think back to it now and I can't even imagine it, and I was there, way back when. Sometimes it's like that, you think back to something horrible and it doesn't seem real, or you wonder how you survived it. Without even knowing it, my aunt always provided the lifeline I needed when I was floundering in the quicksand. I'm not saying I would have ever done anything to hurt myself, but I thought about it. I don't know, I guess I spent a lot of my life feeling worthless and filled with self-deprecation. Maybe not so much when I was little, but there was a time when I thought a lot of things about myself and none of them were good.

When Maggie's second husband, Pete, passed away a year and a half ago, his business assets were transferred to her. She owned commercial property and apartment rentals all over town. When the storefront next to Muddy Waters became vacant, she decided to fulfill a lifelong dream of opening a gift shop. My aunt planned to set me up with a job and a place to live. She was convinced I would thrive once I was away from the drama back home. According to Maggie, it would give me a chance to follow my 'whimsy,' as she put it, and maybe even fall in love. Speaking of which, she mentioned there was a 'nice boy' she wanted me to meet. Good ole Maggie, trying to get me laid before I was even unpacked. As if she could read my mind, she added that she'd wait to set me up with 'the boy' until I had a chance to settle in. I had a pretty good idea she was talking about Kane, at least I hoped so.

Muddy Waters and my aunt's store, Whimsy, were connected by a set of ornate double doors. The businesses could operate as one when the doors were open, and separately when the doors were closed. A long time ago, the entire space housed a bookstore, so an impressive floor-to-ceiling shelf spanned the back wall, complete with a rolling ladder. Whimsy showcased vintage books, items made by local artisans, upscale touristy items, and the works of local authors. The smells of balsam and cinnamon danced around me, and I found a display of jewelry made by a local silversmith. There was a collection of hardwood shelves filled with pottery, candles, and maple candies. My aunt encouraged students at the rec center pottery studio to sell their wares in the store which made for a unique combination of maple leaf ornaments, wonky mugs with awkward handles, and expertly crafted tea sets. Fairy lights wrapped with faux ivy were strung whimsically around the ceiling.

"Someone will be in shortly to open the store. I need to take care of a couple of things, but when I'm done, I'll show you the apartment and you can get settled in."

I decided to stroll around town, and before I went out the door, I tossed an edible down the hatch. Maple Street continued up a hill and storefronts lined both sides. I went into The Meat Boss and the man running the quaint little deli appeared to be in the middle of an argument. The guy was abrupt when he greeted me, and then ditched the woman working behind the counter, leaving her with a line of customers. Even after the man went into his office, I could still hear him growling into the phone at someone named Vin to 'get it done.' If the man had been on a landline phone, I imagine he would have slammed the handset into the cradle. I felt uncomfortable being there, so I left. I recognized the buildings but most of the businesses had changed, and I was surprised how many of the storefronts were empty. I went into a natural food store and bought tea for my emergency stash. Hey, some girls carry around a collection of makeup and receipts from shopping sprees, I carry emergency tea bags, a good luck joint, and spare underwear. Jealous?

By the time I returned, I could feel my edible kicking in, so I stood mesmerized by the ancient brass handle and heavy wooden door at the entrance of my aunt's store. The aroma of candles and balsam spiraled together with undertones of coffee beans and pastries from next door. I spotted an area in the front of the store that was dedicated to kids, complete with a drawing station. A blue cookie tin filled with the broken nubs of well-loved crayons waited for little hands to create art. I stuck my nose in the tin, and it brought back childhood memories. I knelt and looked through a small shelf filled with children's books written by local authors. Built-in shelves held vintage books, quirky oddities, and other odds and ends.

The woman opening the store, made small talk with me as I went from one display to the next. She seemed familiar but after all that time, I doubted I'd run into anyone I knew. When I made eye contact with the woman, she ran around the counter and lifted me off the ground. The woman squealed,

"Oh my God, Amelia!"

I hadn't seen my childhood best friend, Sunny, in almost twelve years. When I moved away, she didn't even have her period yet. I was looking at the adult version of the little girl who clung to me during thunderstorms and built tree forts with me in the forest. The freckles and big blue eyes were that of the little girl I remembered, but she had grown into a beautiful woman. Now, Sunny was a couple inches taller than me, slender, and her loosely curled shoulder-length strawberry-blonde hair was twisted into a messy bun with random locks framing her face. She wore too much eyeliner, but she pulled it off without looking trashy. Sunny was the one I thought I'd stay in touch with, the one I missed the most. But just like everything, memories fade, and life moves on. It had been a while since I wondered what happened to her, or if she moved out of Bunman. My eyes filled with happy tears,

"Sunny!"

She smiled ear to ear,

"What's up, fucker!?"

I met Abigail 'Sunny' Solomon on the first day of kindergarten, and we were inseparable until the day my family left Bunman. Sunny's alcoholic and generally horrible father would beat Sunny's mom almost nightly. My mother was cold, critical, and swept it under the carpet when she found out I was being molested at the neighbor's house. We were wounded little birds who found comfort in each other. Sunny would help me sneak out at night when I didn't want to sleep alone. We pulled each other out of the darkness and built fortresses in the woods, no one could hurt us there. The night before I moved, we sat huddled in a dugout behind the school, smoking Marlboro reds, and hiding from our parents. As we cried in anticipatory grief, we promised to write, but over time, the letters stopped.

Our attention shifted to the door as a handsome twenty-something with a dark pompadour and Italian-looking eyebrows crossed the threshold. He had nice eyes and the energy he radiated made my heart race, I became aware that goosebumps were crawling across my skin. He sauntered in like he owned the place, and I stepped aside. He smelled good, and I wanted to lick his face, I could tell he was wearing expensive cologne, and he seemed like a bad ass. The man leaned on the counter with the elbows of his black leather jacket, and in a sexy Jersey-style Italian accent,

"Hey darling, I won't be going to that thing with you tomorrow night, my Pops needs me to do a job."

Sunny's eyes fell to the counter, and I watched as she swallowed her feelings just like she did when she was a kid,

"I told you about the show weeks ago, and you said you'd make sure you could come with me."

She gestured toward the double doors,

"My cousin Olive is playing with the guys from next door."

The man shrugged dismissively like he had better things to do with his time, he glanced at his watch,

"Sorry babe, my pops needs me to do a job."

Sunny appeared unimpressed and replied flatly,

"A job?"

It seemed like that was code for something and I could see his wheels turning,

"I'll come over after I'm done, and I'll bring whatever you want from my brother's place. Anything you want and its yours."

He winked and she crossed her arms,

"Shrimp scampi, house salad with house dressing, chocolate panna cotta."

She paused,

"And an order of that fried zucchini with the homemade ranch."

He winked,

"After we eat, I can give you a back rub or we can cuddle."

I wasn't stupid, I knew what 'back rub' and 'cuddling' were code for, that guy was securing a blow job or a booty call with some wine sauce and an authentic Italian dessert. Sunny seemed disappointed but it looked like she was used to feeling that way, she replied,

"Sounds good."

The hot guy tapped the side of his face and Sunny kissed him on the cheek before he went out the door.

I sneered,

"Who the fuck is that guy!?"

We both watched as he walked away and I added,

"He's got a nice ass, but he seems like a douche bag."

Sunny waved dismissively,

"That's just my boyfriend, Vinny. He has a stressful job working for his father, but he comes over and spends time with me when he can. He takes care of me, like if I need my car fixed or come up short with my bills, he helps me. We order pizza and watch movies and...things."

I had a good idea what those 'things' were, and I didn't want to tell her that it looked like she was an afterthought. I wanted to ask her if the two of them spent any quality time together, but I hadn't seen this woman in twelve years, and it wasn't any of my business. Sunny grew up with a piss-poor example of what a healthy relationship looked like, and I hoped she wasn't following in her mother's footsteps. I could see in her eyes that she had feelings for him,

"He's really sweet most of the time, his father is just, umm, kind of a tyrant."

Sunny waved her hand,

"We aren't serious or exclusive or anything, but maybe when his job settles down. Vinny works most of his jobs at night."

She leaned across the counter and whispered,

"His family's in the mob."

I shook my head and rolled my eyes like the whole thing was nonsense but wondered if 'job' was code for 'incaprettamento,' mafia slang for strangling an enemy out of retaliation. Or maybe it was Vinny's 'job' to smuggle the guns or brick up the coke or launder the money. Was he the 'Vin' that old meat fart was talking to on the phone? The one who was supposed to 'get it done?' I couldn't believe I was even entertaining any of this, and promptly shoved it into a filing cabinet in the back of my mind. There was no way a legitimate mob family was living in Bunman, Vermont. Let's keep it real, that good looking, nice smelling Italian man was full of shit. For all anyone knew, maybe Vinny's 'job' was to participate in high-stakes BINGO multiple nights a week at a senior center. You never really know people and I wasn't judging; I was just making an observation.

I maintained a level of familiarity with Bunman, and felt like I belonged there, but I also felt like an outsider, if that makes any sense. Once I stopped to take it all in, the only thing that stayed the same was the location. I was on my way to get another latte and another serving of eye-candy from the cute barista next door when my aunt emerged from her office. Maggie waited as I went back to the counter but that time a guy with curly dark hair, mutton chops and a curlicue mustache took my order. Seth Lucerne was a hippie type who smelled like patchouli and weed. There was black polish on his nails, and he was wearing funky plaid pants. He had wool socks, and a pair of well-loved Birkenstock clogs he'd probably had since college. Seth had soulful brown eyes and a nice smile, his forearm boasted a tattoo about better days, and I could tell he was battling his own demons.

Seth's voice was gentle, and I'd have bet money he was a musician.

I followed my aunt to the hallway of the cafe where she unlocked a door that opened to a set of stairs. As we came out in the upstairs hall, she gestured,

"There's an entrance from Maple Street, it's to the left of Whimsy. Those stairs lead to your apartment as well as the apartments on the third floor but I don't remember the last time I went in that way."

She gestured down the hall toward the back,

"And those are the stairs to the parking lot."

There were two apartment doors in the hallway and Maggie unlocked the one on the left. We crossed the threshold into a cute little kitchen with a round table and an L-shaped counter. Mismatched place mats sat on the counter along the short side of the L, accented by a row of mismatched stools with mismatched cushions. A handmade ceramic ashtray and mug sat in the dish drainer. I continued into the main room which had a row of tall windows that looked out over Maple Street and the park across the way. I pressed my forehead to the glass, and I could see the entrance to my aunt's store right below me, the sign swinging gently in the breeze. I wiped the forehead print off the window with my sleeve and opened the front entrance, which led to a landing with an antique white bench. There was a hardwood futon with a thick mattress in the living room, and a large, braided rug in the middle of the hardwood floor. A funky tapestry hung on one wall and there were hooks for plants in the windows. I could detect a hint of incense and stale weed.

The large bedroom was furnished with a round cream-colored shag rug, a dark wood four-poster bed, and the tall windows were accented with flowy lace curtains. The deep claw foot tub was going to be perfect for bubble baths. Most of the buildings in downtown Bunman were original eighteen fifties architecture and that building was no exception. I admired the high ceilings and ornamental woodwork as I ran my fingers over the ornate metal radiator.

We went down the back stairs and exited onto a cute little porch. There were several parking spaces, and I assumed that's where I'd keep my jury-rigged twenty-six-year-old piece of Swiss cheese. The row of cars in the lot included a vintage Bronco, an old looking motorcycle, and a selection of late-model Subarus in varying levels of decay. 'Holly' was going to fit right in, in all her cob-jobbed glory. I probably shouldn't admit this, but I pleasured some mechanic named Steve in exchange for my last inspection. And since I wasn't planning on doing that again any time soon, the clock was ticking down on my time with her, and it made me sad.

I changed the subject in my mind, there was a nice backyard with a stone fire pit surrounded by a circle of wooden Adirondack chairs. Thanks to my aunt, there were lots of bird feeders and a couple sets of impressive wind chimes on wrought iron hooks along the back fence. My eyes continued to the other side of the parking lot where I spotted a row of cars. There was a brand-new Lincoln MKX, a dark gray BMW sedan, and a sharp-looking black Escalade, the backs of the cars pointing in our direction. Maggie gestured,

"That's the lot for the Italian place next door, but it's all connected."

When we got back upstairs, Maggie handed over the keys and held me to her chest. For a moment, I was a little girl again and as she kissed the side of my head,

"You're welcome to stay as long as you want, sweetheart. Once you're settled in, I'll set you up with a job downstairs. I need counter and management coverage at the store, especially when I'm out of town."

Maggie put her finger up like she remembered something,

"Oh, and Kane is always looking for help at the cafe."

Maggie winked and I felt a little flutter when I thought about working with Kane. Can you imagine? I bit my lower lip and then switched gears, I felt the need to explain why I abandoned my life in Roundelay,

"Things back home were unbearable."

I stared out the window at pigeons on the power lines and tried not to cry,

"My love life is in shambles, and I swear my mother has made it her mission to destroy me...I feel so lost."

I paused,

"I thought I'd have my life together by now."

Maggie listened patiently, but I was uncomfortable with my recent memories and the feelings they invoked, so I gestured around the room,

"Was someone staying here?"

"Over the winter, I'd stay here when the roads were bad. I think you'll be quite happy; you can make it into a cute little home for yourself."

I did another scan of the room, my imagination making a list of things I wanted to search for at local thrift stores,

"It's perfect, Maggie, thank you."

"I heard you chatting with Abbie, isn't she sweet?"

I smiled,

"You're not going to believe this, I met her on the first day of kindergarten, and we were best friends until the day my family moved to Roundelay. She's the Sunny I talked about when I was little, I haven't seen her in twelve years."

Maggie hugged me again and said she remembered that someone named Sunny helped me through my tumultuous childhood,

"You know, I used to think you were talking about an imaginary friend when you would mention her and had no idea Sunny was a real person. To think I've known her for years now and didn't make the connection."

I made air quotes,

"She seems to be 'dating' a real tool."

My aunt made an expression that led me to think there was a story to tell,

"That 'tool' would be Vincenzo Moretti, he's the youngest son of the local mob family. At first, he seemed like a dream come true, but lately she isn't much more than an afterthought. They've been seeing each other for a while, and I know they aren't serious or anything, but she's constantly competing for his attention. If it isn't the work he does for his father, it's other women. Sometimes she talks about leaving but at this point, it's easier to stay with him."

Maybe that nice-smelling guy really was in the mob, but at the time, I thought he was just swinging his dick around in some dramatic show of self-importance. The thought that Sunny might be staying with the guy just because he helped with her bills made my guts gurgle,

"How is that easier!?"

Maggie put her hand on my arm,

"She needs to get there on her own, she'll leave when she's ready. Right now, she's willing to put up with his behavior, and his job, and I really do think she loves him. Relationships are complicated sometimes, sweetheart."

Maggie was right, I was dealing with the fallout from my own complicated relationships. But I'd heard just about enough of that real or implied mob bullshit, was everyone around there out of their goddamn minds? Maggie kissed my forehead and left me to spiral around in my brain. I pushed away the nonsense about the mob and shifted my focus to Sunny. I knew she was stronger than most, and would do what she needed to do, but she deserved to be happy.

It reminded me of the guy I dated before the one with the whore and the lovechild. Good old, Richard, more fittingly referred to under my breath as 'that asshole,' claimed to be Prince Charming but ended up chopping me down like Paul Bunyan. He made me feel more desired and more rejected than anyone else ever had. He played head games and scolded me for being 'difficult' if I didn't agree with what he said, or when I didn't fall for his obvious lies. Richard didn't leave bruises, but I feared for my life, in more ways than one. He used hunting knives and police batons as subtle warnings, but it was more about the veiled threats with him, the head games, the psychological manipulation. And as expected, he retaliated when I finally cut ties, you get punished when you leave a narcissist.

I hoped I was wrong but Sunny's relationship with Vinny raised some of the same red flags, with all his gaslighting and diversionary tactics. I wondered if he was a magician like Richard, some master of slide of hand and theatrics, some figurative descendant of Houdini. I sat in that secondhand armchair, spiraling about the colossal assholes I had dated, and wondered if I'd ever find an actual Prince Charming. Deep down in my soul, I knew I was too broken and dysfunctional for all that.

I drifted away to memories of me and Sunny in dresses and bare feet, running through the field behind my house. The blades of tall grass left tiny little cuts all over our legs, and butterflies danced in circles overhead. The two of us had Sponge Bob band-aids on our knees and dirt under our fingernails. We swung nets to catch bugs and filled our lunch boxes with pretty rocks and feathers; we considered those things our treasures. We'd climb into the hollow trunks of ancient gnarly oaks and pretend nothing could hurt us there. The smells of damp rotting wood and moss filling our noses as we twisted green twigs and hay into crowns.

I scanned the apartment and daydreamed. The front room was the largest and I decided to sleep on the futon instead of the bed. There was a six by ten-foot sun porch off the kitchen that looked out over the back yard, a similar sun porch was situated to the right of mine. There was an old metal futon frame with a beat-up mattress and a wobbly spindle-legged coffee table. A chipped end table sat empty, waiting for a couple potted plants, evenly spaced hooks waited over the windows, empty until spring. I imagined wind chimes and a bistro table out there, maybe a cute area rug. I unloaded the car, threw myself dramatically onto the junky sun porch futon and lost myself in thought.

Eventually, I unpacked the rest of the boxes, smoked a joint on the sun porch, and ordered a pepperoni pizza from next door. With my belly full of food and my head full of weed, I moved the furniture around and ordered some area rugs from Amazon. When all was said and done, I felt a little bit more like a woman and a little less like a broken little girl. I had never had my own place, not really, I always had a roommate. And even though my aunt wasn't charging me rent, I had accomplished something by relocating my life, for having the balls to do it. I was far from Roundelay, a place rife with shame and judgment. A place rife with my ex, his whore, their love child, and my mother. I leaned my head back on the sun porch futon and blew a stream of smoke into the darkness, watching as it dissipated into nothingness. I had a nagging panic, a creeping dread and anxiety under the surface, but I was ready to follow that whimsy my aunt was talking about.

CHAPTER 2
WAKE-UP CALL

IN THE MORNING, a bubbly woman in a messy bun, a patchwork dress, and fuzzy Birkenstock clogs made my maple oat latte. Her name was Marlaina Bernardi. She was a college student, and her dark hair was in a French braid, loose waves framing her face. Marlaina had olive skin, big brown eyes, and a beautiful smile. She brought my order to the small table next to the fake fireplace where I was nestled on one of the beat-up leather sofas with my feet tucked under me.

"Hi there, are you Maggie's niece?"

"Yes, I'm Amelia."

I put my hand out and she held it in hers,

"I'm Marlaina, I've heard a lot about you.

She nodded her head at the kitchen,

"Rumor has it you might be picking up a couple shifts over here, let me know if you need anything."

Marlaina waved and walked away. I stared out the window at the park and pondered how much things had changed around there. When the dark chocolate voice wafted out to me from the kitchen, a tingle ran through my body. I rolled my eyes and told myself to chill, lost in my head when I felt a hand on my shoulder. I gasped and nearly jumped out of my skin, my cheeks flushing as I looked up to see Kane standing there. He perched on the arm of the sofa and our eyes met, I glanced away nervously and picked at the skin next to my thumbnail. He broke the silence,

"Morning."

Kane smelled like coffee beans, cedar, and leather, I wanted to lick his face. Alright buddy, take it down a notch. There was energy passing between us and I wondered if it was in my head. I replied,

"Morning."

Maggie strolled through the double doors on her way to retrieve a latte and smirked when she saw the two of us sitting there together. She had a shit-eating grin on her face as she speed-walked in our direction. She hugged me and kissed Kane on the cheek, I could smell that she'd just smoked a joint in the parking lot,

"Once you're through the morning rush, you should show my beautiful niece around town."

Yes, my aunt had just suggested that the handsome barista show me around the town I grew up in...subtle. They were close so I felt comfortable with him right away, and he wasn't hard on the eyes either. Kane replied casually as he swung a bar rag,

"I'm free in a bit. I'll show you around and we can grab lunch."

I sensed that the two of them had planned it, and looking at Kane, I knew something else I'd like to grab besides lunch. Maggie dug around in the pocket of her skirt, handing over two twenties and a zippered snack bag with a pre-rolled joint in it,

"Have fun."

She kissed me on the cheek and winked at Kane,

"Take good care of her."

I shook my head. Kane threw the bar rag over his shoulder and disappeared into the kitchen. Maggie retrieved her latte and disappeared through the double doors into her store, the tiny silver bells around her ankles chiming subtly in her wake. I sat there alone with my head spinning, what the hell was happening? I finished my breakfast and flipped through a book to pass the time, but I wasn't really reading it. I felt like I'd be safe with Kane and as obvious as this sounds, I felt safe with him because he *was* safe. Not hot-safe, but like vanilla ice cream instead of Rocky Road.

I was looking for a fresh start, and it made sense for me to open myself up to new experiences. Every other guy I'd spent time with ended up being a colossal asshole, it's like I was a dick magnet, no pun intended. But underneath it all, I desperately needed to feel like I wasn't broken. I hoped my move back to Bunman would lead me in some direction that would shed light on what I wanted out of life. Maybe without my mother looking over my shoulder, I'd be able to figure out who I was. You know, without all of her pretense, facade, and curtains that looked good from the outside. I reflect back on that time and realize I had no idea just how complicated things would get over the next couple of years.

Right then, I was blissfully ignorant, and I guess it had to be that way. If I had even an inkling of the bullshit I'd get involved in, I would have run for the hills. I had this fantastical ignorance, this confident insecurity, this absolute romanticization of what life would be like in that town. The naivety with which I proceeded makes me cringe, I didn't know the truth and I sure as hell didn't know the rules. Just some dumb ass on a quest for a new beginning. Little did I know that I was at the cusp of something so ruthless and dysfunctional that it sounds less like reality and more like some fucked up psilocybin trip.

When I wasn't helping in my aunt's store, I could learn how to be a barista or work at the food co-op. Maybe I could go to the rec center and make pottery to sell in the gift shop. Maybe I could write poetry and have it made into books for the local author section. For the first time in my life, I could do whatever I wanted, without worrying what anyone thought about it. My mother wouldn't be reminding me I was a failure, a disappointment, or that I'll use 'any excuse to spend money,' even though ninety-nine percent of my clothing was secondhand. She didn't even know me well enough to insult me properly. I'd be able to meet new people who didn't know me, I could reinvent myself. But I'd really be letting people know the 'real me' for a change, instead of playing a part. If it was safe to stop wearing masks around people, maybe I'd figure out who I was, and maybe I could heal the broken little girl tucked away deep inside.

I peed and used a travel toothbrush to delete my coffee breath. I rooted around my bag and pulled out a travel bottle of Alien Elixir. After putting on some peppermint lip balm, I tossed an edible down the hatch for good measure. When I returned to the fireplace, Kane was slinging a well-loved L.L.Bean backpack over his shoulder. I followed him out the back door to the parking lot and he gestured between his vintage Bronco and a fast-looking motorcycle,

"It's nice out, do you mind taking the bike?"

I stood there like a deer in the headlights, my eyes like saucers, adrenaline burning in my stomach. Sensing my possible discomfort, he gestured,

"If you'd rather, we can take the Bronco."

I was having a small panic attack on the inside but tried to remain casual, my voice was a little shakier than usual and trailed off as I spoke,

"Umm, no, that's fine, we can take your bike."

I stood there in the parking lot wringing my hands as Kane went up the porch steps and came back with two helmets. He stopped in front of me, assessing my body language or facial expression or something, or maybe he could tell I was about to shit my pants in the driveway. He pretended to be reconsidering, tapping his chin,

"You know what? We should probably take the Bronco; it looks like it might rain later."

Kane jogged the helmets back inside and I glanced up at the sky, there wasn't a cloud to be seen. I let out a big sigh and shook out the tension in my arms, marching my feet a couple times as if it pushed some sort of imaginary reset button. I had dodged a bullet. And I guess it meant something to me that this man I just met had taken the time to realize I was uncomfortable with the motorcycle. Instead of pressuring me or making me feel stupid that I was scared of his bike, he pretended to change his mind. I wasn't used to being around people like that. We climbed in the Bronco and Kane made a loop through town before heading toward the water.

Clover Lake was where I spent most of my time as a child. Back then, Maggie had an adorable little Airstream trailer at a seasonal site, and we pretended it was our fancy beach front property. The awning was strung with white lights and the upholstery on the cushions inside was sewn from mismatched vintage floral fabrics she had thrifted. We'd sit around the campfire with a stack of newspaper riddles taped to index cards. We'd roast (or burn) marshmallows and make S'mores, while we read books like *Green Mountain Ghosts, Ghouls & Unsolved Mysteries*. We'd watch fireflies blink in the darkness as bats swooped down to take sips from the surface of the lake.

Even though it was the off-season, I smelled waffle cones and hot dogs as we crossed the threshold of The Lakeside General Store. We picked out chips and drinks and subs. Kane and I didn't say much to each other in the store, but we didn't need to. He took a right out of the parking lot, onto Lake Road. A mile up, he took another right and nosed the Bronco along a rutted dirt path with grass in the middle. It led through the woods and reminded me of one of those eighties' slasher films. The arched trees gave way to a clearing with a big rock at the edge of the lake. It was a big deal to me that not a single shred of my being was scared to be out there with him. Alone. I was more comfortable with Kane than I had been with some of the people I'd known for years. Right then, vanilla-safe was exactly what I needed.

My aunt trusted Kane and that gave me a sense of comfort, he'd have hell to pay if he hurt me. He noticed I was nervous about the motorcycle and rescued me instead of making me feel uncomfortable. Trustworthy guys were not something I was accustomed to, at that point in my life. Out of necessity, I tended to be on edge and hyper-vigilant most of the time. Between my mother, and my exes, I was used to feeling a twinge of fight or flight most of the time, but I wasn't feeling any of that with Kane. I've been through some things, and he wasn't triggering any of my red flags, so I let myself forget about life for a while.

We sat at a picnic table and looked at the lake and the mountains while we ate chips and subs. The silences were comfortable, I didn't need to fill the gaps in our conversation. When we were done eating, we moved to the flat shelf of rock at the water's edge and shared the joint Maggie sent along. We just stayed there for a while next to the water, talking. Kane told me about the coffee shop, that he was obsessed with roasting coffee beans, and that he wanted to create unique blends for the cafe. He'd been playing guitar since he was six and was in a band with some friends from college. He was close with his family, especially his twin sister Constance, he didn't mention a girlfriend.

When we got back to Muddy Waters, he was quiet, and then said,

"There's a block party tonight with food trucks, music, and vendors over at the park. My band is playing in the gazebo, you should stop by."

Should I?

I imagined holding his hand or kissing him on the cheek but didn't do either of those things. To be transparent, my story isn't some cheesy romance and I'm not going to ride off into the sunset with Kane

Buchanan. My life after that move was something else entirely but this is how the beginning of that part went. And right then, I was okay with the distraction. Kane hugged me briefly and for a split second, with my head against his chest, all was right with the world. For the first time in forever, the man with his arms around me hadn't hurt me, and I wondered if that would change someday. He waved as he walked away, and with his smooth tenor voice, he casually said,

"Be there or be square."

I did 'finger guns' at him and rolled my eyes at myself. I spent the next couple hours arranging the apartment and felt like a failure for needing a fresh start before my twenty-third birthday. I wondered if my fucked-up childhood would mess up every relationship I ever had, or if I had just been dating assholes. In time, I managed to find someone who held my broken pieces together, but right then, I wondered if I was lovable, or if someday I wouldn't be broken. Eventually, I made my way to the sun porch to smoke a joint and stare at the fence in the back yard, a creeping panic sizzled in my stomach and my eyes felt tight with tension. There was a tap at my kitchen door, the dark chocolate voice wafting into my ears,

"Amelia?"

I opened the door and gestured Kane into the apartment. I could see in his eyes that he knew I had been crying, he didn't ignore it, and he didn't shine a light on it. I put the joint out in one of my aunt's handmade ceramic ashtrays and looked up at him. Kane took my hand and squeezed it lightly; I glanced up at him and then dropped my eyes to the table. He asked,

"How's it going? Maggie tells me you're moving in over here."

I gestured toward the living room, with its tall windows and ornate radiators,

"I think it's going to be cute. I love all the windows, and Maggie already has some nice furniture up here. I just need to make it my own."

Kane gestured at the door across the hall,

"Come on, you should meet your neighbor."

I followed as he went across the hall and knocked on the door. We waited. I finally said,

"Maybe they aren't home."

He pulled a carabiner off his belt loop and unlocked the door. He turned the knob as I screeched,

"You can't do that!"

I scurried back into my apartment and slammed my door. There was a light tap and my door opened, Kane took my hand, and we went across the hall,

"This is where I live, did you think I was breaking in?"

I lied,

"No."

I was impressed with how tidy his apartment was. There were no dishes in the sink and there was a neatly folded blanket on the back of the couch. There was a professional espresso machine on the counter and a large flat screen TV on the wall. I peeked into the bathroom and there wasn't so much as a pair of inside out underwear with skid marks up the ass, this guy was the real deal. I could hear a rapid thumping noise; Kane opened a crate and out bounced the fireplace dog with its wrecking ball tail. I knelt and petted her head.

"This is Lola."

Kane put raw dog food into a handmade ceramic bowl for Lola and threw a plastic takeout container of leftover spaghetti and meatballs in the microwave for himself. He offered to share, thumbing toward the wall,

"It's from the Italian place next door, you can have some if you want."

I declined.

A little before six, I pulled on my favorite jeans, a wool sweater, and my shearling boots. I went over to the park and scanned the faces for someone I knew... anyone. Strings of tiny white bulbs lit the inside of the gazebo, and the vendors had fairy lights decorating the insides of their tents. People arrived with chairs and blankets. I saw young moms with travel mugs and knew they probably contained Swiss Miss and a double shot of Bailey's.

There was a bar cart serving local craft-brew beers and hard cider. People milled around with steaming cups of gourmet hot chocolate topped with whipped cream. I hopped up on a low rock wall and spotted Kane in the gazebo with his band mates, plugging cords into amps, and setting up microphone stands. I stared at my boots and lost myself in thought until I noticed a pair of well-loved Blundstones in front of me, I glanced up to see Kane standing there, smiling.

"I'm glad you decided to come."

I felt my cheeks grow hot as I blushed. He had showered and his hair was still damp. The scents of cedar and leather were stronger now, and I could smell his coconut conditioner. He was wearing a pair of jeans and a plaid flannel shirt over a Sevendust T-shirt. We made eye contact, and I felt it everywhere. In my imagination, he leaned in and kissed me. In reality, he gave me a casual wave and strolled back to the stage to be a cool guy who played in a band.

I spotted Seth and patted myself on the back for knowing he was a musician. He removed a tenor sax from a beat-up case and clipped it to his neck strap as he chatted with the guy next to him. Seth was wearing a pair of crazy wool pants, a funky button-up shirt, and a houndstooth sports jacket that was a little too big. My eyes moved to the man he was chatting with; Dugan was a slender guy a couple inches shorter than Kane. He had a nice smile, and I imagined he was soft-spoken and hard to ruffle. Dugan Van Huzon had dark Italian eyebrows and shoulder-length wavy brown hair. He had a clean shave, but I could see dark five o'clock shadow under the surface. He was wearing jeans, a sweater with leather patches at the elbows, and a pair of Vans. Dugan was systematically sorting out the sound system and I watched as he slung a bass guitar over his shoulder. I could tell he was one of those guys who embodies what it means to be a musician, I pictured him reaching up on tiptoes to play a keyboard when he was a toddler. I wondered how they all met, maybe they had gone to school together.

And then a woman climbed the wide wooden steps of the gazebo in some sort of spectacular fashion that made me feel like an awkward prepubescent. Damn. And then I realized that was Sunny's cousin Olive. Olive Steele was the lead singer and keyboard player of Raising Kane, and I wondered how her dark vibe would blend with the three hippies she shared the stage with. Olive was tied into a corseted black dress, straight out of the eighteen-sixties. She had dark hair that stopped mid-back and a choker crafted from four strands of pearls and a cameo surrounded the pale skin of her neck. She was wearing tall lace-up boots with a fancy heel that would send someone like me into a frantic dance to regain my balance. The whole thing would inevitably result in a broken ankle or two. I followed her with my eyes as she chided the one with the mutton chops for the wrinkles in his secondhand sport jacket. Olive's voice was a combination of Stevie Nicks and Janis Joplin. Her almond-shaped nails were painted blood red, and her aesthetic was Civil War

Vampire. I bet she smelled like hand rolled cigarettes, gunpowder, and sex.

Someone tapped my shoulder, and I looked up to see Sunny. We hugged for a long time and then fell into the type of conversation you have with someone you've known your whole life. She grabbed my hand and dragged me to the gazebo so she could introduce me to Olive. Kane shook his head and smiled, and Dugan told me to watch the cords as Sunny dragged me away. We made it back to the place on the wall before someone stole our spot. The distance melted away as we danced in the same park we played in as children. When the music stopped and people dispersed, Sunny and I sat on the low rock wall and swung our feet. Sunny smoked one of her organic hand-rolled cigarettes and we shared a joint. The moonlight sparkled on the pond and the air smelled like dew. Kane and Dugan were rolling cords and wires when we walked by, the two of us waved and Kane hollered over that I should join him for a fire in the backyard. I played it cool, but Sunny made eyebrows and wide eyes at me before we parted ways.

When I was alone in my apartment, I must admit that I did a little happy dance in the kitchen. I leaned over the sink and devoured a package of stale peanut butter crackers I'd found in the junk drawer. There was something about Kane I liked, something besides his dark chocolate eyes, his dark chocolate voice, and his acoustic guitar, or the fact that he smelled like cedar and leather and coconut. Something more than the fact that he played it safe. I was feeling good and didn't even acknowledge the butterflies as I bounced down the stairs to the back door. I stopped in my tracks when I saw Kane sitting around the fire with a woman, Lola curled up at her feet. The two of them had drinks and were passing a joint back and forth. Crap. I wanted to retreat, maybe they hadn't seen me, he waved,

"Amelia, we're over here!"

Kane smiled and the woman waved at me. I waved back but wanted to crawl into a hole. I opened my mouth to tell him I just remembered I had to go alphabetize my silverware drawer. He gestured me over to an empty chair,

"Come join us!"

I pulled up my big-girl panties, pinched the bridge of my nose, and took a deep breath as I approached the circle of Adirondack chairs. I shifted my eyes between the two of them and stood there staring like an idiot. I finally managed to create a mouthful of words,

"Is this your girlfriend?"

They both laughed heartily,

"Look closer, this is my twin sister."

That was when I realized Constance Buchanan was the female version of Kane. Same beautiful dark chocolate eyes and perfect teeth, same dark wavy hair and smile. She was a couple inches taller than me and athletic. Connie was the kind of woman who could rock a pair of black leggings and a jean jacket with tall leather boots. Turns out, she was a drug and alcohol counselor by day, and a whiskey-drinking, weed-smoking bad ass by night. No judgment here, we all need to drown our demons somehow. I was a little high myself, so my mind took a detour, and I wondered if it was possible to drown your actual demons. You'd probably just need to hold their heads under the surface until they stop struggling.

After some small talk, the two of them told me more about modern-day Bunman. I'm not talking about the seasonal leaf peepers and maple syrup, or the best places to find a good pizza pie or maple creemee. I'm talking about the stuff that goes on backstage, the stuff that happens behind closed doors, the secrets only the locals know about. According to Kane and Constance Buchanan, there was a mob family in Bunman and sometimes things were not what they seemed. Even though that was the third time someone had mentioned the mob, at that point, I was sure everyone around there was out of their goddamn minds. I played like that's the first I had heard of it,

"Wait, there's a mob family living in Bunman!?"

Kane continued and gestured,

"Salvatore Moretti, the old man running The Meat Boss, is the big salami around here, if you know what I mean."

I thumbed toward the deli,

"That old meat fart is in the mob; do you mean like the geriatric version? Watch out or he'll throw his walker at you?"

I leaned closer and kept my voice low, like I was telling a secret, cupping my hand at the side of my mouth,

"Psst, did you hear about Salvatore? He got busted for smuggling laundered money in the lining of his Depends, don't tell anyone."

I shook my head and concluded my rant with a little more sarcasm, once again thumbing toward the deli,

"Yeah, that old fart is in the mob."

I wheeze-laughed, picturing the haggard, leather-faced sixty-year-old asshole from the deli as he tried to run after someone or gather enough strength in his arthritic knuckles to use a piano wire around someone's neck. The two of them looked at each other and scrunched their faces, maybe I wasn't supposed to be high for that conversation. I shrugged and Kane continued,

"This is serious, Amelia. I'm not kidding, Bunman has a strong mafia presence."

Kane had to be shitting me. I lived here when I was little and there weren't any big important Italian men with pompadours and pinky-rings tooling around in black sedans with tommy guns and Cuban cigars. I was over it, but he kept going,

"Sal's sons are involved too. His oldest son Giuseppi is thirty-six, divorced, and runs the Italian restaurant across the alley from Muddy Waters."

Constance chimed in to tell me Giuseppi Moretti was sexy as hell, but intimidating, and that she would 'hit that' if she had the chance. Vincenzo, or Vinny, was twenty-four, spoiled, and one of his father's favorite minions. As you'll recall, Vincenzo is the charmer I crossed paths with at Whimsy. And besides Sunny, I heard he enjoyed canoodling with rich businessmen's wives. Let me interject here, that meant Sunny was involved with a douche bag who really was in the mafia. Who knows, maybe Vinny would get kidnapped by an angry husband.

"Sal and his wife, Mary, run the deli, and everyone around here is pretty sure it's a drug front or something. At one time or another he's been suspected of extortion, blackmail, money laundering, drug trafficking, and contract killing. He has high-priced mafia lawyers, so he's never been convicted of anything."

I thumbed toward the deli again, a statement instead of a question,

"That old fuck."

It was dark but I could see Kane rolling his eyes at me before he leaned forward and squinted across the fire, he talked slow,

"He's only like sixty. Do you need training wheels for this conversation? Yes, Amelia, that 'old fuck' is involved in all kinds of shady shit."

Local businessmen were known to go missing or turn up dead. Mafia money and threats kept the Bunman Police Department busy looking the other way. Sal was one of those people who played nice until someone said no, and then the house of cards would come crashing down. The target would end up taking an involuntary toaster bath or find themselves at the bottom of Clover Lake with a bullet hole in their forehead. I wondered if Vinny's 'jobs' were actually 'hits.'

"My aunt never mentioned any of this."

Connie leaned forward,

"You didn't need to know any of this until you decided to move here, but it's important that you're aware of what's going on. As a woman, you need to know who you can trust, and who you can't. Giuseppi is the second in command of the group, he has a presence about him, and he has nice eyes or something. He's scary but there's something about him, you'll see what I mean when you meet him. I think he means well. And I'm not sure what he's holding over their heads, but Sal works his sons like a couple of marionettes."

Somehow, it felt better hearing that information from a woman. I believed Kane, but I *really* believed Connie, sort of. I felt uneasy about how naive I was when I moved back, but at that point I was able to pretend it was all just some rampant urban legend. Sure, Roundelay, Massachusetts was full of crazies, my exes, and my mother, but I was starting to wonder if I'd made a huge mistake. Was I going to be in danger? No, right? I was in Bunman to find refuge from the bullshit back home, not to get sucked into some other hyped-up crap.

I fell asleep on the futon that night, cuddled up under a tattered quilt, I tossed and turned but finally fell asleep. In the morning, I retrieved one of Kane's lattes and sipped it as I people watched from my living room window. Sunny was meeting me to go to the Farmer's Market in town. I put on my favorite pair of jeans and a Whimsy t-shirt before braiding my hair. I spritzed my wrists with Alien Elixir, dug through my purse for some lip gloss, and shoved my feet into my dingy white Chuck Taylors.

As I sat on a stool at the coffee bar downstairs, sipping another latte, I flipped through the paper. Two women on a walk found the body of Drake Stevens in a pile of brush near the dog park. The Vermont State Police retrieved the body, but the cause of death wouldn't be determined until an autopsy took place. Stevens' car was found in his garage and none of his personal effects were missing. His wife told police Drake left around ten o'clock last night to meet with someone and never returned. Well, that's nice.

Sunny strolled across the threshold with her hair in a French braid and glamorous-looking yellow sunglasses on her head. We ventured across town, and I bought a handmade mug from To The Brim with some herbal tea from Within Apothecary. I picked out a pair of Blue Skye Fringe earrings that reminded me of my vintage denim and well-loved sneakers. Sunny bought CBD caramels from 802 Craft Cannabis and three gorgeous, beaded plant stakes from Creations by Candra. We indulged in some drool-worthy pastries from Stevens Farm Fruits and Market, and the woman running the booth was even sweeter than her cupcakes.

After the market, we hopped up on the low wall at the park and sat there for hours. Sunny smoked one of her organic hand-rolled cigarettes and we shared a joint. I told Sunny about my ex, and she told me a little more about her relationship with Vinny. She had tried to break it off a number of times, but he would turn into a different person. He would rage and make threats and sometimes she would fear what he could do to her as he tantrumed in the loss of control. She didn't go into details that day, but I knew whatever he did triggered her in some way and scared her into staying.

As Sunny stared across the park, I recognized parts of her that hadn't changed, and parts of her that had. I sat cross-legged and braided the loose strawberry blonde curls framing her face. We talked about trying to find 'The Fortress,' a cluster of bent oaks and pricker bushes on the edge of a wildflower field, Mother Nature had formed a shelter to protect us from the scary things and the chaos. That little cluster of bent over branches, broken pieces, and dead things, offered safety in the storm. My mind drifted away to those days, so many years ago, when we were little girls. The times we would huddle together in some hollowed out rotting tree, or play make believe in 'The Fortress,' listening for our mothers to call us from back porches at dinner time.

Sunny was tough and knew how to handle herself but what was going on inside was a different story. It was hard to keep the tears at bay when I realized she was still running from her demons. But then again, I was running from my demons, too. A tear rolled down Sunny's cheek and she rested her head on my shoulder,

"Where did all the time go?"

Tears fought their way to the surface, and I fought with the feelings in my throat,

"I don't know."

I kissed the top of her head and wanted to help her so badly but knew I couldn't save Sunny now, any more than I could when we were little. All I could do was love her no matter what, and make sure she had someone to run into the forest with whenever she needed to hide.

CHAPTER 3
FREQUENT FLIER

I'D BEEN IN BUNMAN for a little over a month and had fallen into a nice routine. Most mornings, I ate in front of the fake fireplace, flipped through the newspaper, and savored a maple oat latte before helping at Whimsy. One thing about Bunman was that it brought back all kinds of childhood memories, the good ones, and the bad. I rolled my eyes at how ordinary my family managed to look from the outside. I grew up in the 'look the other way' and 'sweep it under the carpet' family. Everything was fine as long as our big white farmhouse looked good from the outside, especially the curtains, the curtains had to look good from the outside. Anyone who knew the truth about my life would tell you my family did a bang-up job holding up the facade. My school friends thought I had perfect parents, the perfect house, the perfect life. My school friends, and most of my family, had no idea that the perfect-looking house was responsible for the systematic deconstruction of my soul. Well, it was my mother, not the actual house, who systematically deconstructed my soul, but more on that later.

A while back, I found a therapist and saw her sometimes twice a week. I told her about getting molested at the neighbor's house, my dysfunctional relationship with my mother, and the obsessive compulsions I used to survive my childhood. Do you want to know what I learned? I learned how to set better boundaries with my therapist. She left me standing in the hall with her waiting room locked, because she had issues 'following a schedule,' would completely forget I had an appointment, or would fall asleep in the middle of the day and the five alarms she set wouldn't wake her up. I also know way more about her life than a patient should. Do you know what I didn't learn? How to manage my trauma response to getting molested, my narcissistic mother, or the OCD I used to comfort myself. What a waste of time. I snapped out of my head when Marlaina plopped down next to me,

"Wanna help over here today? We're slammed."

My wheels were turning, and she knew it,

"It's not hard, I can get you started."

I savored the rest of my latte before dressing in a black Muddy Waters T-shirt, a pair of thrifted jeans, and my dingy white Chuck Taylors. I contemplated life as I braided my unruly curls. I wanted my time there to be a fresh start, a blank slate. I wanted to settle in, make new friends, and even though I was perfectly fine with one-night stands, maybe I'd fall for someone. Maybe I'd finally find myself, and maybe I'd slay a couple of my demons while I was at it.

I don't even know how to describe my relationship with my mother. Setting aside everything that happened when I was a kid, I still don't think we would have had a good relationship, some people just aren't cut out for it. Some people follow the rules when they shouldn't. They get married and have babies, even though they never really wanted a husband or kids. And sometimes when people do that, it shows. Sometimes people like that don't know how to love a child or protect them from the bad people. Sometimes people like that are so resentful that they're living a lie, that they try everything in their power to be the center of attention. But right then, I was far away from all of that.

I was sitting by the fake fireplace in a cozy café, sipping a maple oat latte, hours from home. That was the most peaceful I'd been in a long time. I didn't feel a nagging obligation to visit my mother, and I wasn't worried about running into my ex, his whore, and their lovechild. But I was fighting a constant battle between standing up for myself and being a good little girl. Someday I wouldn't be broken, but right then, I was. If you didn't buckle up before, you should probably do it now.

I was grinding beans for an espresso when I heard dark chocolate talking with Marlaina,

"Did you see this?"

My interest was piqued. I tried to glance in their direction but there was a shelf in the way. I finished an order and brought it to the counter. I walked back to the espresso machine, tapped out the spent grounds, rinsed the stainless-steel pitcher for the steam wand, and eavesdropped. Marlaina asked,

"Where did they find him?"

Kane unfolded the paper and put it on the coffee bar, flattening the folds, his bar rag in a pile on the counter,

"His secretary found him in his office at ten o'clock last night. At first, paramedics thought it was a heart attack but when they rolled him over, they found ligature marks."

There was a pause before Marlaina screeched out,

"Ligature marks!? Like you see on the crime shows?"

Kane glanced around the room and motioned for Marlaina to keep her voice down, people had perked up and looked over when she screeched,

"Yeah, somebody strangled him. Rumor has it, Anthony Esposito owed the mob a lot of money. Also, what was his secretary doing there at ten o'clock at night?"

I mean, if we're not fooling ourselves, the lady was probably meeting him there to bang. The rest of the day was filled with customers stopping in for coffee with a side of gossip about Esposito's murder. People talked about who he was, who he worked for, and why someone might want to kill him. Was he cheating? Was he embezzling money? Was he on the hook for a gambling debt? I couldn't stop thinking about the Moretti family and wondered if they were linked to the murder. I wondered if Esposito was routinely making whoopie with his secretary, maybe her husband caught wind of it. That's two dead bodies in a month, maybe I underestimated the validity of the mafia activity in Bunman. But then I remembered hearing about cement slippers and figured if the mob killed a guy, he'd probably be at the bottom of the lake.

You know what they say, curiosity killed the cat. So, during my lunch break, I strolled over to The Meat Boss to see if I could catch another glimpse of Salvatore Moretti. The store was nice enough but bland. There was an obvious lack of decor, and the place seemed like it was going through the motions without really participating. There were long strings of sausage hanging from hooks. Do mobsters who run a deli use those same hooks to hang dead bodies before turning them into sausage? Maybe it was a drug front. Maybe it looked like a deli, but they used the basement to pack bricks of cocaine or print counterfeit money and then launder it. I shook my head as I went on a little vacation to fantasy land. I still wasn't convinced the old fuck was in the mob.

There was a steady flow of customers, shopping for last-minute corned beef and cabbage supplies for St. Patrick's Day. I pretended to look at the jerky and dry rubs and started a subtle conversation with the woman behind the counter. Mary Moretti, or Mama Moretti as she was affectionately known, was in her late fifties and trim. She had crowns and her dark blond hair was styled into a shag. In between customers, Mary sat at the counter in a tall director's chair that said 'MAMA' on the back of the seat. I introduced myself as Maggie's niece and Mary's eyes lit up,

"You must be Amelia!"

Mary came around the counter and hugged me, not one of those half-assed floppy-fish hugs like my mother gave, a real hug. It caught me off guard and then Mary kissed me on both cheeks. Salvatore Moretti emerged and as a man entered the deli, Mary said,

"Sally, this is Maggie's niece, Amelia."

The haggard old fuck flicked his eyes at me and grunted or something. I lifted my hand in some sort of half-assed wave. He greeted the man and that was the end of it, I shifted my eyes back to Mary,

"Are you friends with my aunt?"

She smiled,

"Maggie is good to me, and I am grateful to have her in my life. When I'm feeling down, she lifts me up, Maggie is a true friend."

She leaned forward, winked, and whispered,

"She's the one I'd call to help me bury the body."

What!? I'm sure I made some sort of expression with my eyebrows. Anyway, something about that woman melted my heart. It made me happy to know she had my aunt as her ride or die, and I wasn't surprised Maggie had become friends with her. I told Mary I'd be right back, asked Marlaina about Mary's usual order, and five minutes later, I crossed the threshold of the deli with a lavender rose latte. Mary's eyes smiled when the floral scented steam hit her nose, and I slid the cup across the counter. I told Mary I'd see her again soon and hollered to Sal as I walked away, lying,

"Nice to meet you."

He clenched his jaw at me, and I went back to Muddy Waters. When the cafe closed, I asked Maggie for the full scoop on Sal, but I'm giving you the Readers Digest version. Maggie has lived in Bunman her entire life and first heard Sal's name being thrown around when she was in elementary school, even though he was in high school by then. Salvatore Moretti was always kind of a dick. He was the kid yanking pigtails, stealing lunches, and playing teacher's pet while leaving push pins on their chair. From the beginning, Sal acted like he was better than everyone, knew it all, and could do no wrong. Maggie heard people talking when Sal played baseball in junior high, his father would roll up in a big black Cadillac sedan. Aldo Moretti would talk about himself during the whole game instead of cheering for his son. One time, Sal struck out. Aldo stood up and berated him in front of everyone, including the girl he liked. After the outburst by his father, Sal quit baseball and refused to go back. People felt sorry for him, because everybody knows that if a parent acts like that in public, it's only a whisper of what that kid's getting at home. People like that should pull out.

By the time Maggie was in eighth grade, Sal was married, had a kid, and was blossoming into a carbon copy of the sociopath who raised him. He stepped on people if they stood in his way or declined his advances. Over the next decade he nurtured his familial mafia connections, here and in Jersey, and bragged about being untouchable. Sal surrounded himself with other local mobsters and their associates. Rumor has it, he used the basement of his store to traffic drugs, print money, or whatever other nefarious shit mobsters do. Maggie said all the Morettis have killed people before, including Mary, Vincenzo, and Giuseppi. I hadn't yet laid eyes on Giuseppi Moretti.

"Do you think the Morettis had anything to do with that guy who got murdered?"

She shook her head,

"The mob doesn't leave bodies behind."

I knew she was right, and with that, I'd reached my limit of information for the day. Later that week, Maggie ordered lunch and sent me next door to pick it up. The aroma of fresh garlic knots and Mama Moretti's marinara made my mouth water before I crossed the threshold. Giuseppi's Italian Ristorante had dim lighting in the dining room, and there were oil lamps on the tables. People on lunch breaks feverishly devoured the pasta special. Three men sat at the bar watching a recap of the last night's game. Classic Italian music was playing, and the restaurant had old school Italy vibes crossed with dark mafia energy. As long as that building stood, it might have been my favorite place in Bunman. That restaurant was cozy and mysterious, and everything about it made me happy.

I had been there to pick up pizza before that, but that day was the first time I laid eyes on Giuseppi Moretti, he is exactly what you're expecting him to be. He was about six inches taller than me, stocky but in good shape. Giuseppi Moretti had a presence about him. He was dressed in dark slacks and a white button-up shirt, the top two buttons left open, sleeves rolled up a couple times. He had dark brown eyes and a dark pompadour with a hint of gray at the temples. He had a gold chain and a nice watch. Giuseppi Moretti smelled like Tom Ford Tobacco Vanille, and Cuban cigars. He was sexy and intimidating, like Connie said, and I would also probably 'hit that' if I had the chance. Giuseppi shook my hand and then pulled me in and kissed me on both cheeks. I smelled the whiskey on his breath, and I think I made an involuntary sound of pleasure. My body sizzled with energy when that man touched me, I'm not sure if it was attraction or unadulterated fear. That was the first time I heard his deep, sexy Jersey-style Italian accent,

"You must be Maggie's niece, Amelia. I'm Giuseppi, but my friends call me Seppi."

He winked and even though Giuseppi, excuse me, Seppi, was involved in some shady shit with his father, and had probably killed people, my first impression was a good one. I kind of liked the guy. Even though Seppi was a big shot, he still bagged lunch orders, worked the register, and took dinner reservations. He was extremely good looking but I'm not sure what first attracted me to him. Maybe it was the whole aesthetic I was drawn to, the inner sanctum of it all. I watched his body language and listened to his voice, and none of it raised red flags or made me think that guy was a douche bag. I've been duped before, but I was comfortable around him and felt like Seppi was a straight shooter, no pun intended. I made a mental note not to piss the guy off, I didn't want to end up at the bottom of Clover Lake.

Sunny and I had lattes and went to the food co-op on Saturdays. On Sundays, I'd get two lavender rose lattes and spend time with Mary Moretti. The cafe and food co-op were great places to hear gossip. I rarely saw Sal, but when I did, he was red-faced and smelled like sausage, stress sweat, and whatever kind of aftershave rich old fucks wear. By then, I could manage Whimsy when my aunt was out of town.

Maggie left me in charge while she visited friends in California for a few weeks. Yes, I said a few weeks. It was fine, I could handle it, and if I was drowning, Kane would throw me a rope. I knew how to make the schedule, record payroll, and order supplies. I could man the helm if it wasn't for too long, otherwise I'd panic. I had a twinge of fear the first time she handed over her big set of keys, but I got familiar with the regulars. The newest frequent flier was a hunk who'd been in three times that week, not that I had counted.

If you're wondering about Kane, we worked together and sometimes we hung out by the fire in the back yard. He was a big help when my aunt was gone and carried heavy things up the stairs to my apartment. He hooked up my smart TV and Wi-Fi. We had chemistry and the way he looked at me made me melt. He tucked loose curls behind my ear sometimes, it was this intimate gesture he would do, even when other people were around. It was this indication that there was something going on between us, even though we hadn't talked about it. We weren't something but we weren't nothing. Kane made me feel cared for, and when I was with him, I didn't feel as broken. That might not seem like a big deal to some people, but I know someone listening to this story will understand, and you'll understand if you feel broken too.

Sometimes, Kane would make me a latte on his personal espresso machine and deliver it in his pajama pants. Sometimes, I made homemade bread and left a warm loaf in a basket on his welcome mat. I would kiss my hand and touch his door before walking away, it kind of became a routine, this sly exchange of lattes and fresh bread. When we were near each other, we stood closer than strangers but not as close as lovers, his touch did something to my insides.

I was emerging from the office on my way to retrieve a panini from the café when my frequent flier appeared. He put his hand out to me,

"I don't know if I formally introduced myself, I'm Marco Masiello."

We shook hands. He asked,

"How are you today?"

I gave Marco a once-over and made a mental note of his forearms, and the rest of him for that matter. I told myself to pull it together for crying out loud. I was pretty sure that Marco guy was going to ask me out or something, and I was trying to figure out if I was going to accept. I nervously doodled on a pad of heart-shaped sticky notes but tossed them under the counter because I thought they would send the wrong message. When I looked up, we made eye contact. I wanted to drench Marco in gravy and sop him up with a biscuit. After way too long I replied,

"I'm good, how are you?"

Marco shifted,

"Oh, pretty good. I'm trying to find some handyman work. Sometimes the big guys take weeks to fit you in, but I'm flexible so if you need anything, let me know."

Alright, that's it, I was convinced he was trying to get down my pants. Although, I'd seen him at Muddy Waters a couple times, so I realized maybe Marco was just a nice guy trying to find handyman work. Also, he was too hot to be interested in me, maybe I was the one who wanted to get down *his* pants. I focused. Maggie had a list of little things she wanted done, ahead of some planned renovations. Marco seemed nice but it made me anxious to have people in my space, I'd usually hide. I declined his offer because I'm a big pussy, but knew I'd say yes if he asked again.

"That's OK, doll. I'll check back next time I'm around. Here's my card, shoot me a text if you change your mind."

Doll? I took the card. Marco winked and I watched his ass as he walked out the door. I sighed, if I didn't get a little action soon, I was going to have to dust off my electric ear cleaner, if you know what I mean. I was sitting at Maggie's desk staring at Marco Masiello's business card when Kane walked through the door.

"Your food's getting cold."

He placed my lukewarm panini on the desk, and I handed him the business card,

"This guy has been in here a couple times this week, and today he offered to do handyman work. Do you know him?"

Kane read the front and back of the card nonchalantly, shrugged and handed it back,

"I know of him, but I don't know-him, know-him."

He gestured toward the deli,

"I think he works for Moretti."

OK, buddy. Did everyone around here have to bring everything back to the Morettis? I stayed on task,

"Maggie needs a couple things done around here but I don't like strangers coming into my space."

"Amelia, you're running a store, strangers come into your space all day."

I waved him away,

"I mean, it makes me nervous when people come in to fix things."

"The next time he comes in, text me, and I'll come over and give him a once over for you."

Kane kissed me on the top of the head and retreated to the world of coffee beans and paninis. I wanted him to kiss me somewhere else.

CHAPTER 4
MR. FIX-IT

WHEN MARCO came back a few days later, I texted Kane before greeting him. I poked my head out of the office and waved casually,

"Hi Marco."

"Hi Amelia, I hope you're having a good day."

I saw Kane out of the corner of my eye, and he stood on the other side of the double doors. Marco continued,

"I just wanted to check with you again about the repairs. I've been thinking, and I know the problem might be money. I need the hours for a certification, so I don't mind doing the work for free, I can even come in when the store is closed, so I'm not underfoot."

Kane strolled in like he wasn't standing there all along,

"Hi there."

Kane gestured toward the cafe with his bar rag,

"You're a handyman? I've got quite a few things in the cafe that need to be repaired."

Marco winked at me and disregarded the part about Kane needing repairs,

"You heard that right, I'm trying to get Amelia to let me do some work she needs, free of charge and after hours so I'm not underfoot."

Kane shrugged at me with his face and said,

"I think you should go for it; it's hard getting work done around here and it usually breaks the bank, Maggie would agree. This guy is extending an olive branch, and I think you should take it."

Marco looked at me expectantly, and Kane stood there swinging his rag like I was wasting his time. I rolled my eyes so hard I could see my brain. Was I going to say yes? Sure. Was I going to tell my aunt? Absolutely not. I shrugged,

"OK."

Marco smiled, winked, and said,

"Great! I'll be here tomorrow, bright and early."

Ever the over-sharer,

"Umm, I'm going to New Hampshire with my friend tomorrow, a woman named Sofia will be opening the store at ten."

Marco shifted nervously and blushed,

"Maybe you can let me take you to dinner in exchange for my services."

There it was. I moved my eyes from Marco to Kane and back to Marco. I squinted and pointed to the middle of my chest,

"You want to thank me for letting you do free handyman work by taking me out to dinner?"

Marco shifted, bashfully,

"Just leave a key at the cafe along with a list of the things you want me to do, and I'll be here bright and early tomorrow morning."

Once Marco was out the door, I looked at Kane with both palms up and shook my head,

"What the hell is happening!?"

Kane clenched his jaw. I crossed my arms, looked at him impatiently and exhaled a long dramatic sigh. Annoyed dark chocolate wafted into my ears,

"What is happening, is that I talked you into accepting free handyman work, and apparently I'm trying to get you laid while I'm at it."

Kane threw the bar rag over his shoulder and retreated to the world of spent coffee grounds and muffin crumbs. I closed my eyes and pinched the bridge of my nose. I didn't like this situation one bit. My entire life I'd been called uptight and hyper-vigilant. Well, I'd show them who was uptight and hyper-vigilant. Before I could change my mind, I marched right down to the hardware store and made a copy of the key to the front door of Whimsy.

That evening, Kane invited me over and I sat anxiously on the couch, watching him putter around in his kitchen. I played with Lola's ear as he poured lemonade, and we moved to the sun porch I could see from mine. I'm not sure what time we went out there, but the sun set, and we watched the stars blink to life. We ordered Chinese and Kane pulled out a bottle of liquor. We ate egg rolls and rice noodles. And then we smoked weed and drank tequila. He told me about his friendship with my aunt,

"After Maggie's husband died, she stopped going on her casino trips, so I offered to go with her, and over time, we became close. She moved into the store next to mine and the rest is history. Your aunt came into my life at the perfect time, and I think we're good for each other."

Kane and I listened to records, talked about life, and shared stories about Maggie. The electricity bouncing between us was insane. At the end of the evening, He walked me to the door and tucked a loose curl behind my ear. Our eyes met, and soon after, our mouths found each other for the first time. It was the most intense kiss I'd ever had. He gently scooped the back of my head, leaned down and our noses touched briefly. Kane rubbed his nose against mine playfully, and I could feel the warmth of his breath. Our lips parted and our tongues danced delicately, stopping for smaller kisses so we could taste each other's lips. That kiss was not a means to an end, but it was confirmation that we both wanted to take things to the next level.

Bright and early the next morning, I was savoring a latte at Muddy Waters when Marco moseyed in wearing jeans that showed off his ample package. His t-shirt clung to his chest and arms in all the right places. A chain hung around his neck. He had olive skin, deep brown eyes, and a scar through his right eyebrow. Marco was sporting a fresh shave, and if he had cigarettes rolled into his sleeve, he would have resembled an Italian James Dean. That was the first time I'd seen him fresh out of the shower, and if he smelled as good as he looked, I'd be in trouble. I shook my head at myself. For crying out loud, don't be a slut. I thought I'd be at Sunny's before he got there and I contemplated hiding under the coffee table. Instead, I took a deep breath, pulled up my period-stained granny panties, and greeted him,

"Good morning, Marco."

Kane's eyes followed Marco as he detoured from the order line to the fake fireplace. He put his toolbox on the table and came close to me, he smelled like warm spices and musk; I made an imperceptible sound low in my throat. Oh my God, he was hot, and I wanted to lick his face. I tried to play it cool. He winked,

"How are you this morning?"

Marco's eyes were gentle, and his dark hair was damp and tousled into waves. I dropped my gaze and picked at the skin next to my thumbnail while wrangling the ball of nerves in my throat, I hoped my voice didn't crack when I spoke,

"I'm leaving shortly, if you're done before the store closes, you can give the key to Sofia. If you leave after that, please lock up on your way out and I'll get the key from you when you're done. I appreciate this."

Kane rolled his eyes and then waved his hands and apologized to the woman at the counter, who thought he was rolling them at her. She flipped him off, pivoted, and sauntered out the door. Smooth. I made eye contact with Marco again and my nipples got hard.

"You're welcome, doll."

He touched my hand, and my hackles went up. If there's one thing I don't like, it's feeling like I'm being worked over. If it wasn't for Kane thinking this was a great idea, I would have put the kibosh on the entire thing a long time ago. For a second time, I told Marco I was going to be two hours away and handed him the key to my aunt's store. I know, I'm an idiot. I told Marco, if he needed anything, Kane would be next door until the cafe closed.

I didn't have bubble-gut or the nervous shits at Sunny's apartment, but as soon as we were on the highway, I felt like I'd made a huge mistake. I was riding along to an estate sale to bid on a large collection of vintage books my aunt wanted for the store, so I wasn't going to make Sunny go back. She could sense I was ruminating on something because I wasn't saying anything,

"What's up, fucker?"

I shrugged, but if I had been alone, I would've turned around. My aunt would kill me if she knew I gave some stranger a key to her store, what was I thinking? Sofia wouldn't be opening Whimsy for another two hours; I spiraled with panic. Something was off, why was that guy so insistent on doing free repairs? Why had he started coming around after Maggie left? Sunny told me to smoke a joint, so I did, and then I tried to enjoy my day with her. Before I put it out of my mind, I asked Kane to check on Marco.

Kane waited an hour or two and then nonchalantly popped in, under the guise of bringing Sofia some lunch. Marco was busy removing big storm windows, and said he was about to run to the hardware store. He told Kane he needed access to the electrical panel so he could change an outlet. Kane told Marco he'd have to wait until I was around to unlock the door to the cellar stairs. According to Kane, the two of them talked for a few minutes, the guy appeared to know what he was doing, and I should go enjoy my day. Kane asked Sofia if she was comfortable being alone with Marco, and she replied with an expression that made him feel like it was a stupid question. With that, he retreated to the world of steamed milk and caramel swirls with a bar rag over his shoulder.

As soon as I got home that evening, I dragged Kane downstairs so I could make sure everything was as it should be. The store was locked, and the list of repairs was on the counter under a note written in purple on one of my heart-shaped sticky notes. 'Hey Doll, I'll be finishing my chores tomorrow...your place or mine?' With a winky face. Wonderful. I threw the purple pen in the trash and washed my hands. I walked out of the bathroom and threw the pad of sticky notes in the trash on top of the pen. I sprayed the entire counter with disinfectant and wiped the surface with a rag. Kane stared at me,

"What is happening!?"

I stopped wiping the counter, looked up at him, and barked,

"WHAT!?"

"You are very clearly having some sort of an episode, what are you trying to accomplish?"

I threw the rag on the counter, flipped Kane off with both hands and stomped up the stairs to my apartment. I couldn't shake the cooties coming from that note. Kane did his best to distract me, but I spent the evening pacing between both apartments, moving things around, and feeling uneasy. I put my tea bags in alphabetical order by flavor. After I ate, I went to Kane's, and we shared some tequila before binge-watching Psych. Don't get me wrong, my TV was fine, but Kane had a freaking surround sound system. When I watched my show there, it felt like I was standing right next to Shawn Spencer as he pretended to be a psychic detective. I could only imagine what happened when Kane watched porn in there.

In the morning, I clomped downstairs dramatically and ate cold pizza while chatting with Sofia. She had long dark curly hair, big brown eyes, and a Spanish accent. She was short like me, a little curvier, and at that moment she was four or five months pregnant. I knew Kane had asked her, but I wanted to make sure Sofia was comfortable around Marco. She moved her eyes from her romance novel to my face,

"I have uncles who traffic drugs, and counterfeit money. I've seen some shit, I'm not afraid of that asshole."

Sofia lifted her dress and revealed the handgun strapped to her upper thigh; I choked on a mouthful of pizza. She let out a bark of laughter and dismissed me to the office. I am not ashamed to say that a pregnant woman with a Glock was preventing my day from involving bubble-gut, the shits, and a Valium.

It wasn't long before Marco came strolling through the door with his toolbox and a coffee. This time, I didn't fall for his winking, his cologne, or his nice forearms, I was all business. I thanked him again for doing the work before he said,

"I need to get to the breaker box and the door to the basement stairs is locked."

I texted Kane so he'd pop in unannounced. I scooped up the basket of miscellaneous keys under the register, and Sofia patted her gun. I rolled my eyes and stomped down the hall, seriously, I was starting to wonder if I was in the Twilight Zone. What the hell was happening? Thirty seconds later, Kane called my name. I told him we were down the hall, and he casually strode toward me with a to-go cup.

"Here's your latte, I didn't want it to get cold, so I figured I'd deliver it."

Had I ordered a latte? I shrugged. Kane winked and put his hand on the small of my back. I thanked him and he asked what we were doing. I sucked steamed milk through the lid and found that it was a scalding hot cup of fucking coffee. I, in fact, had not ordered a latte. I didn't know what to do. I proceeded to swallow the lava creeping its way through my esophagus, tears coming to my eyes. Marco gestured at the cellar door,

"I need to get to the electrical panel so I can install the breaker for the new outlet, I'm hoping to finish up today."

Marco turned to me and winked,

"And then we can schedule that dinner."

I rolled my eyes again, snagged a set of two keys to the basement stairs, and handed one of them to Marco. He unlocked the door, and we followed him down the stairs. We came to the landing with the electrical panel, and controls for the sprinkler system. While the three of us stood there, my gaze drifted to the metal door leading to the basement. The handle was secured with an Abus Granit padlock. I wondered if the big metal door was from its days as part of the deli. If you ask me, it gave off major Chainsaw

Massacre vibes. Marco couldn't get any further than the bottom of the stairs, so we retreated to the world of avocado toast and cappuccinos. The whole situation was making Kane uneasy, or jealous, or something. We went to his office and Kane pushed the door shut, leaning on the edge of his desk with his arms crossed. I paced,

"Something is off about that guy. I know you think I'm overreacting, but I'm telling you, there's something not right. I'm going to thank him, give him a hundred dollars, and call it even. I am not going to dinner, or anything else for that matter."

Kane gestured for me to come to him. Our eyes connected and his gaze softened. He held out his hand and pulled me in. I stood between his knees and when I got close, I could smell coffee beans, sugar, and six-dollar coconut conditioner. Kane tucked a curl behind my ear and I felt electricity. He kissed the top of my head and then my cheek. We stood nose to nose and when I grazed his lips with mine, I felt his breath catch in his throat. I kissed his cheek and looked up at him, when I touched his face, I felt butterflies.

We stood nose to nose again, and this time I was more deliberate when I touched his lips with mine. We kissed more deeply that time and I ran my fingers through his hair, he whimpered. His hand moved along my side and his thumb brushed my breast. Kane unbuttoned my shirt as we kissed and my body was on fire. He kissed my throat and then my collarbone. My bra came off, and Kane was kissing his way to my chest when there was a knock at the door, it was Marco,

"Bro, you know where Amelia's at? I'm all set."

We looked at each other and Kane put his finger to his lips. I held my shirt closed and hid in the closet laughing, tears streaming down my cheeks, praying I wouldn't squeak. I leaned out at the last second to grab my bra from the top of Kane's desk. He opened the door with his hair a mess and his shirt half untucked, and I'm sure he had a boner. He tried to hold it together,

"Haven't seen her, bro. She might be running errands. If you're all set, I'll take the key."

Marco dropped the key into Kane's hand, gripped the door frame, and leaned into the office,

"Dude, you got a girl in here?"

Kane replied, making a muscle,

"No, dude, I was just doing some push-ups."

I held my breath and hoped this conversation was going to wrap up, or else I was going to explode. I was wheeze-laughing as I peeked through the crack at the two of them.

"I'm all set, tell her I'll be in touch about my payment, if you know what I mean."

Marco winked at Kane and walked away. Kane closed the door and locked it, he flailed his arms,

"I was wrong, I hate that guy."

I came out of the closet,

"Why are you all of a sudden agreeing with me?"

Kane sat on his desk,

"He's got an angle, and I don't like it. I think he's trying to get down your pants."

I went palms up,

"That's what I said!"

Kane was pacing. He gestured dramatically and raised his voice,

"Did you hear that? He's looking forward to his 'payment,' and I know what that's code for! It means he did something for you, and now you're obligated to 'put-out,' as payment."

My mouth fell open and I wrinkled my nose, excuse me? Left hand on my hip, bra hanging from one finger, right hand holding my shirt together,

"Put-out!?"

And then I spiraled. I matched Kane's dramatic hand gestures, buttoned my shirt, and raised my voice,

"Oh, do you think he's expecting me to go necking down on Lovers' Lane?"

I looked at him and narrowed my eyes,

"And then, maybe we can work our way up to some heavy petting."

I paused and threw my hands in the air,

"What the hell are you talking about!?"

I gestured at nothing. What on earth was I going to do? Seriously, I was not going on a date with that guy. I was done, he was canceled, swipe left. I dwelled on it all day but managed not to let it ruin my night. I did, however, take a shot of whiskey and an edible and stress-cleaned both apartments while listening to a song on repeat for three hours. Let's see, what else? I ordered a seventy-dollar pillow and a new fitness tracker because I should start exercising. Later that night, I put a sheet mask on my face and ate a pint of Ben & Jerry's with a fork, while standing in the front window with the light on like an absolute fucking psycho. So, you tell me, maybe I did let it ruin my night.

CHAPTER 5
A BUMP IN THE NIGHT

MARCO CAME AROUND a few days later, and as expected, he was sweet as pie. I was afraid I'd end up freaking out or flee like a feral cat, but I held it together. The more I looked at him, the more I hoped he would ask me on that date. Instead, Marco thanked me for letting him do the work and had me sign an official-looking piece of paper where he tallied up his hours. He gave me another business card, winked, and walked his sweet ass right out the door. That was the end of it? I stood there holding my breath, staring at the business card, and Sofia barked from her stool at the counter,

"HA! That's it!? That's all he's got!?"

I rolled my eyes. I don't want to tell you how much time I spent running through scenarios and conversations, so I would be prepared for every possible situation if he persuaded me to go to dinner. Then he just came in, asked me to sign a paper, and left. I mean good, but what!? Sofia chimed in again,

"You dodged a bullet, that one's got a small pee-pee anyway."

I locked eyes with her, raised an eyebrow, and smirked,

"If the bulge in his pants is any indication, I'd say you're way off on that one."

She waved me away dismissively and returned to her romance novel. I spent most of that day shut in the office doing payroll and playing on my phone. When I was sick of being in Maggie's office, I went next door and sat with Kane.

Most nights we ate at his place, but that night seemed different, it felt like he was asking me on a date. After a candlelit dinner of homemade lasagna, garlic bread, and salad, Kane came to me and held my hands. He kissed me differently that time. We sipped tequila while we talked and cuddled. Our mouths came together passionately, and I could feel him pressing against me. He pulled off my shirt and kissed my chest. I rubbed his stomach and teased at his waist. We discovered each other with our mouths and fell asleep in each other's arms...until two in the morning.

Lola stood up on her blanket and barked. Kane slid out of bed, pulled on the jeans he had thrown to the floor, and shoved his feet in his sneakers,

"She doesn't bark."

Kane told me to get up and I didn't question it. I put on his sweatpants and my t-shirt. He unlocked a safe in his nightstand and pulled out a Ruger,

"I don't like guns."

His eyes were dark. I squeaked,

"Kane?"

He put his finger to his lips and moved silently across the apartment. He put his ear to the door, went into the hall and paused for a beat. He unlocked the door that led to the cafe and traipsed down the stairs with me trailing behind him. We came out in the hallway across from his office. Kane removed the safety, opened the doors to Whimsy, and listened. Someone was at the bottom of the cellar stairs.

We could see shadows and movement. Kane had the gun out in front of him, my hand was on his back. That is when I realized Marco had plenty of time to make a copy of the key to the store. There was a loud hissing sound. As Kane was advancing to the stairs, we smelled something burning, sparks flying. A loud crackle caused me to make a high-pitched screech. The torch turned off and I peed a little in Kane's sweatpants. Marco called out,

"Amelia? Is that you? Sorry to startle you, doll, I forgot to finish something when I was here,"

Kane swung the door open, advanced, and pointed the gun at Marco. Sarcastically, Kane's voice going up at the end of the question,

"Whatcha doing?"

Marco jumped,

"Jesus!"

Marco was wearing a welding mask and thick suede gloves. Kane moved to him, safety off, gun in front of him. Marco put his hands up, Kane shoved him against the wall, and he slid to the floor. He told me to see what Marco had been doing. I looked between the two of them. Kane gestured toward the door. I stepped over Marco's legs and toolbox, picked up the flashlight, and shined it on the door to the basement. Marco had been trying to cut through the Abus Granit padlock with a torch. Kane unclipped the carabiner from his belt loop and dangled keys in front of Marco,

"What's the problem, can't get into the basement?"

"I was just finishing the work I'm doing for Amelia. I realized I didn't finish something and wanted to come back when the store was closed so I wouldn't be underfoot. I'm just trying to help Amelia, I swear."

"It is two o'clock in the fucking morning, and this is breaking and entering. You're lucky I'm not calling the cops; you need to leave."

Kane lifted Marco by his armpit and marched him up the stairs. I noticed that Marco wasn't resisting, and I was glad Kane had his gun. Kane put his hand out and Marco fished the duplicate store key out of his pocket. Kane pushed the door open and sent Marco into the night, locking up behind him. I spiraled,

"Why was he here!? What was he doing!? Why does he want to get into the basement!?"

Instead of answering my questions, Kane threw his arm around my shoulder, kissed the top of my head, and said,

"You're safe now, I'll protect you."

I said,

"First order of business is getting a new lock on the front door, and I'm not calling Marco Masiello to do it!"

In the morning, I went over for my latte. As I was chatting with Marlaina, I heard Kane's office door open. I glanced up expectantly as someone walked out, and instead of Kane, it was Marco. He stopped in his tracks when he saw me and then couldn't get out of there fast enough. My stomach turned, I clenched my teeth, and then I got pissed. What was going on? I left my coffee on the counter and stomped over to Kane's door. I knocked hard enough that it hurt my knuckles. As the door opened, Kane's eyes were focused on the place Marco's eyes would have been if it had been Marco, except it wasn't Marco, it was me. My blood boiled and I yelled,

"What the fuck is going on here!?"

Kane pulled me into his office and shut the door, he gestured for me to lower my voice. Yeah right, buddy. I put my finger in his face and continued,

"You have a lot of explaining to do. Were you just trying to distract me? Are you in cahoots with Marco? Because that's what it seems like to me and

I'm over it."

I started to cry, Kane reached for me, and I swatted him away,

"And I just did down the pants stuff with you!"

By itself, maybe seeing Marco come out of Kane's office wasn't a big deal but the addition of the down the pants stuff made it sting a little more. My mind raced, I was in a new place and had responsibilities. I really liked Kane and thought he liked me. My past relationship PTSD and fear of abandonment kicked in, so I started sobbing and impulsively said,

"I never want to see you again!"

Kane reached for my arm, and I pulled it back. He was hurt and confused and had tears in his voice, pleading,

"Amelia..."

My eyes overflowed, I was triggered. I grit my teeth and slapped him across the face before storming out of his office. Even then, I knew I wasn't just slapping Kane, I was slapping every man who'd ever hurt me.

When I returned to Whimsy, Sunny and I talked about everything except what was going on in our lives. During her lunch break, we ate greasy hamburgers and salty fries. In the afternoon, once Sunny talked me down from the ledge, she led me to a room down the hall filled with boxes of books from estate sales. She left me to blissfully sniff the bindings and pages of old novels and told me she'd come get me after she tallied up the register. I was sitting alone with my thoughts when I heard her on the phone,

"I can't tonight, I have a headache."

I had no idea what was being said on the other end of the line, but I gathered it was Vinny and he was expecting some attention,

"You'll have to be patient, good things come to those who wait."

Sunny ended the call and shortly after, we went to her apartment. I was in the bathroom when someone came through the front door. She seemed surprised but not like she thought someone was breaking in. I held my breath and put my ear to the door, it was Vinny. He was telling Sunny how much he loved her and that he couldn't stand another minute without her. They had a thing going on, because it seemed to do something for her that he was practically begging her. It was like they were playing a game of cat and mouse,

"I changed my mind, baby. I decided I'd come to you if you're not feeling like going anywhere tonight."

"Vin, I said I have a headache, you'll have to be patient"

His voice got all sexy,

"I don't wanna wait, and I know how to make that headache go away."

I couldn't wait to see what kind of smart-ass response she had for him and when Sunny giggled, I rolled my eyes, oh for crying out loud. I mean he was hot, but did she just call him, Vin? I sat in the bathtub with the curtain drawn, knees tucked to my chest, listening to them have sex. It didn't take them very long. You'd think the guy would have been battling impotence as a result of his guilty conscience. You'd think whacking people would eat you up inside, but what do I know about anything? If I made it a habit to whack people and dump their bodies, I don't think I'd ever sleep again. And what kind of a person does that? I'll tell you what kind, a fucking psychopath. I mean if the rumors are true then we're talking, serial killer material. Either way, they had an arrangement, and I was no one to judge. Even before I got to know Vincenzo Moretti, I knew he had a sweet side, but he also had a dark one. He could be nice but wasn't always. And at that point, he was known to canoodle with other people's wives.

Sunny and I took edibles and ate spaghetti and sauce off paper plates. We made a box of brownies and ate them out of the pan with glasses of milk while they were still warm. She let me borrow pajamas and we curled up in her bed, talking about Kane and Vinny. Sunny thought Kane really liked me, and I thought Vinny was a bad boy with a soft side. We fell asleep cuddling like we did when we were little, under the same quilt Sunny had when she was five years old.

The next two weeks were not great. Sunny's relationship with Vinny ramped up again, she was pretty sure something was going on. They had an agreement of sorts and were not exclusive, but the more Sunny pulled away, the more Vinny tried to convince her he was Prince Charming. He seemed desperate to keep Sunny in his life, presenting her with gifts and over-the-top displays of affection. At the time, it felt to me like he was doing all that while lying, cheating, and playing head games. She had been there before; Vincenzo Moretti tended to view life as one big dick-swinging contest. I did my best to be there for her as she maneuvered shark infested waters but tried to focus on my current situation with Kane.

Kane texted me several times over the first couple days and pleaded for me to let him explain. Maggie told me he was miserable but didn't know why. He left a maple oat latte in a to-go cup outside my kitchen door every morning, and every morning I dumped it down the drain. Then one morning, I opened the door and instead of dumping the maple oat latte down the sink, I drank it. I wrapped my fingers around the cup, knowing he had done the same. Then I curled up under a quilt and sobbed as I drank it.

I really liked Kane, and I thought he liked me back. I was smarter than that. I shouldn't have gotten involved with someone I worked with, and I shouldn't have allowed myself to think things would go anywhere between us. But maybe we were meant to be together. I wrote a note telling him I was ready to talk, and before I could slide it under his door, I tore it into tiny little pieces and flushed it down the toilet.

I decided to give up on men, nothing good ever came of it, I'd just get taken advantage of and manipulated.

I sat on the couch staring at the empty cup and wrapped my fingers around it again. I have a track record for going zero to sixty if I'm hurt or angry, and I was pretty sure that's what I had done. I knew Kane had feelings for me, I could see it in his eyes when I was crying in his office. I felt it every time we locked eyes, or he tucked a loose curl behind my ear, I felt it every time we kissed. I missed him and wanted to know his side of the story because maybe I had it all wrong. What did Marco do besides give me free repairs and try to blow-torch a lock? I went through the motions of doing miscellaneous tasks in my aunt's store but couldn't concentrate. I stopped what I was doing and walked through the double doors to the cafe with Maggie's eyes following me.

I went to Kane's door and leaned in, empty. I peeked into the kitchen. Seth and Marlaina were busy making lattes and lunch specials. I asked,

"Do you know where he is?"

Marlaina leaned into my line of sight,

"Alex stopped by, and they left together. I'm sure they'll be back soon."

I had no idea who Alex was. No big deal, what's another hour or two? By that night, I'd be curled up on Kane's couch watching shows on the big TV with the surround sound system. No problem, I went back to the store and when Maggie didn't have anything for me to do, I helped at Muddy Waters. I made paninis, bagels, and avocado toast before washing dishes and making napkin rolls. I was trying to kill time, where the hell was he? In those moments of solitude, I went through the motions. I imagined what that evening would be like, thought about curling up with Kane and smelling his six dollar coconut conditioner. I evaluated my past relationships and the fact that none of the other guys I had been with were anything like him. Maybe I was changing, maybe I was growing, maybe my taste in men had evolved into some healthy. I thought about shaving my legs and wearing my cute pink panties, maybe we would fall right back into a rhythm. I was feeling lonely but that's not why I wanted to talk to him, I guess I had realized I'd made a hasty decision and maybe it was time for me to own up to it. Maybe it was time for that broken little girl to act like a woman.

But as time ticked and he hadn't returned, I wondered if Kane had been in an accident or if he had been kidnapped by whoever this Alex guy was. How did they know each other? My mind spiraled like it always did but none of the catastrophic scenarios I invented amounted to a fart in a hurricane when it came to what happened next. And none of the imaginary scenarios I invented involved a beautiful woman. I was making small talk with a couple of regulars as I wiped a high-top table in the corner, that's when Kane crossed the threshold with Alex. Time stopped and my heart flew into my throat, I wanted to become invisible. I saw Kane but he didn't see me. I froze and held my breath. He made sure Seth and Marlaina were all set, and then he and Alex disappeared up the stairs to his apartment. If you're wondering, Alex was short for Alexis. Alexis was blonde, beautiful, and Kane seemed to like her. My knees got weak, I sat down hard, put my head in my hands, and completely fell apart. People just sitting there socializing over last night's episode or the latest book they'd read and there I was, crying my little heart out.

CHAPTER 6
SLIPPERY SLOPE

THE TIME FOLLOWING the incident in the cafe was filled with crying fits, bouts of depression, and self-deprecation. Since he had no idea, I wanted to talk to him, he wasn't pressing the issue. There was a maple oat latte outside my door every morning. Some days I drank it and some days I dumped it down the drain. Kane was spending time with Alex, they had been together in college, and from what I heard, he had loved her. I didn't know if they were spending time together as friends, or as lovers, and most days it almost killed me to imagine him with someone else. He had a history with her, so maybe I was a fool to entertain the idea that he would choose me. I was surviving on caffeine and edibles, and if something felt good, I was sure as hell going to do it. Right then, that's what I needed.

Maggie went out of town briefly, and Sofia reminded me that I didn't need any free repairs from, 'needle dick.' I won't tell you what else she called him. She must have manifested 'needle dick's' presence because five minutes later, guess who came through the door. I'm not kidding. I was at Maggie's desk paying invoices when I heard Sofia shout,

"No, you go! We don't need you here!"

I went to investigate the situation and found Marco standing awkwardly on the other side of the counter. He was in belted jeans, a tucked-in henley with the buttons open, and a leather jacket. I kept it professional, maybe he was looking for a gift. I went around the counter,

"What can I do for you?"

He took a deep breath, held it, and exhaled like a pressure cooker letting off steam,

"Can we talk?"

I could tell he had something on his mind, but I wasn't in the mood for his shit. I waved him in,

"Sure, come into the office, I'd love to know why you were blow-torching my lock in the middle of the night."

Marco shifted nervously,

"Can we go somewhere else?"

I went palms up and he could tell I wasn't feeling very friendly. He seemed desperate, pleading,

"I promise, I'm not trying to do anything creepy, I just need to talk to you. We can go wherever you want, preferably not in Bunman."

I was curious what the hell was going on,

"Fine, give me ten minutes."

I finished what I was doing, peed, and met Marco in the parking lot behind the store. We hopped in my car and Marco directed me to a diner twenty miles away. I noticed that even though we weren't saying much, I didn't feel nervous or like I had to fill the silence with pointless small talk. He smelled like warm spices and musk, and he had the perfect amount of stubble. Marco motioned toward his cigarettes, and I nodded. He lit one and cranked the window down a couple inches, blowing smoke into the wind. Part of me felt like I was going behind Kane's back, and part of me knew that if Kane and I were together, he wouldn't be spending time with Alex.

We went to a booth in the back of the diner and Marco sat facing the door. The waitress poured waters, filled our mugs with burnt coffee, and took our orders. We sat there in silence, and I felt my face flush, I am not a fan of wasting my time. Nothing was being said, we just sat there. I worked the wrapper from my straw into a chain of folds. I put cream and sugar in my coffee...I stirred my coffee...I sipped my coffee. I couldn't stand it, threw my spoon down, and stared at him,

"Alright, what is happening!?"

Marco sat straight as an arrow, and it looked like he was going to bail.

"If you run away, I'm not going to look for you, I will leave you here."

He squirmed in his seat,

"I don't know if we should talk here."

I went palms up and shook my head,

"Look, do you have something to say to me, or did we come all the way here so I can watch you wring your hands?"

Marco appeared deflated and couldn't sit still,

"I need to tell you something."

I gestured dramatically and opened my eyes wide,

"Great, we've established that. Could you get to it? I have shit to do."

Tears formed in Marco's eyes as he stared at his napkin. And because I'm not a complete monster,

"OK, how about this, we eat our pancakes and find somewhere else to talk."

A single tear fell onto his napkin and without looking up,

"Thank you."

Breakfast wasn't a complete bust because I love blueberry pancakes with home fries, and I didn't have to pay the bill. Marco seemed to feel a little better once we were back in the car. I drove around until we found a pond with National Forest hiking trails. Even before we got out of the car, I felt like something was going to happen between us. I didn't know this guy from Adam, but I know a person's eyes tell us all we need to know. Marco looked like he had the weight of the world on his shoulders and was ready to put it down.

We walked along a path that led to the pond and climbed onto a boulder that looked out over the water. I pulled out my thrifted flip top tin and shared a joint with Marco Masiello, a stranger, but not. We sat there getting high, looking at the green mountains, the pond, and the birds flying around. I wondered if he ever did things like this to soothe his soul. Sometimes, being in nature is all you need. Marco looked like he needed to be taken care of, and I wanted to take care of him. We faced each other and sat cross-legged, I looked up at him and put my hand on his knee,

"You're safe."

We made eye contact,

"You're not."

I scurried off the big rock and ran toward my car. I was a third of the way there when Marco started gaining on me. I didn't even glance over my shoulder, I just ran as fast as I could. If I got to my car, everything would be okay. With about five hundred feet to go, Marco wrapped his arms around my waist and lifted me off the ground. I kicked and squirmed and tried to scream but he clamped his hand over my mouth, so I licked it.

"Gross, Amelia! I'm not going to hurt you, you're okay!"

My kicks and squirms lost steam, and tears streamed down my cheeks, he was holding me more than restraining me,

"Shh. You're safe, deep breaths, I am not going to hurt you."

He lowered me to the ground, my PTSD had kicked in, so I tucked my knees up to my chest and sobbed. He squatted down in front of me and put his hand on my arm,

"I am not going to hurt you; do you understand that?"

I shrugged and my crying tapered off. I was alive, he hadn't murdered me, I wasn't sausage, I was safe. Marco helped me up, looked around, and held my shoulders,

"The reason I want to talk to you is because there are some things you need to know, but if anyone finds out we had this conversation, I'm dead. I'm risking my life to help you."

Marco positioned himself so we were eye to eye, I saw the softness again,

"I'm not here to hurt you."

I went back to the boulder with Marco, wrapped my arms around my knees again, and stared across the pond. Marco told me everything, he went all the way back to the first time he came into Whimsy. He told me he worked for Salvatore Moretti. A while back, Marco had a conversation with my aunt to warn her that Sal had ordered him to threaten her. But because Marco warned her instead of hurting her, the two of them had become friends. Marco told me they still had coffee sometimes, somewhere besides Bunman.

The first time Maggie left me for a long period of time, she asked Marco to keep an eye on me because Sal was on high alert. I came into the picture and suddenly Sal was giving Maggie a hard time about getting into the basement, she worried he'd do the same to me while she was out of town. I mentally skated over the fact that my aunt was friends with a mob wife, and a known associate of Salvatore Moretti. I couldn't imagine.

"Yeah, but what's down there? Can anyone even get in there with that lock on the door?"

"Kane can."

I wasn't sure what to make of that. Why did Kane have the only key to that lock?

"How did you get into the store that night?"

"I made a copy of the store key while you were gone, and when you handed me the key for the cellar stairs, I kept it."

"Why were you torching the lock in the middle of the night?"

I could tell he was looking for words,

"A long time ago, Sal had access to both basements. He used the one under The Meat Boss for storage, and used the one under Whimsy for equipment, freezers, and other things."

And because I was totally naïve at that point in the story,

"Like storing holiday decorations?"

Marco shook his head and scrunched his eyebrows like I was asking a stupid question,

"No."

The possibility of reality sinking in,

"Like chopping up bodies?"

"You're getting warmer."

I'm sure I had a look of disgust on my face as I recoiled. He continued,

"When your aunt took over that storefront, Sal had us move things out of the basement. Lately, he's been insisting I get down there to make sure nothing was left behind. I want to look around and reassure Sal there's nothing left. If we find something down there, we can destroy it, I know people who can do that. Then I can tell him there's nothing left, and maybe he'll drop it and move on. Until then, anyone standing in his way is a threat and I would never forgive myself if something happened to you."

Somehow, I believed him. He shook his head,

"How can we get in there?"

A light bulb went off in my head,

"There's a door connecting the basement of The Meat Boss to the basement of Whimsy, so maybe there's a door connecting the basement of Whimsy to the basement of Muddy Waters."

I had access to Muddy Waters through the double doors so it would be easy to sneak down there to look, and that's exactly what we planned to do. We went back to Bunman, and I dropped Marco off a quarter mile from town. Sofia asked where I went and what happened, so I reassured her that he was just apologizing for being pushy about the repairs. She waved me away, shook her head like she didn't really care one way or the other. She went back to her romance novel and muttered something under her breath about the size of his penis.

Night fell and I could hear Kane's favorite show when I put my ear to his door (don't judge me) so I knew he was in for the night. I gave Marco the green light and met him at the front door of Whimsy. We went through the double doors to Muddy Waters, made our way through the cafe's kitchen, down the stairs, and into the basement. We used the flashlight on our phones to light the way and found ourselves standing in a room that smelled like coffee beans and sugar. We located the connecting door behind a storage rack and once we moved the rack, we could see there was no lock on the door. I smacked Marco's arm with the back of my hand and pointed,

"Look!"

I turned the knob, and the door swung open, that was easy. Was it too easy? The space under Whimsy was empty other than a couple of stainless-steel tables in the middle of the floor and some deli equipment pushed against the opposite wall. We looked in every inch of the basement and didn't find so much as a hair. The reason Sal couldn't get in through the deli's basement is because there was another Abus Granit padlock on that door. Marco took pictures to prove there was nothing in the basement besides abandoned equipment.

We backtracked through the door to the cafe's basement, returned the storage rack to its spot in front of the door, snuck up the stairs and through the double doors to my aunt's store. I pulled the doors shut, click. Mission accomplished. We heard footsteps on the stairs and I pulled Marco into Maggie's office. We sat against the door in the dark and I wondered if Alex was trailing behind Kane in a cute little nightie and panties he bought for her. My heart pounded in my ears. Two minutes later the footsteps went back up the stairs and then Kane's apartment door shut. I exhaled the breath I had been holding.

We were sitting in complete darkness. For a second, I wondered if I was sitting there alone, maybe I had dreamt all of it. I slid my hand across the floor until I felt Marco's hand. I squeezed and he squeezed back. My body reacted to his, maybe it was something, maybe it was the adrenaline and stress receding. That day was just one more ride on the emotional roller coaster. There had been one hurdle after another since I got here, and it felt like things were going to be okay. Sal would be off my aunt's back, and we wouldn't have to worry about getting whacked by the Moretti family for knowing something we shouldn't. I squeezed his hand again; the adrenaline was dumping, and I swallowed the tears in my throat. I managed to squeak out,

"Thank you."

His voice was soft and sexy,

"For what?"

I paused for a beat before moving from my position against the door. Fuck it. I put one knee on either side of him and wrapped my arms around his neck. He whispered,

"What are you doing?"

I whispered back,

"Shh."

He smelled so good.

Marco scooped his arms around my butt, pulled me closer, and I rested my head on his shoulder. I closed my eyes and stayed like that for a long time, I took that kind of comfort any time I could get it. I inhaled deeply and released another layer of the fear and stress I had been holding. Marco rubbed my back, and spoke into my hair, cigarettes and cinnamon gum on his breath,

"You're okay."

No one else existed, it was just the two of us. His skin smelled like warm spices and musk. I brought my lips against his and ran my fingers through his hair. I wondered if he had ever been loved before and I wanted to make him feel loved. I wanted to tell him how I was feeling but couldn't find the words.

I unbuttoned his shirt as we kissed, and we rubbed noses like we'd done that before. He responded to my touch and my body grew eager to be closer to him. I was a sucker for hero worship, it was one of my things, I guess. I led Marco to my apartment up the front stairs instead of the back ones, pushed him against the wall as soon as we were inside, unbuckled his belt and pulled it out of the loops. Marco's breathing quickened and his eyes grew hungry, like I was his prey, even though I was the one doing the hunting. We lost our cloth barrier and kissed as we danced our way to the bedroom, tumbling onto the four-poster bed in a pile of bare skin and lust. Marco made love to me in a way no one else ever had, and when we woke up in the morning, we did it all over again. As an aside, I was right about the bulge in his pants.

In the morning, I made eggs and toast. Marco wasn't interested in a latte, so I made some sub-par pour over coffee. Something was different about him; he was passionate and loving and I felt content when I was around him. He was rough around the edges in all the right places. I started to realize that sometimes good people do bad things, and maybe Vincenzo Moretti and Marco Masiello fell into that category. Marco was involved sin things I didn't think I'd ever understand but he touched me in a way that made me feel whole. I went to him, and we stood nose to nose. I knew it was probably a one-night stand and I wanted to make the most of it.

While Marco showered, I snagged the maple

oat latte from the hall. When he left, I went with him down my front stairs and gave him a lingering kiss. I smacked his ass as he walked away and then rolled my eyes at myself. I laid on the couch staring at the ceiling. First things first, I liked how I felt when I was with that guy. Second, I had a feeling we missed something when we were in the basement. There had to be something more, or Sal wouldn't be threatening my aunt, and demanding that one of his men snoop around. How was I going to get down there without sneaking through Muddy Waters? Eventually, Kane would catch me. While I was in the shower, I realized I knew enough about Kane's routine that I could probably get my hands on his carabiner and remove the key for the padlock.

I opened the store that morning and as soon as Sunny got there, I told her about Marco. The last thing she knew; he had been caught trying to get into the basement, and here I was telling her I slept with him.

"You said all along that he was trying to get down your pants, you were right!"

I bit my bottom lip and blushed,

"I started it."

She smacked me and her face lit up,

"You did not!"

"I did."

Her eyes went wide,

"What got into you!?"

"I like him."

A smirk formed,

"You're in a love triangle."

I wrinkled my nose at her. I had feelings for Kane, but my relationship-PTSD had caused me to turn on a dime at any sign I might get hurt. Marco was involved with the mafia, which I found sexy and scary, and he was fantastic in bed. I felt safe with both of them but my time with Kane was like steppingstones and my time with Marco was like fireworks,

"I like them both."

Sunny sympathized,

"I've been there, follow your heart. You can't tell me 'Dark Chocolate' over there isn't banging that blonde. Sorry, but there's no reason why you shouldn't have fun too."

"It's more than that, Marco can protect me. I thought Kane was safe, but he isn't connected, and he wasn't being honest with me."

I shrugged,

"I always end up with cheaters or jerks, but Marco feels different, and that was the first time in my life I made the first move. Something about him made me feel safe taking that leap without being scared that things would be weird if he said no."

She shrugged and went palms up,

"What are you going to do?"

"I'll probably panic, not text him, and he'll end up screwing his ex.

CHAPTER 7
A TWEED SPORTS JACKET

MAGGIE RETURNED three days later and while she was in her office doing paperwork, Sunny and I unloaded boxes from a vintage book auction in Maine. I hadn't said a word and that wasn't like me, so Sunny nudged me with a shoulder,

"What's up, fucker?"

I paused for a beat,

"You want a coffee?"

She flicked her eyebrows,

"Yes. Yes, I do."

Sunny didn't know what I was up to, but she knew I was up to something. We chatted with Marlaina, and I made sure to talk loud enough that Kane would hear me. We took our lattes to a leather sofa and sat by the fake fireplace. I could see Kane's office door from where I was sitting. We were carrying on a bullshit conversation when I caught movement out of the corner of my eye. We were laughing and carrying on and pretending we didn't see him, real junior high shit. Kane stopped when he saw me, but I kept talking to Sunny. He kept standing there. An eternity later, Kane walked over and stood in front of me,

"Can we talk for a minute, please?"

When I heard Kane's voice, I remembered how much I missed him. Anger and jealousy do crazy things to our hearts, love can turn to hate in the blink of an eye. And then I couldn't talk because if I said anything, I would cry. Sunny squeezed my hand, and I let out a big sigh, I tried to shift gears or compartmentalize or anything that would make me not feel my feelings, but my feelings flooded in anyway,

"Amelia."

I glanced up at Kane and his eyes were pleading with me. I made eye contact with Sunny before following him into his office. Sitting on the edge of his desk, my stomach churned with anxiety. He closed the door and stood there looking at me like I might be a mirage. Our eyes locked and I remembered why I sobbed in the corner of the cafe when I saw him with Alex. I wrapped my arms around his chest and released a big sigh as he rested his lips on the top of my head. I let myself cry.

I cried for a bunch of reasons...because I missed

Kane, because he had probably slept with Alex, because I had slept with Marco, and because feelings are unpredictable. Love doesn't always travel in a line, sometimes it does all kinds of loops and turns before you get to your destination. Maybe that's what was happening here. When I pulled away and moved my eyes to his, he kissed me, deeply.

I pulled away and looked up at him,

"What are you doing?"

I could tell he was hurt, shifting from one foot to the other,

"What do you mean?"

I went palms up and shook my head,

"I mean, what are you doing? Aren't you with what's her name?"

He looked confused,

"Who?"

And then I got pissed because he was playing games,

"Don't play stupid, Kane. I came down here to talk with you a month ago and you were off with 'someone' named Alex. I was at the table in the corner when you came through and took her up to your apartment. I asked around, I know you were with her in college, and I know the only reason you broke up was because her job transferred her. She's back now."

Kane stared at me, speechless. I gestured toward my aunt's basement,

"And why are you the only one with a key to the

basement?"

He sat down hard and put his head in his hands, his voice broke,

"You wanted to talk?"

"Yes."

When Kane looked up at me, he had tears in his eyes,

"Why?"

I was done with the bullshit and wasn't afraid of what I had to say, but my hands were on my hips as a defense mechanism,

"I'm not making any assumptions about your feelings for me, but I was catching some major feels for you. I decided enough was enough and came over to talk to you, but you weren't here. I helped around the café so I would be here when you got back."

I gestured toward the wall,

"I was wiping the table in the corner when you two came in, you didn't see me, but I saw you. You had your arm around her and went up to your place."

He met my eyes briefly,

"Amelia..."

My voice trembled,

"Do you want to know what I did when I saw you with her?"

He didn't say anything, I watched him breathe and I let him sit in it. I gestured at the wall again,

"I sat there with my head in my hands and sobbed in the corner while people drank coffee around me."

My tears started again,

"I thought we were going somewhere together, but I was just a detour."

He glanced up at me,

"Amelia, I spent time with her because I thought we were done. If I thought we were together, I would have taken Alex to lunch, caught up on life, and wished her well."

We stood there awkwardly and after a long pause he said,

"I want to show you something."

Kane held out his hand. I followed him up the stairs, and he opened the door to his apartment. I stood in the kitchen as he poured lemonade, Lola bouncing around waiting for a treat. When Kane put the pitcher away, I noticed a picture of us on his fridge. He left the glasses where they were and stood in front of me. He tucked a curl behind my ear and lightning shot through my body. I looked up at him and put my hand on his face, I rubbed his beard. Our kisses were salty from tears. He lifted me onto the counter and stood in front of me. We made up for lost time with our mouths. He was on his way somewhere and he was going there with me. He had to finish his work, and I had to finish helping Sunny, so after one more long kiss at the top of the stairs we went back down to earth.

I insisted Kane let me into the basement, and

he did, no questions asked. He even sat down there with me for a while but eventually he got bored and went upstairs. When I pulled the appliances and equipment away from the wall, I could see the door to an old walk-in freezer. I propped the door open and looked around. The dark space was musty, there were storage totes on the wire shelves, and everything was neat and organized. I shook my head, this seemed like an incredibly stupid thing to hide.

I pulled the bins from their shelves and dug through various items. I noticed it was clothing, mostly business wear and expensive shoes. I found a silver Omega watch and even though it was probably fake, I tried it on and decided it was the classiest thing I owned. Maybe that stuff was a hodgepodge of dress clothes and shoes that had been mixed in with some vintage books my aunt brought back from an estate sale. I pulled out a plaid tweed sports jacket and it fit perfectly. There were a couple of brown stains near the pocket but as a thrifter, I knew all the secrets for removing stains.

Later that evening, I put my magic stain concoction on the tweed jacket and noticed the peroxide mixture bubbled like when I bled through my pants and needed to remove the stain. The clothes looked like they were from high rollers, so I surmised that the stain was from the dried juices of a rare filet mignon, served to the man at a fancy country club. I was sure the guy enjoyed it with a starter of oysters

Rockefeller and a tulip-shaped whiskey glass of Lagavulin neat. I was sure he worked as an executive and I bet he liked to gamble, but not bingo or slots, I'm talking like blackjack or poker. I bet his wife was thirty-six but looked twenty-four, and I bet they had a vacation house at the beach.

Bringing myself back to reality, I wondered why the walk-in had been used as a storage space and why the equipment was blocking the door. I realized there was nothing in the freezer that Salvatore Moretti needed to worry about in the first place. Who cared about any of that stuff? There were suit coats, blazers, and a tuxedo jacket with long tails. I checked the pockets of the tux jacket and came out with a set of keys. The fob was for a BMW, and that, along with a couple of other keys, hung on a Bulgari key ring. I planned to add my car and apartment keys to the ring and carry it around like a 'fancy pants.' I could push the lock button whenever I saw a BMW and eventually, maybe I'd come across the car, and could return the keys to their rightful owner.

At the bottom of the tote with the tuxedo and keys, I found loose change and a unique maple leaf pin. I set the pin aside to put on my purse. Not one part of me thought these things might belong to murder victims. Before I knew how this story was going to end, I was pretty naive. I proceeded, blissfully ignorant, believing that I was simply looking through some random crap in an old freezer. I found a tote full of shoes, including a pair of women's Tom Ford loafers that retailed for over two thousand dollars. Some of the shoes had mud splatters from commutes on spring days but nothing I couldn't fix.

Some of the mud scraped off with my fingernail but didn't turn to powder like mud usually does. For shits and giggles, I grabbed my peroxide and used a cotton swab to dab the brown spots on the two-thousand dollar loafers. Some of the spots fizzed. Mud doesn't fizz, blood does. So now I had a tweed sports jacket and a pair of loafers with blood on them. Did I get nervous about that? Nope. I tried on the pair of suede loafers with the fancy fringe and fizzy spots. Obviously, it was filet mignon juice, like on the jacket. Score. I had a new watch, a stylish sports jacket, and a pair of expensive leather loafers.

In retrospect, I realize that not one shred of my being thought I should ask my aunt before snooping around the basement. Once I saw there was nothing incriminating or mob related, I didn't worry about any of it anymore. I proceeded, without a care in the world, assuming I was digging through unwanted clothes. Not one part of me was concerned that this stuff had belonged to people who'd been whacked by Salvatore Moretti. Don't worry though, I got the blood stains out with a little elbow grease. Did I mention that I planned to work the watch, the tweed sports jacket, and the loafers into my regular wardrobe rotation? Looking back, that was a glaring example of my innocence in the eyes of evil.

CHAPTER 8
A SHOT IN THE DARK

SEPPI GAVE ME nothing to worry about, and even delivered my lunch a couple times over the next week. He would kiss me on both cheeks and when I opened my lunch, I'd find an eleven-dollar piece of tiramisu. So, I wasn't worried about the all-mighty Giuseppi Moretti anymore, but I was on high alert and my nervous system was on overload, which caused me to smoke more weed and drink more whiskey. When I returned to Bunman, I was trying to escape the stress and anxiety back home, and I was just dealing with different stress. Quite frankly, I was sick of being on edge all the time.

I asked my aunt about the garage on the other side of town, and she told me she owned that too. That's right, my aunt owned the mafia garage where

Sal may, or may not, have moved his 'operation.' Maybe Maggie knew something, but I didn't push. I planned to snoop around the next time she went out of town. She had been making frequent trips, so I knew it was only a matter of time. And the next time Maggie went away, she didn't have an ETA for her return. Before she was even in her car, I was looking through the well-labeled keys and found three tags that said 'Garage.' The garage at her house had a keypad, not an actual key, so the keys were not for the garage at her house. Adrenaline triggered and my heart rate quickened. As soon as the taillights to the little blue VW Beetle faded, Kane and I drove to the other side of town.

We passed what used to be Stanley's Service Center, turned around, and parked down the street. From afar, the building looked secure. As we got closer to the garage, I dug around my bag for the keys. The building was constructed of painted cinder blocks and once upon a time, it functioned as a gas station where you could get an oil change and a pack of smokes. I tried all three keys on both doors and none of them worked. I checked the key tags again, they were labeled 'Garage' on one side and clearly said 'Stanley's' on the other. I handed the keys to Kane so he could give them a try, and he couldn't get any of them to work either.

"Do you think someone changed the locks? Why would someone who doesn't own the property change the locks on an empty building?"

Kane went palms up and we went back to the car. We went home and I pestered him until he agreed to go back with me after dark, so I could snoop around some more. The time crawled. I made taco dip and Kane came over to eat it. We ordered pizza and after we ate, we dressed in black. The two of us sat on the sun porch waiting for night to fall.

Once the cover of darkness descended over Bunman, it was time for a stroll to the other side of town. As we approached the garage, we could see there were lights on inside. It was possible we didn't notice the lights during the day, but I was ninety-nine percent sure the building had been dark. Maybe someone was living there. Kane led me in a wide loop, and we ended up next to a low rock wall in a wooded area about fifty feet from the rear of the building. Light and shadows were reflecting through a window on the side that faced a row of trees.

I was relieved when Kane told me he didn't have his gun. Since I hadn't been in the garage before, I had no idea what the layout was. We didn't get any closer on that attempt. I stood up and Kane pulled me behind the low wall as headlights approached. A dark Lincoln Continental pulled into the driveway and came to a stop behind the garage. My heart was pounding, I wanted to look so badly but knew I couldn't. The engine went silent, someone got out of the car. When I couldn't stand it anymore, I peeked over the wall and saw a man that looked like Sal entering the back door.

"Why is he here?"

Kane shrugged. I persisted,

"Yeah, but what is he doing in there?"

Kane shrugged again but his shoulders went up more this time. I got more agitated,

"Do you think he's doing something illegal in there!?"

Kane's eyes got wide, and he did another exaggerated shrug, his shoulders going up to his ears. He put his palms up in the air and shook his head, I got the point. We couldn't see what was going on, but Kane verified the black Lincoln was Sal's. There was no way we were going to find out what was going on in there, so we looped back around to the buildings across the street and made our way home. I was getting used to compartmentalizing tidbits of information into tiny little boxes and stacking them in the back of my mind. I'm not sure that's a skill to be proud of, but what I am sure of is that it's a trauma response I invented to save myself from uncomfortable realities.

As soon as we were home, Kane called his college friend, Mike, to see if he could help us with our fact-finding mission. Mike Quinlan is ex-military and up for anything involving tactical maneuvers. We made plans to meet at his house the next night. Kane told me Mike was obsessed with old spy memorabilia and collected vintage Maxwell Smart devices. I wondered if Mike was going to bring his shoe phone and pen camera when we staked out the garage.

The next evening, we picked up a four-pack of craft beer and plugged Mike's address into the Garmin suction cupped to the windshield of the Bronco. Mike's house was fifteen minutes away and I got the chance to see Clover Lake by moonlight as we made our way to Quinlan's Landing. Mike's property consisted of an old farmhouse with a barn, chicken coops, a vegetable garden, and what looked like a sizable crop of marijuana. I was excited to see how Kane introduced me to his friend. I knew this guy was in his life when he was with Alex, and I wondered if she would come up in conversation.

"Mike, this is..."

Mike didn't even wait for Kane to finish his sentence,

"You must be Amelia!"

He picked me right up off the floor in a bear hug. Mike was built like a brick shithouse and was wearing a tactical belt in his living room. Do you know what I wear in my living room? Sweatpants and a t-shirt littered with whatever ice cream dribbles I can't manage to get from the container to my mouth. I sighed. I realized I might need to evaluate my life choices. Kane handed the beer to Mike, who disappeared to retrieve chilled Pellegrino, and a charcuterie board piled high with olives, berries, cheeses, and fancy-looking nettle crackers from Frog Hollow Farmstead. I eyed the brick fireplace as I sipped my bubbly water and tried to snoop without snooping.

I excused myself to use the powder room, and you guessed it, had gotten my period. My purse was in the Bronco. Wonderful. The way Mike looked, I figured he had girls there all the time, so I opened drawers and cabinets looking for a stash of pads or tampons and all I found was a shit load of Magnum condoms for Mike Quinlan's monster dong. Damn. I ended up MacGyvering something out of toilet paper. At least that guy got the fluffy stuff and not the kind that dissolves into shreds and gets stuck to your lady bits. Also, since I know you're wondering, the only cool thing I found during my scavenger hunt was a taser taped under the sink and an impressive handgun in a holster that was hanging on the outside of the toilet tank.

I also found that in the amount of time it took me to pee, snoop around every inch of Mike's bathroom, and cob-job a pad, the plan to stake out the garage had been put into place. Nice job Amelia, and thanks Mother Nature, you bitch. I followed the two of them into Mike's garage. There were six-foot tall gun safes, rolling tool cabinets and generators that could run all of Bunman, and then some. The two of them changed into dark clothes before strapping guns to their thighs and knives to their ankles. They packed lock picks and zip ties. At that point, I didn't even bother to ask, I had a pretty good idea what the plan was. I dug an edible out of my pocket and tossed it down the hatch along with a swig of some of Mike's Grey Goose, right out of the bottle, when no one was looking.

We piled into Mike's Hummer, went around the lake and back into Bunman. We parked a hundred yards from the garage, walked the tree line, and came out in the spot behind the low wall. I knew the only reason I was invited along was because Kane knew I'd pitch a fit if he left me at home. I knew I was dead weight, no pun intended. Kane kissed the top of my head and jumped over the wall, jogging to catch up with Mike. The moon was full, and I could see their silhouettes as they moved to the back of the garage.

There were no cars in the driveway and the lights were off. I knew the two of them had gained access when I saw the light from the exit sign briefly before the door closed again. I waited. And I waited. Eventually, I climbed over the wall and went a little closer. In retrospect, I realize I was probably being extremely impatient. I knew they were trying to figure out what was going on in there, but I wanted them to hurry because I didn't like being alone in the dark. Another five minutes went by (it was probably actually thirty seconds) and no one had even driven by. It looked dead around there, again, no pun intended.

I approached the door and prayed they'd left it unlocked. My clammy fingers touched the cold metal knob a split second before a hand clamped over my mouth and an accompanying arm snaked around my waist. I smelled warm spices and musk. I tried to scream but it was only a squeak. My mind raced. Why was Marco here? Had he done something to Kane? Why hadn't he called me after we slept together? Why hadn't I called him? Was Marco part of whatever was going on in there? Was he going to hurt me? Had my cob-jobbed toilet paper pad made its way into my pant leg?

I squirmed and flailed as I kept trying to scream, Marco lost his grip, so I dragged the sole of my Doc Marten down the length of his shin and slammed the back of my head into his mouth. Marco cursed, threw me away, and grabbed his mouth. My feet hit the ground, and I tried to run away as he desperately scooped me to his chest again. I screamed and Marco clamped his hand over my mouth again, that time I could taste pennies. Just then, Mike threw the door open to the commotion and when I squeaked again, Kane shouted,

"Amelia, I'm here!"

Mike shined his flashlight in Marco's eyes. Marco dropped me and moved towards Mike with blood dripping from his nose and split bottom lip, pleading,

"Dude shut it off, shut it off!"

Mike pulled his taser and closed the distance, Marco's voice was trembling and frantic,

"Shut it off! I beg you, man, please shut it off!"

My voice was trembling just like Marco's, I was pissed and scared. I kicked in his direction,

"Screw you, Marco!"

Mike had Marco's hands together behind his back, Marco pleaded, scanning the property nervously as he panicked,

"For the love of God, shut off the fucking light! You guys CANNOT be here!"

I panicked and swatted for the flashlight. Mike made a face and lifted the flashlight out of my reach. Marco squirmed,

"Sal is on his way, you guys need to get out of here, especially you, Amelia."

Mike sat Marco in the driveway, and as if he didn't have time for Marco's bullshit, he said,

"You're trespassing."

Marco spoke quickly and scanned the street anxiously,

"I'm not trespassing! I work for Sal, and he's on his way. I'm supposed to walk the perimeter and give him the all-clear. Sal's right-hand, Franco, has been waiting, and if he doesn't hear from me, he'll come to see what's causing the holdup. This is bigger than you guys, please go."

Marco's gaze shifted to my face, tears teetering at the brim of both eyes, a wet spot forming in the crotch of his jeans. He pleaded,

"Amelia, please go! Even if these clowns stay, please go! Sal will kill you if he finds you here!"

I had another adrenaline rush, and my mind flashed to our day together, the trust, the intensity, the way he was with me that night. Just then, a pair of headlights approached. Kane and Mike made eye contact, Mike cut the light, and the two of them lifted me by the pits. We stood flat against the side of the building that faced a line of trees. An SUV swung into the driveway as the three of us ran for the cover of the pines. We climbed over a section of the low wall that camouflaged us from the garage and watched as the driver exited the vehicle,

"What's the holdup, Coco?"

Marco stuttered a little,

"I, I was just going to text you; I was checking the...the perimeter."

The large man tried the knob and swung the door open,

"Why is this door unlocked, Coco?"

Marco's voice was high and squeaky,

"I don't know Franco, I swear."

Franco slammed Marco against the cinder block wall of the garage, hard enough that it knocked the wind out of him. Franco sounded nervous and pleaded,

"Dude, what the fuck is going on!? He's coming, what the fuck am I supposed to tell him!?"

While Marco caught his breath, the man shined a flashlight in his face,

"What the fuck happened to you? And why is your lip busted!? Who was here!?"

We couldn't see Marco, but we could hear him,

"I don't know, Franco, I swear!"

That was the last thing Marco said before we heard a single gunshot. We ran the opposite direction into the woods, in the dark. I clotheslined my shins, catapulted into the air, and landed with a thud. We held our breath to listen, and I threw up hot vomit that splattered my boots. I sipped bubbly water on the way back to Mike's and no one said a word. That's when I knew for sure that my toilet paper pad had worked its way out of my underwear. I pulled off my sweatshirt and sat on it. Once the adrenaline faded, I cried quietly in the back seat. Poor Marco, I had never been with anyone who was killed by the mafia.

When we got home, I took a bath and an edible, and then ate most of a pint of Phish Food. At that point, I did not handle situations like that with finesse or level-headedness. Situations like that gave me the nervous shits and triggered my OCD, and not the kind of OCD people ignorantly boast while posting reels of kitchen organization. I'm talking like I was convinced I needed to have certain things a certain way so people I cared about wouldn't die in some catastrophic fashion. I thought killers were after us. I slept on Kane's couch and ran to the window every time a car approached. I woke in the middle of the night and did the three dishes in Kane's sink because according to my brain, if I did that, we'd be alright. After a horrendous night's sleep, I ran down to Muddy Waters and grabbed the newspaper. I scanned the front page and then every other page. Nothing, not so much as a missing persons announcement. I kept my mouth shut and my ears open, no one was buzzing about some hot guys getting shot behind Stanley's Service center. No one was gossiping about some guy who didn't make it back home. Had I dreamt the entire thing? At that point, anything was possible.

CHAPTER 9
THE GUILT TRIP

I KNEW I NEEDED to go back home to get my things, but I didn't want to do it alone. My relationship with my mother was tense, at best. Given that I had moved hours away, I knew the visit would be full of comments about how I was going to fail out there in the 'real world.' The following Saturday, I asked Kane to come with me to get the rest of my things, and he said he'd love to. Little did he know what a shit-show my life was before I came here. With my luck, we'd run into my ex, his whore, and their lovechild. I was clenching my jaw and rolling my eyes before we even left Bunman.

I tossed an edible down the hatch, kicked off my dingy white Chuck Taylors, and tucked my knees to my chest. My fingers were laced around the white paper cup holding my maple oat latte. Kane tried to keep my mind occupied with stories of his life. We stopped at scenic vistas and sang to hair bands from the eighties. I told him a little bit more about my family and my ex. I was glad I never really settled into my old apartment. The things in my room had already been boxed up because someone else moved in the week after I left. I needed to get my things but while I was in Roundelay, I knew I'd also need to see my mother. Obligatory visits are the worst visits, they give me panic attacks, the nervous shits, and trigger my mommy issues.

Before we got to Roundelay, I took an edible so I wouldn't be a complete ball of nerves. I explained that my dad was kind and caring and loved his girls more than anything. I loved my dad and took pride in the fact that I inherited his witty sense of humor. Maxwell Birch made pickles and pies and chicken and dumplings. He built model airplanes and tended to his gardens. My dad worked hard and took pride in the things he did. He was the kind of person who'd pull over to help a snapping turtle across the road so it wouldn't get run over. My dad prided himself in giving meaningful gifts and would excitedly tell the story of where he found it, or why it made him think of you. He was one of the good ones, and he was one of my favorite people in the world. Deep down, I hoped that someday he would get to experience life without my mother.

My mother was the Happy Meal toy that broke while you were still eating your fries. She was the gumball machine ring that cut your finger, the fortune cookie with no fortune inside. My mother was a bitch. She didn't have the mental or emotional capacity to parent a human. If you were one of her cats, you would get treats and cuddles. When you were an actual human, she pushed out of her womb, you were dog shit. Every single time I tried to tell her something bad had happened to me, I'd get shushed, criticized, and the issue was swept under the carpet. Over time, the lump under the carpet grew so tall that I couldn't see my mother over the mountain of shame and rejection.

No one was there when we got to my apartment, so it was an unceremonious visit. Kane loaded up the four plastic totes filled with my things. I went into the bathroom and gathered my toiletries and perfumes, tossing them in Ziploc bags. I didn't bother with my shampoo and conditioner, but I grabbed my box of contacts and remaining pads. We stopped at the cafe in town and like a good boyfriend, Kane said the coffee in Roundelay tasted like burnt feet. I procrastinated as long as I could and then we went to my parents' house.

That was the house I lived in when we moved to Massachusetts, and it had a lot in common with the house we had in Bunman. It was a beautiful farmhouse with a wrap-around porch and a two-car garage with a hay loft. There was a garden, a well-maintained yard, and a hundred feet of landing strip for my dad's remote-control planes. A long-empty chicken coop and fence from my pony still stood in the backyard.

My trip down memory lane was interrupted when my mother came onto the back porch and hollered for me. Nails on a chalkboard. I grabbed Kane's hand and dragged him toward the house. Before we got to the steps, my dad came jogging out and picked me right up off the ground,

"Boo-Boo Bear, I've missed you!"

I kissed my dad on the cheek,

"I've missed you too, dad."

I gestured toward Kane,

"This is Kane. Kane, this is my dad, Max."

My dad gave Kane a hearty handshake. Maxwell Birch is tall and fit and handsome, and I'm not just saying that because he's, my dad. He has a curly salt and pepper crew cut, and a favorite pair of chinos. He has a nice smile, a dimple in his chin, and a stellar sense of humor. He has hazel eyes like mine and can grow one hell of a beard.

The three of us followed my mother into the living room, she didn't so much as offer us a glass of tepid water, or some of her shitty spigot wine. We sat on the couch and my parents sat in their chairs. The TV was on. As always, my dad asked about my apartment, my job, and my car. I told him about the apartment and that I was working in his sister's gift shop and that the twenty-six-year-old piece of Swiss cheese was still getting me from point A to point B. I told him all about my life in Bunman, but I left out the part about Salvatore, Seppi, and Vincenzo.

As always, my mother judged my life choices and humiliated me in front of my boyfriend. She couldn't understand why I broke up with my last boyfriend, even after I reminded her that my ex got someone pregnant and broke up with me. Marta Birch is about what you think. She's kind of preppy but not, thinks her shit doesn't stink. Dark chin length bob with a good number of wiry grays. She smelled like nice perfume, her nails were manicured, and her breath smelled like shitty chardonnay. My mother criticized my expensive (thrifted) purse, reminded me I'd 'use any excuse to spend money,' and then showed me five pairs of shoes she ordered from QVC. Like I gave a shit, what a fucking hypocrite.

My mother ran off to fetch a bulk pack of bungee cords she found at a discount store,

"Since you aren't making enough money to replace that rust-bucket, I'm sure you can use these to hold your bumper on or something."

What a bitch. And then she added,

"I hope you can establish yourself someday, Amelia, you can't drive around in that thing forever."

My mother told me about someone else's twenty-three-year-old daughter who owned a beautiful home, married a successful man, and had two perfect kids, a boy and a girl. How wonderful, she said they were like a Norman Rockwell painting. When I couldn't stand it anymore and felt my moral obligation to visit my parents was fulfilled, we worked our way toward the door. My dad hugged me again, I kissed him on the cheek and told him I loved him, he slipped me a twenty-dollar bill and whispered,

"Get yourself something nice, Boo-Boo Bear."

My dad retreated into another room so he wouldn't have to watch me walk out the door. My mother and I were not huggers, but sometimes, like when I had moved several hours away, I felt like it was necessary. Those were the most insincere hugs I had ever received, hugging her was like hugging a floppy fish. Kane followed suit and received an equally awkward embrace; he said it was like hugging a flounder. Before the two of us walked out the door, my mother said she had something for me and ran off to the other room. I rolled my eyes in anticipation. My mother returned, carrying a familiar looking gift bag with some things she 'didn't have any use for.'

I took the gift bag and put it on the kitchen table. Inside, there were some gift-exchange gifts from her co-workers, including votive candles and some wine glass charms to use with her shitty spigot wine. Then I saw some wax melts that looked familiar. I removed the next piece of tissue paper, and my eyes landed on a beautiful, unused, handmade ceramic wax melter. You might think I'd found a treasure amongst the trash, and you would be right. My eyes filled with tears and

Kane looked on helplessly. I moved my gaze from the wax melter to my mother's face, my voice trembled with hurt and deep rejection,

"I made this for you in my college pottery class as a Mother's Day gift a couple of years ago. I didn't have money to buy you anything, so I made something I thought you would like. I'm glad to see it meant something to you, it doesn't even look like you took it out of the bag."

My mother had the balls to wave me away,

"No, that can't be right, I got that thing from one of my friends for Secret Santa. And anyway, I don't use wax melts, I prefer candles."

I showed my mother the bottom of the melter, my initials. I turned back, left the other trash on the table, wrapped the melter in tissue paper, and nestled it at the bottom of the bag. You know, I wrapped the melter in the same tissue paper I put in there several years ago, when I gave it to her. I told my mother it was a mistake to come over and went through the door with Kane trailing behind me. Kane jogged over, carrying the box of crap from my bedroom. I pointed to the garbage can and he dumped the contents of the box in the trash before getting in the driver's seat of my car. I held it together until we got out of the driveway, and then in an instant, I was sobbing so hard I couldn't catch my breath. Kane pulled into a little gas station, and I almost threw up in the parking lot. He ran inside and came back with a ginger ale. I hated my mother so much that it made me want to vomit.

"Why didn't you want the box of stuff from your room?"

"Because I know it was filled with old love letters, dried-up nail polish, and the cigarettes I hid under my mattress in twelfth grade. I'm sure all that stuff was a veiled attempt to shame me in some way. It was a mistake bringing you here, I only went to see my dad, and so my mother wouldn't make me feel guilty."

I continued to sob for a long time and when I finally stopped, we went to a snack bar to devour greasy burgers, salty fries and waffle cones full of maple soft serve. We made our way around town, and I showed Kane where I worked as a teenager. We strolled through the park and went to the library. The two of us were circling back to the car when I spotted a familiar black Ford F-150 with metal testicles hanging from the tow hitch. It felt like I was trudging through marshmallow fluff while being punched in the gut. I grabbed Kane's hand, stopped walking, and held my breath. The driver's side door of the truck opened, and my ex stepped out. I moved my eyes to the passenger door and waited. The door opened, a skinny blonde with milk jugs slid out, and opened the back door to retrieve a rear-facing infant seat.

I pulled Kane back and we stood close to the building until my ex, his whore, and their love child entered the Chinese restaurant across from the park. I dragged Kane back to the twenty-six-year-old piece of Swiss cheese, got in the passenger seat again, and had a complete and total mental breakdown. It's not an exaggeration when I tell you I cried for most of the trip home, and only stopped when I momentarily ran out of tears. Kane detoured to his sister's house to pick up Lola, and when we got home, he ordered dinner from Giuseppi's.

I took a long shower and let the water hit my swollen eyes. I went to Kane's and found him in the kitchen waiting for me. We sipped tequila as we stood at the counter, eating pepperoni pizza and chocolate fudge cake. When I was getting ready to leave, he kissed my neck, and my breath caught in my throat. I looked up at him as he tucked a damp curl behind my ear. Our mouths found each other the way they always did, I felt vulnerable, deflated, and rejected by my mother. I needed to feel love, connection, and acceptance.

I kissed Kane harder than usual and felt my body losing the battle between letting him in and crying alone in my bed. He took my hand and led me to his room. He unbuttoned my pajamas and kissed the newly exposed skin. He sucked my nipples and kissed his way to my belly button. He hooked his finger in the waist of my panties and tossed them to the floor. I pulled his shirt over his head and untied his pajama bottoms. There was both a tenderness and an urgency to what we were doing. We made love that night, replacing the criticism, rejection, and pain with pleasure, acceptance, and connection. When I woke, Kane was already up. I padded into the living room to see the wax melter on the coffee table, the scent of roasted pine cones filling the air. Through swollen slits for eyes, I saw that he was admiring my work. He said he loved the melter and asked me how much I wanted for it. Right at that moment, that is exactly what I needed to hear.

CHAPTER 10
DIMPLES

AFTER THE MARCO DEBACLE, it was a little more talk and a lot less action. I all but managed to push the whole thing into the back of my mind. I mean let's face it, if Sal knew we'd been there, we'd be pushing up daisies. Seppi would deliver my lunch sometimes, and sometimes he'd stay to eat with me in Maggie's office. I never asked why, and I guess it didn't matter. But I had this strange, unspoken trauma-bond of some sort with Giuseppi Moretti. I guess even way back then, underneath all the darkness and mystery, something about that man both disarmed me and made me feel untouchable. Maybe it was utter naivety but maybe it was the possibility that I'd finally met someone whose soul was as broken as mine.

And just for the record, that's when I knew Seppi was a good one who does bad things sometimes, and not just some deranged asshole with no conscience. You might not think good people are capable of evil, or maybe you just don't have the courage to admit that you're capable of it. Either way, nothing in life is black and white, nothing. As we get a little further into this rehashing of my last twelve years, please remember how you feel about me right now. I'm just some normal girl with broken bullshit and skeletons shoved in my closet, right? I'm not some monster, I'm just some broken little girl. Telling this story brings up a lot of feelings for me because at this point, I was blissfully ignorant. I had a fantastical picture of some happily ever after.

To everyone else in my life, I kept my radar up and probably came off as standoffish and snappy, but at that point, it didn't matter. When I look back, I don't think being standoffish and snappy while under extreme stress will be one of my big regrets in life. I went through the motions but everyone who knew me, knew I was sinking. I was spiraling in my head, waltzing with dark demons who plied me with weed and empty promises. After much convincing from Sunny, I set off for the nice salon up the street, gift certificate hot off the printer. I'd never done anything like that, but maybe 'treating' myself would pull me out of the slump. A pretty woman in a black apron delivered a latte and retrieved a basket of lotion samples. The place smelled like people who could spend money being nice to themselves and I wondered if I would ever be one of those people. I held some of my hair to my nose and concluded that I smelled like dry shampoo, disappointment, and stale weed.

I got chunky caramel highlights and squoval gel nails with a French tip. It felt nice I guess, even though I wasn't accustomed to doing things like that back then. It was nice to pretend I was someone else for a while, even if deep down I wanted to burn the costumes and all of the masks. I hadn't yet learned that if you walk the walk, most of the time, it's pretty easy to fool people into believing what they see. Sometimes masks are used to hide, and other times they are used to trick people. I spent the walk home admiring my fingernails, which were usually chewed down and unpolished. But that day I could have convinced someone I was a woman who had money to take care of myself. As I was getting ready to unlock my door, Kane leaned into the hall,

"Hey, I made a dinner reservation, be ready a little before six."

He closed the door halfway and then opened it again,

"Your hair looks nice, I like it."

Our normal rotation was Chinese food (in or out), soup and sandwiches at Bolson's Deli, and pizza from Seppi's or the place up the street. The only place Kane ever made a reservation was at The Roof, a top-notch steak place on the other side of town and I wondered if the rib eye was on special. It would be nice to go out, most nights we'd eat on the sun porch while we swallowed fire and smoked Maryjane. It had been a productive day, and the clouds of depression were lifting a little. It seemed like we were moving in the right direction with our relationship.

I couldn't stand the stiff goo the salon woman put in my hair, so I hopped in the shower and wiped the slate clean. I dressed in cute panties, a push-up bra, and a form-fitting white eyelet dress. Instead of smashing my curls into a disaster on the top of my head, I worked curl cream through the strands and scrunched my ringlets to life. The highlights made me look cool or something, like one of those girls who had French kissed by the ninth grade. I slapped on winged eyeliner, mascara and a plummy mauve lipstick. I tossed an edible down the hatch, put on some earrings, and strapped the Omega around my wrist. A couple sprays of Alien Elixir and then I finished the look with a pair of low-heeled booties I bought secondhand.

I gave myself a once over in the mirror, I looked good, damn good. I felt sexy and romantic and daydreamed about Kane dancing with me in the parking lot of The Roof, spinning me like a princess, kissing me passionately, and maybe more. I twirled and my reflection revealed that I was wearing a disguise, just some ragamuffin masquerading as a pretty woman. I had to remind myself I could pull it off, I was perfectly capable of being pretty, of wearing an outfit that some girly-girl would wear on any given Tuesday.

We went out the back door and instead of unlocking the Bronco, Kane led me up the alley to the street. I didn't think anything of it, maybe we were walking to the fancy French place around the corner. Nope. When we reached the sidewalk, Kane took a sharp left and opened the ornate wooden door of Giuseppi's Italian Ristorante. That's when I wondered why Seppi had been eating lunch with me, and why I hadn't mentioned it to Kane. Too late now, maybe Seppi was gone for the day. There's no way the owner of a popular Italian restaurant was still at work at six o'clock on a Friday night, right?

We were seated in a cozy booth in the corner, and I positioned myself so I could watch for Seppi. I ordered my first glass of wine. The waitress delivered a basket of warm bread, and a smashed bulb of roasted garlic drizzled with fancy olive oil and Italian seasoning. We shared an appetizer and enjoyed our meals with no sign of Giuseppi Moretti. I relaxed a little and ordered a second glass of wine. As we were waiting for coffee and a piece of torta barozzi, I heard his voice. Crap. I stared at the table and fluffed my hair, so it was obstructing my view. You know, the whole 'if I can't see you, you can't see me.'

When Seppi got close, I contemplated sliding under the table or retreating to the powder room while he finished his rounds. I tossed back the last of my second glass of Cabernet Sauvignon and my hand was on the stem of the empty glass when Seppi came to our table. I froze. Maybe if I didn't move, he wouldn't notice me. Why did I wear a push-up bra? Anyone? He made eye contact with Kane,

"How is the chicken parmesan tonight? Did you enjoy your meal?"

Kane nodded but I could tell he was one of the people who believed the rumors.

"And who is your beautiful companion this evening?"

Shit. Seppi's eyes moved in what felt like slow motion from Kane's side of the table to mine. When he recognized me, he immediately slid into my side of the booth. He kissed my cheek and his eyes fell to my cleavage. A drop of sweat rolled down my back, into the crack of my ass. I was praying Seppi wouldn't say anything about our lunches. My breath caught in my throat when he reached out for my hand and rubbed the back of it with his thumb. I was distracted by the fact that he was touching me like that, and then he said,

"That's a beautiful watch, where did you find it?"

I swallowed hard and paused for way too long. I smelled whiskey and Cubans on his breath. The pocket of energy between us was charged with body heat, nerves, and the knowledge that I was in trouble.

I tried to keep my voice from shaking as I lied,

"It was my grandfather's watch, he left it to me when he died."

My grandfather was still alive, and I was definitely going to hell for that one, but it sounded believable. I exhaled slowly, in an attempt to calm myself, because my heart was beating in my ears and I was starting to feel sparkly. I couldn't read Seppi's face,

"Someone I used to know had a watch like that, that person has also passed."

That's fine, everything was fine, nothing was fucked. And then Seppi's arm slid across my shoulders. Electricity shot to my nipples; I could feel them pressing against my fancy push-up bra. The side of his thigh touched the side of mine. Hmm. My you-know-what got all tingly and confused. I panicked and reprimanded myself for being a whore. Seppi's voice was sexy and a little too familiar, he flashed perfect white teeth as he smiled. He winked, and out of the corner of my eye, I saw Kane make a face of displeasure on the other side of the table. When Seppi leaned in, I smelled a hint of sweat and what was left of that day's Tobacco Vanille. Deliberately, and in a low breathy voice,

"I've enjoyed our lunch dates, Dimples."

Our eyes met, Seppi winked, and his eyebrows did something sexy,

"I hope we can do it again sometime soon."

Dimples? My face flushed, I held my breath, and felt two sets of eyes on my burning hot cheeks. Seppi leaned in a little more and kissed me on the cheek again, his five o'clock shadow scratching my skin. That time, I avoided eye contact, but I glanced at Kane, who was holding his breath. As Seppi retrieved his arm, he grazed the back of my neck with his fingertips and warmth spread across my skin. Jesus. Seppi thanked us for coming, finished his lap around the room, and retreated to the inner sanctum.

I made the walk of shame back to the apartment and had the nervous shits before going over to Kane's. I hesitated at my kitchen door before going across the hall, I had a feeling it wasn't going to go well. I crossed the threshold into Kane's apartment and joined him on the sun porch. Maybe he forgot about it already, or maybe it didn't bother him the way it would have bothered me. He was standing, silent, and didn't put his arms around my shoulders or kiss me. He didn't spin me like a princess or make the first move or lead me to the bedroom. He put his hands on his hips, his face tense and angry, he'd had a couple glasses of wine too, so the gloves were off,

"You see the hypocrisy, right!?"

Maybe he wasn't talking about what I thought he was talking about. My voice went up an octave,

"What?"

He got a little louder,

"Do I need to remind you how you responded

when you saw Marco come out of my office!?"

I shook my head. If I didn't say anything, I wouldn't risk saying the wrong thing. Where was he going with his line of questioning? He continued, talking with his hands,

"I just want to make sure I understand. It wasn't OK for me to have a conversation with Marco, but it's perfectly acceptable for you to have secret lunch dates with Giuseppi fucking Moretti!?"

I scrunched my face in a 'yeah, but' kind of way, and shrugged. I meant to tell him, I just hadn't.

"He has a nickname for you, and seems pretty comfortable getting in your space, are you sure you two are just sharing lunch?"

Seppi hadn't called me Dimples before that night, and we certainly hadn't done anything together, I was offended. I stood and put my hands on my hips, getting in Kane's face,

"Excuse me!?"

I knew I had made some questionable decisions, but screwing Giuseppi Moretti wasn't one of them. He was intense, sexy, dangerous and intimidating, all of which are a huge turn-on for me, but I wasn't stupid enough to do anything about it,

"Nothing is going on between me and Seppi, he's just looking out for me."

Kane threw his hands up,

"Why!?"

That was a good question, I shrugged. Kane

kept talking with his hands, trying to get through to me,

"If one of the Morettis is being nice, there's a reason. None of them do anything without a motive, they've always got an angle, have you not been listening to how things work around here? Are you fucking nuts!?"

And then I said what most men have no problem saying to a woman whilst she is being hysterical,

"Calm down!"

In case you're wondering, that wasn't the right thing to say to a man either.

"Amelia, you slapped me across the face and didn't talk to me for weeks, because you saw Marco walk out of my office. What would you do if I was having secret lunch dates with a powerful member of the local mob family, and conveniently forgot to tell you about it? Let's not forget that you decided to talk to me, and then changed your mind because you saw me walk across the cafe with another woman. Things seem a little lopsided."

I didn't have an answer for him because he was right. Whatever, that didn't mean my feelings weren't valid. This was different, I hadn't slept with Seppi or been in a relationship with him, and I didn't love him. For whatever reason, ulterior or not, Seppi seemed to be on my side, and that meant something,

"OK, but nothing is happening between me and Seppi. I go over to pick up lunch all the time and sometimes we talk while I wait. Occasionally, he delivers my order and stays to eat with me, it's perfectly innocent."

Kane squinted at me like I was missing something important,

"You don't find it strange that Giuseppi Moretti, member of the mob, takes time out of his busy day to deliver your lunch!? You don't think someone like that has more important things to do!?"

Well, when he put it that way, it did seem kind of strange but what did I know, I wasn't inside Seppi's head. He was a little flirty, but he was like that with everyone, and he hadn't tried anything that made me feel uncomfortable or like he was hitting on me. Although, if we were in a bubble, I would have licked that man from head to toe and fucked his brains out. Kane threw his hands up,

"Well, aren't you going to say something!?"

And because I couldn't seem to hold it together to save my life, I started to cry. Goddammit. What could I say? Sorry, I didn't mean to have lunch with Giuseppi Moretti five times? I was a fucking idiot, and I knew it, but I didn't want to mess things up with Kane,

"Kane, I…"

But he wasn't buying it,

"So, it's OK that there's a double standard, and now because you're in trouble, you're turning on the waterworks?"

I looked up at him and our eyes met, I squeaked, "That's not what I'm doing."

But really, who cares. Seriously, who gives a shit? I inadvertently ruined what should have been a nice night. That time, he needed a break from me for a while, and I retreated across the hall with my tail between my legs.

CHAPTER 11
BACK AGAINST THE WALL

SINCE THERE WAS NOTHING mob-related in the basement, I figured maybe we could host local bands and open mic nights. If I made it a nice space for Kane to do gigs with his band, maybe he would forgive me. I moved the storage totes of clothes into the third-floor storage space and arranged the kitchen equipment neatly on the shelves of the walk-in freezer. I pushed the two stainless steel worktables into a corner for cake or gifts or merch, depending on the occasion. And then I had the bright idea to ask Seppi if he'd be interested in having someone sell pizza during some of the events.

The next time I went to Giuseppi's Italian Ristorante to pick up lunch, I should have just opted for a cup of soup from the crock of shit. Seppi came out of his office when he heard me. He put his hands on my shoulders and kissed me on both cheeks like usual,

"Dimples."

So far, so good. Well, buckle up. I told Seppi I wanted to show him something, and you should have seen the twinkle in his eye. I'm pretty sure he thought I wanted to show him my tits or something because he appeared very excited. He made sure there was a piece of tiramisu in my order, but little did I know, I wouldn't be eating it.

Seppi followed me up the sidewalk and through the front door of Whimsy. He greeted Sofia casually and she narrowed her eyes at him. She's not a fan of men in general, but she really has something against Italians for some reason. Seppi went into Maggie's office and put the take-out containers on her desk. That time, instead of sitting in the extra chair, he turned and looked at me in a way that made me both excited and terrified. Seppi is sexy for a lot of reasons. First off, he is very attractive physically, not like a model, like someone who could kill you or make you cum in the blink of an eye. He's wealthy and powerful, he could have been eating with any woman he wanted. I broke the silence,

"I want to ask you something."

And that, folks, is when I knew I'd made a huge mistake. Sofia could see me but couldn't see Seppi. I made eye contact with her, and she patted the gun under her dress. Once Sofia returned to her book, Seppi walked me backward until I was against the wall, and out of Sofia's line of sight. My breath caught, was this really happening? Was Giuseppi Moretti making a pass at me? Yes. Yes, he was. He pressed his body against mine. I inhaled sharply and closed my eyes, his voice had an intimate quality,

"I enjoy sharing lunch with you, Dimples, you should let me take you to dinner sometime."

I opened my mouth to tell him that wasn't what I had in mind, and he kissed me. Like, really kissed me. Our tongues touched and I almost had an orgasm. Oh God, I could feel it everywhere. He tasted like espresso, Cubans, and expensive aged whiskey. Just for a second, I gave into it, I kissed him back, and his touch set my body on fire. In Bunman, the Morettis did whatever their little hearts desired and I knew it, I was just one of a long line of woman this man had backed against a wall. I walled it off somewhere deep inside, slammed the door on the whole idea, simultaneously dreaming about kicking him in the balls and fucking his brains out. Did people ever tell this guy no without getting punished? If I kicked him in the balls, would I end up at the bottom of the lake with a bullet hole in my forehead? Seppi ran his thumb across my left dimple and my nipples got hard. Nice going nipples, you traitors. He made a sound low in his throat and sucked my neck. I whimpered in submission and my knees went weak, so he leaned into me with his body.

Someone came through the front door of Whimsy and the bell distracted him enough for me to come to my senses and pushed him away,

"I'm flattered, but that's not what I had in mind."

My panties were wet, and I wanted to push him onto the desk and have my way with him. Seppi took a deep breath and collected himself,

"That's OK, Dimples, what is it you'd like to ask me?"

I glanced at Seppi's crotch and there was a bulge pressing against his zipper. I didn't back down,

"I want to show you the basement."

His eyes were hungry, and I ignored it as I strolled toward the door and bounced down the stairs, no turning back now. And then I led a Moretti into the basement of my aunt's store, where the walk-in freezer stood wide open. Completely oblivious, I told Seppi about my idea to hold events with live music and vendors and asked if he'd want to sell slices of pizza down there. His face did something I'd never seen it do before, his voice was scary and not like when we would share meatball subs and antipasto. He threw his hands around as he barked,

"What the fuck are you doing down here!?"

I swallowed a ball of nerves and explained that I thought it would be cool to host events so people could mingle, listen to local bands, and eat local food. Once I knew people were interested, I could bring it up to Maggie. I realize now that it sounds like I wanted to have a junior high dance in the basement of my aunt's store. Seppi's gaze moved to the open freezer and that was the first time I saw darkness in his eyes, I know now that it was the look of unadulterated fear. He appeared to short circuit. He clenched his jaw, his voice frantic like Marco's had been, he grabbed my shoulders and screamed in my face,

"What did you do!? Where's the stuff that was in there!?"

Just to be clear, I'm an idiot, and figured if I pretended everything was fine, then everything would be fine. I gestured nonchalantly toward the freezer, but my voice was a little higher than usual,

"In there? The only stuff in there was kitchen equipment, and all I did was move it around so it would take up less space."

I thought I was doing a pretty good job keeping my cool, asked again about the pizza and knew I was in trouble. Seppi took a step toward the freezer, and I watched as his body stiffened, his breathing quick and shallow, his hands balled into fists at his sides. He was enraged and terrified all at the same time,

"What the hell are you doing? You shouldn't be down here, you can't be down here, Amelia!"

And then Seppi moved toward me differently than he had upstairs. That time, there was nothing sexy about it, and I was crapping my pants. I decided it was time to mosey on out of the basement and he decided it was time to stop me. I saw him coming, a split second too late. The fear and anger in his body was coming out of every pore. Seppi's hand flew up to my throat and I stumbled, my back slamming against the wall. I hit hard enough that I lost my breath, and I panicked, gulping for air with my back against the dirty brick wall. He leaned in and put his mouth to my ear, I could feel the heat of his breath as he growled through clenched teeth,

"My father isn't going to like this!"

He was breathing in my face and hot tears ran down my cheeks as I sobbed. The tough girl who wanted to kick him in the balls five minutes ago was shitting her pants. What's weird is that in the middle of all this, something happened. While Giuseppi Moretti had me pinned to the wall by my throat for the first time, I saw something soft in his eyes, like he was apologizing for something. I held my breath as energy passed between us, and noticed Seppi wasn't breathing either. I didn't know what it meant, but I was mesmerized for a moment in time. I was looking into his soul, and he was looking into mine, but maybe it was in my imagination. It startled me when a voice came from the bottom of the stairs,

"So, what are you going to do, estúpido?"

I turned my head to see Sofia standing there with her pregnant belly and a handgun. She had the Glock leveled at Seppi's chest. He removed his hand, smoothed his shirt, and disappeared up the stairs. We heard the front door open and close, and I ran to Sofia,

146

she wrapped her arms around me tightly,

"You want Kane?"

"He might not come."

My hands were shaking when I handed Sofia my phone. We were in the age of texting unless it was serious. I could hear Kane, and he sounded worried, even before he knew it was someone else on the other end. All she said was,

"Come to the cellar, OK?"

Sofia ended the call, handed the phone back, and like fifteen seconds later, Kane was running down the stairs two at a time. He looked back and forth between me with my red throat and tear-stained cheeks, and Sofia with her pregnant belly and handgun. He wrapped his arms around me, but my adrenaline dumped, and my legs gave out, I sat on the floor and dry heaved into a trash can. He kept asking what happened but I couldn't get it out. Sofia put her gun back in the holster on her thigh,

"Estúpido was pushing Amelia around, I told him what are you going to do? I should have popped a cap up his ass."

She gestured like a magician making something disappear,

"I could snuff him out just like this."

Kane glanced in her direction,

"Sal?"

Sofia waved him away and pointed at the wall facing the ristorante,

"No, the pizza one."

Kane charged toward the stairs with his hands in fists, and fire in his eyes. I knew he thought he was going to save the day by confronting Seppi, but he wasn't. Through my tears and sore throat, I managed to squeak out,

"Please don't go."

He stopped on the bottom step and got himself under control. He ushered me upstairs and started the shower. I was alone in the bathroom, but Kane promised he would stay in my apartment. I wrapped myself in a towel and went to my room to find a pair of pajamas and some slipper socks waiting on the bed. While I changed, Kane made a pot of tea and got me some ibuprofen. Right then, that was the scariest thing I had ever experienced, and I was a little surprised I hadn't pulled my fainting goat routine. Kane and I cuddled on the couch, and then ordered pizza from somewhere besides Giuseppi's. I had a couple shots of tequila with my edible, mediocre pizza, and garlic bread sticks.

Kane tucked a curl behind my ear and saw Seppi's faint hickey. His eyes moved to mine as he ran his fingers over the patch of red skin,

"How did you do this?"

I told him I burnt my neck with a curling iron, and he bought it. We kissed and I felt safe. I laid on the futon with Kane on top of me, my legs wrapped around his waist, and I felt him pressing against me. I pulled his shirt over his head and tossed it across the room. I ran my hands over his chest and stomach and put my fingers inside the waist of his pants. He kissed my chest and worked his way down. We took our time and when the release finally came, there were tears in my eyes. Sometimes a little bit of closeness goes a long way to mend the wounds on the inside.

Let me clarify something, because I'm sure there are quite a few of you wondering why we didn't call the police after Marco got whacked. I'm sure you're also wondering why we didn't call the police after Giuseppi Moretti physically assaulted me. You don't call the police on the Morettis unless you want to take an eternal dirt-nap. And at the time, the police department in Bunman was in Sal's back pocket, the entire judicial system in that broken little city was corrupt. But shortly after the Seppi incident, Kane took me shooting at Mike's, and registered me for a Concealed Carry certification course. Eventually, I'd feel like a bad-ass, but right then I felt vulnerable and scared.

I wasn't about to throw rocks at the hornet's nest. You do what you want in that situation, but I chose to do nothing. If you don't know what kind of person Salvatore Moretti was, I haven't been doing a very good job telling this story. Regardless, I attempted to keep my nose clean. It was going to be a while before I went down to the basement again. A huge part of me wanted to run, things were off the rails.

To add to my anxiety, I hadn't heard from my aunt in a while. And while that wasn't entirely out of the ordinary when she was traveling, something felt off and I was starting to worry.

I laid low for a while. Kane managed Whimsy and I didn't even come out of my apartment. Looking back, I'm not really sure what I was hiding from. I mean, in the big picture, nothing had actually happened. I soon realized that the basement situation with Seppi was just a fart in a hurricane compared to what happen next. But I didn't meet Sunny for the farmer's market or bring Mary her latte and muffin. I spent a couple days in bed with Lola, burning cozy scented candles and watching mindless rubbish. I lived on whiskey, edibles, cold pizza and Ben & Jerry's. When I finally emerged, it was only to stare at the fake fire and drink one of Kane's lattes. He thought we should check on Maggie's house and fill the bird feeders later.

Besides filling the feeders, I wanted to check Maggie's fridge for anything that might go bad so I could bring it home. It felt like something was going on with my aunt and I was hoping I'd see clues at her house that would give me some answers. I knew she traveled a lot, but that trip seemed excessive. I usually heard from her every couple of days, and it had been longer. It's not that I didn't believe she was in California, but she was oddly incommunicado. I wasn't receiving pictures of the ocean or selfies at funky restaurants. She wasn't video calling me while walking on a boardwalk eating ice cream, just an odd radio silence. Once inside Maggie's house, I kicked off my high tops, put them on the doormat, and slid my feet into her slippers. Kane pulled his Ruger and proceeded through the house with Lola trailing behind him. She was calm and her tail was wagging but my hackles were up.

I went into the living room and could tell someone had been there. What were they looking for? Tea bags and a roach clip? A bar of all-natural goat's milk soap and a handful of psychedelic mushrooms? Mystery novels and a pair of cheaters? I was so confused that I didn't even get upset about it. I knew it was probably Sal's goons, and I was giddy knowing they wasted their time. Unless they wanted to enjoy canned soup and diet ginger ale. And that's when I realized it smelled like chicken soup in the kitchen. I had no idea what was going on, was someone staying there? Why did the house smell like chicken soup? It didn't look like the place had been ransacked, it just seemed like someone had been there. Quite honestly, it was one of those houses where things had a high sentimental value and a low cash value. Like me, my aunt Maggie prefers to furnish her home with secondhand belongings. I scanned the counter for soup clues. I wasn't sure, but there might have been a different mug in the dish drainer then there had been the last time I was there.

I took all the semi-perishables out of the fridge

and packed them in a box. I took some tea bags and a handful of shrooms. Before we left, I maneuvered the cramped garage and squeezed around the front of the VW to get to the can of wild bird food, the place was like one big booby trap. Once the feeders were topped off and the bird bath was filled with fresh water, we locked up and headed home.

CHAPTER 12
A SHOE BOX FULL OF EYEBALLS

THE REST OF THE NIGHT was unremarkable; we ate burgers and fries and fell asleep on the couch. I woke and sat straight up with a jolt of adrenaline. The shower was running so I threw the covers back and padded to the bathroom,

"I wonder if those bins of clothes I found are what Sal is looking for. I didn't see anything incriminating, but maybe something in there would connect him to someone he whacked. I didn't go through everything, maybe there's a smoking gun or a duffel bag filled to the brim with counterfeit bills."

I was spiraling. My voice went up another octave and I waved my arms around while I talked, even though Kane couldn't see it through the shower curtain,

"What if there's a shoe box full of eyeballs!? Or like some guy named Ken's clothes. You know, because Ken was wearing the clothes and then Sal whacked him, stripped him down, and made him into sausage."

He stopped me,

"Breathe, Amelia."

I stood there with my hands on my hips,

"Well!?"

Kane responded as any sane person would, after a crazy bitch interrupts a perfectly peaceful shower with nonsense. He peeked out of the shower curtain,

"Amelia, I promise you, Salvatore Moretti is not looking for the shoe box full of eyeballs he forgot in your aunt's basement."

I peed and then sat on the lid of the toilet, waiting in silence for Kane to get out of the shower. He jumped when he threw the curtain open and saw me sitting there. I tossed him a towel. As he was drying off,

"I need to work the counter in the cafe until noon, why don't you come down and help me, a change of scenery will get your mind off things. Sofia has the store covered."

He stepped out of the shower, and I crossed my arms like a child,

"Fine."

I watched Kane shave and do his hair before I got in the shower. I threw my towel-dried ringlets into a half-assed messy bun without looking in the mirror. Who cares? Seriously, who gives a shit? I pulled on a pair of black pants, a Muddy Waters T-shirt, and my dingy white Chuck Taylors. I took an edible for good measure, don't judge me. I grabbed an apron and went behind the counter. When it was slow, I delivered lemonade and muffins to Sofia. Luckily, it was steady over there, but not so busy that she needed help. You might be wondering why I was bringing someone lemonade and muffins when I was the one who needed to be taken care of, and I might be wondering the same thing.

To go on a bit of a tangent here, let me tell you a little more about myself. I'm always the one who moves over when I pass someone on a sidewalk. I'm the one who holds the door, or lets you back out of a parking space. I'm the one who waits patiently as the oblivious idiot in front of me talks non-stop for five minutes about their shit job or sick cat after the cashier asks, 'How are you, today?' I'm the person who wasted a birthday evening waiting for a friend who was two hours late and then complained about their life for three hours. And let's not forget the times I've spent an entire day doing something I didn't want to do because I didn't want to hurt someone's feelings.

I think there is something about being neglected as a child that sets you up for selflessness to the point that it becomes a detriment. Hardwired to accommodate other people while never allowing anyone to accommodate you. Feeling guilty for putting people out or feeling like your interests aren't as important. In my case, maybe it's some learned mindset from years of criticism and negativity, years of being made to feel like a burden. Let me tell you something else about me, I'm working on those things. I'm working on holding my ground, setting boundaries, and standing up for myself, that's why this situation was bothering me so much. I was supposed to be in charge but had no control over anything going on around here, and I'd about had it. The low rumble of anger I'd pushed down deep inside my entire life was gaining steam and eventually I was going to lose it. I pitied the bastard who took the pin out of that grenade.

I was annoyed that Kane felt the need to babysit me, even though it was well past noon, and I had decided to stay. I was grinding beans for a latte when a light bulb went off. I stopped breathing. I'd watched my aunt drive her Beetle down Maple Street on her way to the airport. It took everything I had to cash out some basic bitch, and finish making her latte, before speed-walking into Kane's office. I stood there with my back against the door, my eyes like saucers.

He scrunched his eyebrows, a little too nonchalant,

"What's up?"

I just stood there with my eyes bugging out of my head. Kane leaned forward and then stood up from his desk. He snapped his fingers at me,

"Amelia, what's going on!? Did something happen!? Did you see Giuseppi!? Are you OK!?"

I stared at the wall, but it wasn't in focus,

"Something's wrong."

Kane moved toward me and tried to make his voice sound calm,

"In the cafe?"

I shook my head and tears came,

"You saw Maggie drive down Maple Street on her way to the airport, right?"

He looked confused,

"Yeah?"

I pulled the hair tie from my disaster of a messy bun and put it on my wrist. I pulled the hair tie back off my wrist and made another messy bun. I moved the papers on Kane's desk into a neat little stack. I pushed his chair in. I gathered all the loose pens and put them in an empty coffee mug. I wiped the dust off the filing cabinet. I grabbed a half-empty glass of water and dumped it into a hanging plant in the window. Kane stood in front of me and put his hands on my shoulders,

"Amelia, what happened?"

"When we were at her house, the car was in the garage."

I was numb as we drove to Maggie's house. Part of me thought she was OK, maybe she left her car at home and got a ride to the airport. Maybe she had a boyfriend she didn't want me to know about. My mind bounced from one thing to another, reasoning, bargaining and disbelief. I circled the perimeter of the house with Kane at my heels and then sat on the porch swing and stared at the woods. We locked up once we had checked every square inch of the house. The place was secure, and my aunt was not in there somewhere chopped into tiny little pieces.

We were down the street when I remembered she had cameras at her house. If I got her laptop off the kitchen table, we'd be able to see who parked the car in the garage and find out who made the house smell like soup. Kane made a U-turn, and we returned to my aunt's house. I was shocked when I opened the door and saw Maggie in the middle of the kitchen in the slippers I had just been wearing.

In normal Amelia form, I fainted like a goat, and since I didn't come back to the car, Kane came to see what was taking me so long. When I opened my eyes, the two of them were standing above me with worried looks on their faces. I blinked a couple times to clear the cobwebs and didn't understand what I was looking at. I sat on the couch with one of Maggie's cans of diet ginger ale, trying to comprehend what was happening. She was teary-eyed and anxious, trying to feed me oyster crackers. I couldn't put two words together,

"What..."

There was a long pause before Maggie sat next to me on the couch and put her hand on my knee. I looked up at her and then at Kane, he said,

"I guess we know who's been making soup."

Once I was finished with my impersonation of a fainting goat, she began to explain,

"There's a lot you don't know about my life."

Yeah, no shit. Maggie was my favorite aunt, and I thought we were close. She said she was going to California, but I was sitting next to her on the couch. She had been acting oddly ever since I got to Bunman. I stared at the hole in the top of my soda can. We stayed there for hours so I won't recount it word for word, but I'll give the Cliffs Notes version for anyone who is scratching their head as much as I was.

When the deli took up two storefronts, Sal was renting from Maggie's husband. After Sal downsized the deli, he and his associates maintained sole control over the basement under what is now Whimsy. Shortly before they married, Pete became paranoid, insisted on selling his five-thousand square foot federal-style home, and moved in with Maggie. Pete grew increasingly anxious and installed cameras. He built a bunker in the basement with everything a person would need to hole up, indefinitely. It seemed he was preparing to hide from someone or go to war. There was a room full of canned items, jugs of water, and MREs.

After Maggie took ownership of the properties, things were a little tense with Sal and eventually, she started receiving threats. Sal started moving his 'operation' out of her basement and into the garage on the other side of town. She would be able to use her basement, and he would have his privacy. Out of the blue, while Sal was still in the process of moving his things, he entered the basement through the connecting door and caught Maggie snooping around down there. She was putting the pieces together and he didn't like it one bit.

Since Sal didn't like to get his hands dirty, he had Marco sniff around. Instead of intimidating her or delivering threats, the two of them bonded over the whole thing, just like he said. Late one night, Marco asked if he could talk with her somewhere besides Bunman. She drove twenty miles outside of town to meet him in a diner parking lot and I assumed it was the same place we ate the blueberry pancakes. He had been pressured by Sal to threaten or eliminate Maggie, but he didn't have the heart to do it. Somehow, he and Seppi convinced Sal that my aunt was nosey, but not a threat. By that time, Kane had secured the deli and stairway doors to the basement with the Abus Granit padlocks. Things were rocky but no one died, and my aunt wasn't looking over her shoulder as much.

Things ramped up when I came into the picture. Mary introduced me to Sal and suddenly there was someone new in the equation. If I was anything like my aunt, I'd be snooping around and sooner or later I'd uncover something. Yeah, like the bloody sports jacket and loafers I cleaned with peroxide and a little elbow grease. I'm an idiot. Sal approached Marco a second time about delivering threats to Maggie. Just like the time before, Marco tried to convince Sal that my aunt was harmless. He also helped her plan a subtle dry run, in case she needed to go into hiding.

Everyone around there knew enough to shut their eyes and mouth when it came to the mob activity. Then one day, along came a dumb girl with a motor mouth, who had too many questions, and suddenly there was another problem. My saving grace was that apparently, Sal thought I was dumb as a box of rocks and decided I couldn't add two and two together with a calculator.

Ultimately, Marco convinced Sal I was so dumb that they could go in and out of the basement right under my nose if they wanted to, that one hurt my ego a little. Maggie took a couple of test trips and did go visit friends in California, but while she was there, she was in close communication with Marco. She had him come into the store a handful of times to make sure I was OK, and that led to offering free handyman work so he could keep tabs on me for Maggie. Sal saw Marco going in and out of Whimsy and told him to do a sweep of the basement to see if there was anything left down there. My aunt swore him to secrecy about the whole situation and honestly, I wouldn't have believed him anyway. I replayed the day with Marco, and how he risked his life to let me know what was going on,

"Marco came in to talk with me a while ago and told me some of this."

I looked from Maggie to Kane,

"We went through the basement of the cafe one night to make sure there was nothing down there."

Kane smirked,

"I knew it!"

"When you came down to see if someone was in the cafe, we were hiding in Maggie's office."

I left out the part about how Marco made sweet, sweet love to me that night. But I teared up when I thought about Marco's eyes, the way he smelled, and how his hand felt in mine.

Maggie made sure I was comfortable running the store for an extended period. She told everyone who would listen that she was going back to California indefinitely to be with a sick friend. No one suspected a thing. Ever since we saw her drive away, she had been living in the bunker. The reason it looked like someone had been in the house was because she had been up there in the middle of the night to get books or heat a can of soup. The flaw in her plan was that you can't delete the smell of chicken soup, and filling her feeders would require me to go into the garage.

I asked about Seppi, Vincenzo and Salvatore, she told me the rumors were true. Seppi had tried for decades to distance himself from the reputation of the Moretti family. There had always been pressure for Seppi to follow Sal's orders or lose his restaurant. Now that my aunt owned the properties, I wasn't sure what Sal meant by that, but I wouldn't put it past him to burn the place to the ground in an assertion of his dominance. According to my aunt, people made constant comments about his mob ties or that he was a young Tony Soprano. I smirked to myself at that one because that's the first thing I thought when I laid eyes on him. Turns out Seppi was a good guy, wrapped up in a perpetual battle with his narcissistic father. I had no idea what was going on in the garage, or what happened to poor Marco, but now all that mattered was that Maggie was safe and I knew where she was.

We ate freezer-burnt chicken nuggets with spaghetti, canned pasta sauce, and freezer-burned garlic bread before we tucked Maggie into the bunker. If I decided to stay with her, it wouldn't look weird for me to bring groceries in on a regular basis. She had enough food in the bunker to feed herself for another year, but she wasn't eating fresh fruits and veggies, everything was processed trash. I couldn't even imagine how inflamed her body must have been from all the sodium and preservatives she was ingesting. Most days, she consumed instant oatmeal, canned soups, instant coffee, diet ginger ale, and powdered milk. At that point, the shrooms and marijuana were the most natural things she was putting into her body.

I wanted Maggie to be able to eat homemade meals. I told people I was going to sleep there occasionally so the house wouldn't sit vacant for so long. I loaded my car with a duffle bag and made a pan of stuffed shells. Kane made a dozen coffee cake muffins. I bought a burner phone and some minutes at a Walmart, two towns over, and stopped to load up on fruits and veggies at the grocery store. I went to my aunt's before it was dark and made several trips from the car to the house. I didn't look over my shoulder, I just acted like I belonged there.

Luckily, my aunt was a private person who already had blinds in all her windows. We could stay up all night, watching TV while smoking weed and shoveling ice cream into our faces. Since her husband had installed a signal booster in the bunker, the burner phone could send and receive texts when she was locked away in there. I told her I'd make sure the bird feeders stayed full, and we talked about how long we could feasibly continue this charade. Eventually, I'd have to get back to my life, but I didn't want to leave my aunt alone any more than I had to. I wondered if I should sneak her into my apartment, but I knew my aunt had a good setup in the bunker. She could check the cameras and then sneak upstairs to watch TV or heat a can of soup in the middle of the night.

We talked about Marco possibly, maybe, getting murdered, and I told her about the people coming in and out of the garage. My aunt thought Marco was hiding somewhere and confirmed that Sal was renting the garage but said she didn't think it was being used for anything nefarious. I disagreed and I thought she was trying to protect me. My imagination had decided the mob brought bodies in to grind them into sausage that they then sold in the deli. I threw up in my mouth thinking about it. I told Kane not to eat sausage ever again, you can never be too safe. Maybe it was drugs or counterfeit money, but the way things were going, anything was possible.

As we sat at the kitchen table sharing coffee, there was a timid knock at the door. It was my aunt's neighbor, Agnes. Maggie tiptoed out of the kitchen and went down the stairs to the bunker. I took my time answering the door. The adorable old woman standing there said she had seen my car and wanted to bring me a strawberry rhubarb pie. I thanked her profusely before she retreated to the world of parakeets and individually wrapped butterscotch candies.

By the time Agnes was back on her porch, Maggie and I were shoveling warm strawberry rhubarb pie into our pie holes. In that moment, I realized how much my life had changed. In summary, my aunt's properties were wrapped up in mob shit. I found a guy blow-torching a lock on a basement that probably contained the personal effects of people who were eliminated by the Morettis. I slept with the blow-torch guy and then possibly witnessed him get whacked. I had been having secret lunches with Giuseppi Moretti. Let's not forget about my on-again, off-again relationship with Kane, and reconnecting with Sunny.

The latest development was realizing my sixty-year-old neighbor was in the actual mob, and was spraying his venom at my aunt. No worries, Sal's goon made friends with her, instead of delivering his threats. Let's not forget that I was only perceived as a threat until the weaselly mobster decided I was two marbles rattling around in a tin can when it came to deductive reasoning skills. At that point, I knew things were fucked but I had no idea bow badly. And I had no idea how close I was to the fire, I should have felt the heat but I didn't. Just for the record, if someone told me this story, I would tell them they're bat shit crazy.

CHAPTER 13
TO COMPLICATE MATTERS

SUNNY THOUGHT Vinny had gotten himself into hot water. He'd been more irritable, preoccupied, and seemed nervous. He was more attached to his phone, and when he took calls at Sunny's place, he'd talked outside while pacing in the street, so she couldn't hear him. He would come inside, red-faced, worked up, and tense. He was lost in thought and my guess was, he was either talking to Sal or whichever rich businessman's wife he was screwing. The upside was that with Vinny so preoccupied, he wasn't being possessive or controlling, and Sunny wasn't getting the third degree if she wanted to spend time without him. Sunny told me she would be happy if she never heard from Vinny again, but I knew she didn't really mean it. They fought hard and they loved even harder, maybe someday they would be exclusive. Right then though, I was worried Vinny was in trouble, and hoped he wouldn't end up at the bottom of Clover Lake.

I was staring at the park through one of the big front windows of Muddy Waters when my sister nosed her VW Van into a space in front of the cafe. My sister Opal was beautiful, mysterious and marched to her own drummer. I knew she would be coming into town but didn't know when. Opal slid out of the driver's seat and stood on the sidewalk with sunglasses nestled in her crazy dark curls. I tapped on the window but even though I could see her, the sun was hitting the glass, and she couldn't see me.

I pushed through the door and wrapped my arms around her. Opal Magnolia Birch was a romantic who believed in love at first sight. She was an old soul with a sharp tongue and the ability to build you up or tear you down in an instant. Once I had my arms around her, I didn't want to let her go. I introduced Opal to the baristas before making her a latte and a bagel. Once we were settled into a booth, I sat with my chin in my hands as my twenty-seven-year-old sister described her adventures on Route 66. Kane strolled out of his office and stood there smiling, he knew how much I had missed her. They had heard so much about each other that they hugged like old friends, he was a foot taller and lifted her right up off the ground.

Opal and I walked around the modern-day version of the town we grew up in, and we reminisced about the lost landmarks. We got maple creemees and shared a joint, and then sat by the duck pond and braided each other's hair. Opal told me she'd been in Vermont for a little while, reconnecting with old friends as she made her way to Bunman. Opal said she was planning to stay for a week or two before hitting the road again, and I hoped she meant it. The more Opal thought about returning to Roundelay, the more she wanted to keep driving but, just like me, I think deep down, my sister knew she couldn't run forever.

We had horrible relationships with our mother. Opal hadn't had a positive interaction with Marta Birch in a decade. My sister spent two years in intense psychotherapy, and after her wanderlust journey cross-country and back, she was tinkering with the idea of finding a place to call home. Opal was drawn back to Vermont, but once she got back to Bunman, I was afraid it would stir up a bunch of old shit. Maybe she could see past all that. Maybe she could pack the bad stuff away in a filing cabinet in the dark recesses of her mind, that's what I always did. I didn't tell Opal what happened with Marco, or that there was currently a black cloud of impending doom hanging over Bunman. If I told her that, she wouldn't have stayed, and I needed her to stay.

Kane invited us to join he and Connie for dinner. I had only been around Connie twice, but from what I could tell, she and Opal would hit it off. The two of them are free spirits who follow their hearts and don't care what people think. I talked to Opal about dinner, and she was looking forward to hanging out with Kane and Connie. Opal enjoyed meeting new people, that's where we differed. I invited Sunny to join us and told her she was welcome to bring Vinny. Prince Charming must have been off boning his other lady because Sunny accepted but said she'd be alone. I told Maggie I'd be home late, and that I'd bring home some leftovers.

The four of us piled into the Bronco to meet Connie at a hibachi restaurant on the mountain, me in the front with Kane, Opal and Sunny in the back. The two of them chatted like sisters, I spent the drive gazing longingly at Kane as he drove. I was anxious because I'd never been to a hibachi place, what if I didn't catch the flaming hot shrimp the chef threw at my face, what if it flew right down my throat and I choked on it? Or what if the hot shrimp bounced off my forehead and left a grease spot on my shirt, or in the crotch of my pants?

Despite my protest, Connie made a reservation and the six of us sat right at the hibachi. The chef made a volcano out of an onion but didn't throw hot shrimp at my forehead, my shirt, or my crotch. Connie's boyfriend, Jeff, was good-looking and in his forties, and the two of them seemed like a good fit. The group of us shared saké, dumplings, and fried noodles with duck sauce. We exchanged stories of childhood hijinks, and spent most of the evening either laughing, or laughing so hard we were crying. I excused myself to use the restroom, and when I came out, I slammed right into the chest of Giuseppi Moretti. Crap.

I attempted to avoid eye contact, staring at the ugly red carpet as I weaved around him. Just when I thought I made a clean getaway, Seppi's fingers wrapped around my wrist, and something snapped. Triggered by some combination of saké, feelings, and the fact that I'd about had it with the dumpster fire burning around me for the last six months. Fueled by some unrestrained rage, I looked him right in the eye. I never subscribed to his brand of self-importance. Looking back, I never regarded him as some larger-than-life and it somehow nurtured the bond we have. Most people regard Giuseppi Moretti a certain way, out of necessity. It eliminates any amount of authenticity in the exchange, his interactions with most people were bullshit and he knew it, but here I was getting in his face. A pendulum swung and while one extreme was his status in the mob, the other extreme was a broken little boy, and I knew it. That was the part of me that didn't give a single shit who he was or that he was a Moretti. My heart was pounding in my ears, I was incensed, and my voice was shaky,

"Let me go!"

Tears filled my eyes but just so you know, I didn't back down, screw that guy. I was seething under the surface for so many reasons, the situation with Seppi was just one of them. I swung back and slapped him across the face. Whatever. It felt good and, in the moment, I wasn't the least bit worried about ending up at the bottom of Clover Lake. He was caught off guard and just stood there staring back at me, the hand-shaped red area on his cheek becoming more pronounced by the second. I locked eyes with him again as he rubbed his face. Maybe it was overkill, but I took a step closer and jabbed my finger into his sternum,

"Fuck you!"

Seppi stood there doing nothing, and I stood there hyperventilating, big fat tears falling down my cheeks, the storm of rage had passed. I got lightheaded and sat on the floor with my back against the wall, I wasn't conditioned for this bullshit. That's when I saw the return of something gentle in his eyes. Seppi squatted down in front of me and put his hand on my knee, more gently this time, but I swatted it away. He was close enough that I could smell his cologne and when he spoke, I smelled the whiskey on his breath, a sentence in just one word,

"Dimples."

Seppi was genuinely emotional under the surface, and I could feel it, emotions made the Jersey-style Italian even more pronounced,

"I'm sorry for what I did to you. I don't have an excuse, it's not your fault. I'm mixed up in my father's shit. The beef is between me and my old man, it has nothing to do with you."

He smiled a little, but I could tell he was faking it to see if I'd smile back, he continued,

"I've given you some space and notice you haven't been ordering lunch."

Seppi paused, staring at the ugly carpet like he was finding his words, and then he stood up and shook his head. He put his hand out and I let him help me up, he gestured with his other hand as he talked,

"That's not even the point, I just want you to know that I miss having lunch with you."

I caught movement out of the corner of my eye and shifted my gaze, Kane was storming down the hall with clenched fists, flared nostrils, and fire in his eyes. He reached for the holstered Ruger and Seppi raised his hands,

"I mean no harm."

And then, my brave, and perhaps drunk boyfriend, shoved Giuseppi Moretti against the ugly wallpaper in the hallway of a hibachi restaurant. Like, hard. Kane got in Seppi's face, and I saw spit fly out as he hissed,

"How do you like it, asshole!?"

Kane took a deep breath as he geared up for more,

"If you so much as look at Amelia again, I'll fucking kill you!"

Seppi took a deep breath and stayed under control as Kane bent so they were nose to nose, Seppi reasoned,

"I was just apologizing to Amelia. I went too far, and I'm sorry, I never meant to scare her."

Seppi paused for a beat, Kane backed up an inch or two, but his expression didn't change. Seppi moved his eyes to mine, gesturing,

"I still want you to call me if anyone gives you trouble."

Kane puffed up a little more, very matter of factly,

"So far, you're the only one giving her trouble, pal."

I stood there with the palm of my right-hand stinging, hoping Kane was done with his anger outburst, eventually he would cross a line and end up at the bottom of the lake. He started to turn away, but then turned back to Seppi and continued,

"Oh, hey, we haven't seen Marco in a while, you wouldn't happen to know anything about that, would you, tough guy?"

I really hoped Kane wasn't making it worse. That was when we were going to see if Seppi was actually sorry for how he treated me. I was pretty sure we were also going to see how tolerant he was of Kane's bullshit. I focused on Seppi's facial expressions, his body language, and whether his hands were relaxed or balled into fists. Seppi's hands were open, he used them as he talked,

"I don't know where Marco is, he's a loner, sometimes he drops off the radar."

Somehow, I bought it. Am I the most naïve person on the planet? Possibly. But Kane believed him too. As we were dispersing, Opal and Constance came strolling toward the bathroom. With no idea of the current situation between me and Giuseppi Moretti, my beautiful and charming sister squeaked by and made sure to rub up against him a little while she was at it. I rolled my eyes at the entire shit show unfolding in front of me and returned to my seat. Jeff glanced across the table and I'm sure he had no idea what was going through my head. Sunny made eyebrows at me, and I shook my head. I didn't make small talk; I just drained the rest of the saké into my mouth and let the heat, fear, and anger go back to baseline.

Kane came back from the bathroom and took his place in the seat on my left, his adrenaline receding. He stared at the side of my face with wide eyes, probably shitting his pants as he realized what he'd just done, there was no way I was talking about any of that at dinner. I ignored Kane's gaze and tossed back the rest of his saké. Constance and Opal returned to the table, my sister giddy, waving a piece of paper. I was tempted to slap her with salmon, or squid, or whatever the fuck this shit was. She leaned in,

"I got that Tony Soprano guy's number. It looks like he just got slapped across the face, whoever he came here with must be a crazy bitch."

Seppi hadn't come there with me, but she had the crazy bitch part right. Opal continued to gush,

"He is so cute, and so powerful looking."

She clutched her thrifted pearls and grabbed my arm,

"Oh my Gosh, do you think he's, like, in the actual mob?"

Kane and I looked at each other, I nodded and replied flatly,

"Yeah, I think he's, like, in the actual mob."

Deep down, I was conflicted about Seppi. Looking back, we hadn't seen anyone do anything to Marco. I was the one who scraped my heel down his shin and smashed his lip with the back of my head. Maybe Marco was alive and well. Maybe Seppi was nothing more than one of his father's minions. I'd heard the rumors, but I'd just looked into Seppi's eyes, and there was something vulnerable in there somewhere. I knew he could be scary, but the way he grabbed me in that hallway didn't make me feel threatened. Seppi seemed more like a big brother, or like a person who could keep someone safe. Don't get me wrong, it's not like I wanted my sister involved with a mobster. But if she was going to be with a mobster, I'd want it to be Giuseppi Moretti.

Shortly after the hibachi incident, I decided to get lunch from Giuseppi's. I was alert and hyper-vigilant. Seppi probably wasn't killing people and feeding them to a meat grinder, but that didn't guarantee he wasn't evil. I know what you're thinking, make up your mind, is the guy a good one who does bad things or is he really just a bad one? I guess I was wishy washy for a while but you would be too, this isn't something you expect, that you'll cross paths with some Tony Soprano type on the daily. But that time I didn't see Seppi when I waited for my order, and to tell you the truth, I was kind of disappointed. Something about him was mesmerizing to me, and none of it had to do with his place on the food-chain. That day, I didn't see him, but when I unpacked my food, there was a piece of tiramisu.

Opal spent a day exploring Bunman and visiting dispensaries. You think I'm a pothead, you haven't seen anything yet. Opal is the poster child of a sixties hippie. She was a free spirit, loved animals and flowers. She had a couple of hobbies and one of them was enjoying a big fat spliff with her feet in a body of water. When she got back that evening, I asked about her adventures. She leaned against the counter eating cold pizza,

"I went to lunch at that sandwich place on the other side of town and then looked around in some of the shops near the lake. You know, those boujee ones with the seventy-five dollar socks."

Opal scoffed and when she got close to me, I smelled weed, patchouli, and Tobacco Vanille. I did an olfactory double-take of sorts, took a big sniff. It was that cut scene in a movie where things go from confetti to an off-key pipe organ playing suspenseful tones. I was sure more than one person in Bunman wore that cologne. Maybe Opal had been with someone who happened to wear Tobacco Vanille. Opal hadn't spent the day with Giuseppi Moretti, had she?

Twenty minutes later, as an afterthought, while changing into sweats,

"Oh, and I met up with that guy from dinner, that Tony Soprano guy. His name is Seppi, and he owns the Italian restaurant next door. He asked if I've ever waited tables or worked as a hostess and told me he'll hire me if I decide to stick around. We're going out again on Sunday night. He's not really my type but there's no harm in having fun, it isn't like I have to spend the rest of my life with him."

I closed my eyes and pinched the bridge of my nose. Awesome sauce.

CHAPTER 14
COVERT OPS

FOR THE NEXT MONTH, I went through the motions at work and even managed some planned renovations during my aunt's 'absence.' I took care of all the paperwork and bills and hated that I was spending hours a day in Maggie's office. I felt vulnerable and anxious. Like a big baby, I leaned in the door of Kane's office and gestured toward the gift shop, my voice a little whinier than usual,

"I don't like being in there alone, do you mind if I move my desk in here?"

Kane smiled to himself before looking up from his own pile of paperwork,

"Are you asking if you can move in with me?"

I got flustered, blushed, and backtracked. I waved my hands in surrender,

"No, I just meant that…I just thought…"

Kane motioned for me to come to him. I stood in front of him, his left hand caressed the side of my face. He kissed my forehead and nose and neck. I could feel the warmth of his tongue and the heat from his breath. I felt my nipples against my shirt. I made a sound low in my throat and kicked the door shut. Kane's hand scooped the back of my head, and our tongues danced in a deep kiss that made my knees weak. I ran my fingers through his hair and nuzzled my face into his neck, taking in the scent of coffee beans and six-dollar coconut conditioner. We stayed like that for a long time. I felt safe and I let it flood over me and let myself be free in his arms. He kissed me on the nose and winked,

"You can move in with me but I'm not sure how much work we'll get done in here."

I was relieved and excited to share space with him. I was scared I had overstepped, or presumed we were committed to each other when we weren't. I knew this wouldn't be forever, and once Maggie could return, the desk would go back where it came from. My move into Kane's office put a spring in my step, so I decided to treat everyone to lunch from Giuseppi's.

I sauntered into the ristorante to see Opal waiting tables during the noontime rush. It was foreign to see her in black pants and a white button-up shirt, her crazy hair tied back in a tidy bun. She was someone who lived in broomstick skirts and bohemian dresses, bare feet or Birkenstocks. Her hair was long at the time, and her curls tended to be out of control, in a good way. I noticed how comfortable she seemed and how happy she looked. I was pulled away when Seppi leaned out his office door,

"Dimples."

Oh boy, I couldn't wait to see what this was all about. I pinched the bridge of my nose and let out a big sigh. The woman at the counter told me it would be another fifteen minutes; I gave her a finger wave and went down the hall. Once I was in Seppi's office, he closed the door and moved his eyes to mine. I looked back at him like he had three heads, I didn't have time for this bullshit. I crossed my arms and glowered at him,

"What do you want?"

He waved me away,

"We need to get Maggie out of there, now!"

I raised an eyebrow, inquisitive,

"Out of California?"

Seppi ventured over to my side of the desk, leaned in, and spoke quietly,

"Cut the shit, Amelia, my father knows Maggie is in Bunman."

I panicked and thought of my aunt in the bunker, at least I hoped she was in the bunker, and not cutting her toenails on the couch or something. I swallowed the lump in my throat. Through tears, I mumbled,

"I, I...need to go."

Seppi's fingers clamped around my arm, and I spun around as my body came to a stop, he kept his voice low,

"This is serious, do you want me to send someone to get her?"

That didn't seem right,

"I'll be right back."

He released my arm and moved out of the way. I threw the door open and went to the dining room to find Opal. I stood in front of her, and she put down a handful of cloth napkin-wrapped silverware. She looked at me and I took her hands,

"Do you trust Seppi?"

She nodded,

"Yes."

I kissed her on the cheek and went back to Seppi's office. I closed the door and sat in the big leather armchair across the desk from him. I took a deep breath,

"I trust you. Here's the thing, she's probably in her bunker and won't come out for anyone but me. She's watching the cameras, and she has guns."

Seppi gestured toward the door and asked,

"Where did you go just then?"

I gestured in the same direction,

"To ask my sister if she trusts you."

He smiled,

"Your sister is here? I want to meet her!"

I looked at him like he had three heads and then

gestured through the wall at the dining room,

"Umm, Opal Birch is my sister, the girl you're dating or whatever, the girl wrapping napkins around silverware."

Seppi made a face I couldn't decipher and nodded his head. I threw my hands up, and all he said was,

"I didn't know."

My beautiful sister must have given him her alias in case she wanted to ghost him,

"McNamara?"

He nodded,

"Yup."

Seppi leaned out and told the girl packing orders to deliver the food to the café. He shouldered his leather jacket, snagged his keys out of the top drawer of his desk and went to what looked like a closet. When he opened the door I could see that it was an access point for the secured garage. We climbed into the fancy black Escalade and drove off into the noontime sun to save my aunt. Even though we were in the middle of a crisis, I took a second to appreciate that I was in a small space with Giuseppi Moretti, member of the mob.

To my surprise, Seppi pulled into the driveway of Stanley's Service Center and said he needed to get something. I thought I was going to shit my pants while I waited in the parking lot where Marco may, or may not, have been whacked. Seppi shoved a large handgun into the cup holder and threw his arm over the back of the seat. The tires chirped as he reversed course, a tinge of stress sweat radiated from the armpit of his designer dress shirt. I stared at the gun, my voice went up an octave,

"Is that thing loaded!?"

Seppi ignored me, and I'm pretty sure he rolled his eyes. About a mile from the garage, Seppi pulled into the parking lot of an apartment building. He sent a text. My stomach gurgled, I was sweating, and squirmed around in my seat. Seppi told me to calm down, and when I glanced at the side mirror, I saw a man walking toward the car. The man was dressed in black sweats. The hood of the sweatshirt was obscuring the man's face, but his walk seemed familiar. He had a backpack, probably full of guns, piano wire, and eyeballs. I tucked my knees up to my chest, hugged my legs, and squeezed my eyes shut. I didn't like what was happening and it was making me feel icky. Seppi said one word,

"Dimples."

Seppi unlocked the car, the man in the black sweatpants and hoodie slid into the seat behind me. I smelled warm spices and musk, and when the man pulled his hood down, I could see that it was Marco. He leaned forward and reached between the seats to touch my left arm,

"Maggie's gonna be OK, we'll get to her before Sal does."

I turned around and stared at Marco with my mouth gaping open,

"You're alive!?"

Marco went palms up and looked at me like I was crazy,

"What!?"

"The night I smashed your face, I heard you get shot!"

He shrugged, patted his chest all over and kept looking at me like I was crazy,

"Nope, I'm in one piece."

I turned around and grit my teeth. Feet on the floor, arms crossed in front of my chest, what the fuck was going on around here!? I went palms up and shook my head. Marco put his hands over the seat and squeezed my shoulders,

"You're tight."

Was everybody in this town out of their goddamn minds!? I tried hard to bite my tongue but couldn't do it. I stared straight out the windshield, threw my hands around, and exploded,

"I'm TIGHT!? I wonder why that is! Hmm, maybe it's because my aunt is in trouble! Maybe it's because I wanted a fresh start, and it's been one thing after another since I got to this God forsaken place!"

I raised my voice some more, I'd reached my limit of bullshit,

"Maybe it's because I thought you got killed... AND YOU'RE SITTING RIGHT IN FRONT OF ME!"

Marco chuckled to himself,

"I'm actually sitting right behind you."

I felt the heat rise in my face, and barked,

"THAT'S IT!"

I threw off my seatbelt, spun around so I was kneeling on the seat, and swung my open palm in Marco's direction. I was halfway in the backseat, lost my balance around a corner, and slammed into Seppi. Once he was done shaking his head at my outburst, he glanced over casually,

"Seatbelt, Dimples, you're going to get yourself hurt."

I sneered at him, rolled my eyes, and pointed at the side of his face,

"*You're* going to get hurt if you don't shut the fuck up!"

I made what I thought was an angry Italian hand gesture,

"Capiche!?"

Seppi's lips curled ever so slightly into a smile, he flicked his eyebrows,

"You're feisty, Dimples, I like it."

"Go fuck yourself!"

I cocked back and punched Seppi in the arm, and all he did was smile with his eyes. I moved my gaze to Marco and swung at him again while I was at it,

"I slept with you, and you never called me!"

Seppi choked. When I looked over at him, he

was biting his bottom lip and had a shit eating grin on his face. I jabbed my finger into Seppi's bicep, right where I had just punched him, and sternly ordered him to,

"Stop talking!"

I sat back in my seat and put on my seatbelt, I gestured at nothing,

"Could someone please tell me what the fuck is going on!?"

Nope. No one told me a thing. Marco and Seppi appeared amused with my temper tantrum, and I sat there with my arms crossed, pouting like a child. Seppi pulled into another garage and handed Marco the big handgun and the keys to a nondescript Nissan Xterra with Mississippi plates. The fifteen-minute ride with Marco from the garage to my aunt's house was filled with more crossed arms and dramatic sighing,

"Did you not have a nice time!?"

Marco looked over at me,

"What!?"

"You know, you didn't like it?"

"Of course, I liked it, Amelia, I like you. I've just never had a one-night stand before, and I didn't know what to do after. And aren't you with Kane?"

On one hand, Kane and I were in the process of something, but we weren't exclusive, and at the time I slept with Marco, Kane was bumping uglies with his ex. It was all kind of a complicated mess. I didn't know how to answer his question, but I tried,

"It's complicated."

That's it, that's all I had for him. Marco pulled into my aunt's driveway and when I unbuckled my seatbelt he grabbed my hand,

"I didn't mean to hurt you; I was caught off guard. I've never had a girl take charge like that."

I met his eyes,

"I've never taken charge like that."

He rubbed my hand with his thumb,

"I didn't want to read into it if you intended it to be an adrenaline-fueled screw. Just so you know, I almost called you."

Situations like that make me crazy. How can someone have feelings for two people at once? Kane felt safe and comfortable because of his relationship with my aunt. We had chemistry, but there were muddy waters involving his ex-girlfriend and their loose ends. Marco was dark and dangerous, but I felt confident and assertive when I was with him. Given the chance, I thought me and Marco would be happy together, and I knew for a fact we had intense sexual chemistry. I was jolted back to reality when I remembered we were in the middle of a rescue mission to save my aunt from Salvatore Moretti. I squeezed Marco's hand in return and felt warmth pass between us. I leaned over and hugged him, taking in the smell of warm spices and musk, a scent I connected to our night together, my body reacted. I kissed him on the cheek and stayed there longer than I needed to before I pulled away. My you-know-what tingled. Before I got out,

"Maybe if the time is right someday, we can see where this goes."

He smiled, but his eyes looked sad,

"That sounds nice."

I went into Maggie's house, and Marco waited in the driveway. She saw my arrival on the camera and came out of the bunker. I explained that Marco was going to take her somewhere and she didn't hesitate for a second. She put it together more quickly than I had, she figured he was alive and had been hiding. Maggie trusted Marco which made me feel better about sleeping with him, for some reason. At least Marco was an upstanding guy, even if he had probably whacked people. I gave Maggie the clothes I was wearing, and she piled her hair under a hat.

We swapped handbags, transferring our wallets and other purse items. She shouldered her duffle and my purse, and walked right out the door to the Xterra. I peeked between the blinds in the picture window and noticed she was doing a decent job walking like me. From afar, anyone who saw her would think they were looking at me. I had even given her my shoes and was glad I hadn't been wearing my dingy white Chuck Taylors.

I locked everything up tight, went out the back door, and traipsed through the woods on overload. Before long, I could see the headlights of the Escalade through the trees. There was a moment when I wondered what he would do if I never showed up at our agreed upon rendezvous spot. Would Giuseppi Moretti, member of the mob, take the time to look for me? At that point, I didn't know the answer to that question.

Seppi unlocked the doors as I approached, and I took my spot next to him in the Escalade, this time maybe I wouldn't punch him in the arm and tell him to shut the fuck up, what was wrong with me? On our way back into town he looked over at me,

"Can I give you some unsolicited advice?"

I glanced over at him,

"About?"

"Kane and Marco."

What did this guy know about anything, but I gave him the benefit of the doubt and shrugged,

"Sure."

Seppi kept his right hand on the steering wheel but moved his fingers as he talked,

"I don't think you'll be happy with either of them. Marco's a loner and I've never seen him with a long-term girlfriend."

He thought for a second before glancing over at me again, I happened to be glancing back, so our eyes met,

"The barista comes off as too vanilla and he doesn't take risks, people like that have skeletons in their closets."

I was pretty sure Seppi was the epitome of skeletons in closets, and I thought this was a prime example of the pot calling the kettle black. I was already starting to learn that things aren't always what they seem but Seppi had no idea how right he was about the bony blonde skeleton in Kane's closet. She came in and out of the picture and I was confident that if Alex said 'jump,' he'd ask, 'how high?' My mind wandered away from the conversation and I jumped when he snapped his fingers,

"Jesus, where the hell did you just go?"

I waved him away,

"I was...thinking."

Seppi had one more thing to say, and I should have known then that someday things would become complicated between us,

"Listen, Amelia."

Amelia? What was happening? I looked over at him again, and after a silence, he continued,

"When you look in the mirror, your perception of reality is skewed."

I had no idea where he was going with that, he shook his head and waved it away but I interjected,

"It's not my fault, I found a vintage fun house mirror at the second hand store."

He glanced over with a line between his eyebrows, not yet accustomed to my brand of bullshit, I continued,

"You might be rich but I'm not, it was only five dollars so I couldn't pass it up. The guy even helped me put it in the back of my car, and I managed to get it home without breaking it."

He scrunched his eyebrows even more so I added,

"Good thing too, do you know what they say about breaking a fun house mirror? Sixty-nine years of bad luck."

He shook his head but his eyes smiled a little,

"I'm just saying, you're not a woman who needs to settle for a hippie who runs a coffee shop, or someone who sleeps with you and doesn't call the next day. You deserve a better man than that, Dimples."

I felt like I was getting a lecture from my protective older brother, and I didn't like it. He had no idea how right he was though, and I wasn't about to tell him. Screw that, I was an adult, I could make my own decisions and what did Giuseppi Moretti know about anything? The rest of the drive into town was silent. Seppi nosed the Escalade down the alley between Muddy Waters and Giuseppi's Italian Ristorante. We were swallowed up by the garage behind the restaurant, the door closed automatically behind us and an alarm engaged. We returned to Seppi's office, and someone was pounding on the hallway door. I stood there wondering what the hell was going to happen next. He swung the door open to Kane, who was standing there all frantic and jealous,

"What is going on in here!? I couldn't find Amelia; she left her phone in the office."

Kane gestured at me, his voice went up another octave,

"Are you wearing different clothes!?"

Kane bristled. Seppi pulled him into the office, closed the door, and put a finger to his lips. I took a step closer to Kane,

"Sal knew Maggie was at her house."

Kane threw his hands up,

"How!?"

I kept my voice calm in hopes it would calm Kane,

"I don't know, but he did. We had to get Maggie out of there before she ended up dead. We switched clothes so if someone sees her, they'll think it's me."

Kane stood speechless for a minute and then hugged me and thanked Seppi. I was grateful for Opal, because I trusted her implicitly. If she didn't trust Seppi, I wouldn't have accepted his help. I didn't let myself think too much about what was going on with Marco. I was just glad to see him in one piece, even if he did kind of ding-dick-dash. Yes, I know, I started it. Kane asked Seppi,

"Where's she going!?"

Seppi reassured him,

"Marco's taking her to an out-of-the-way place on the lake until it's safe for her to come home."

Kane moved his eyes to me and then to Seppi, his mouth hanging open,

"Marco!?"

Seppi explained that Sal wanted Marco to be

eliminated for being sloppy, but instead, Franco shot his gun into the air and told Marco to run. Sal demands that there's no evidence left behind when someone's whacked, so he wasn't looking for a body. Marco had been lying low at his mother's, and now he and Maggie would be safe at a secluded house on Clover Lake until everything blew over.

"What does that mean, until everything blows over?"

Seppi didn't answer that question, but he told some stories from his childhood that made Sal look like father of the year. Elaborate birthday parties with ponies and bouncy houses. He described being showered with toys and food and told us about growing up with a narcissist for a father. Everyone on the outside thought Sal was a good guy and would immediately take his side if he disparaged someone, it had to be the other person who was in the wrong.

Salvatore Moretti had countless stories to tell about throwing someone a rope or paying off a debt to save someone's neck. If someone does something out of the kindness of their heart, they don't feel the need to tell a single soul about it. But if someone feels the need to tell everyone that will listen, that they've done something kind, then they only did the good deed because they wanted a pat on the back. That's the definition of an attention-whore.

The thing with narcissists is, eventually they burn all their bridges, and everyone sees the truth. Eventually people stop subscribing to their self-importance. At some point, they've sucked the life out of everyone who used to give a shit about them, including their children. After the retaliation for perceived slights, the bullying, and gaslighting, eventually every morsel of the mask falls apart. That's when people see a narcissist for what they are, which I've determined, is close to an actual piece of shit.

"Look, I know there are people in this town who think I just go around killing people. I've worked for my father since I was fifteen, and that doesn't always end well, but I'm not the person everyone thinks I am. It's a facade I built to appease my father; I know there's zero chance of having a normal life as long as he's around."

Excuse me!? What was Seppi saying!? Was he going to kill his father!? I started sweating and my vision narrowed. I shook the cobwebs out and had something very important to say,

"I have to go."

I walked my ass right out of that office and back to Muddy Waters. I made a latte and sat at my desk, deep breathing and rubbing my temples. Eventually, Kane returned and closed the door,

"What do you think he's going to do?"

I shrugged and unwrapped my cold meatball sub. I thought about the suits and shoes and watches I found in the basement. I bet all that stuff really did belong to people who had been whacked. My mind was spiraling out of control, I had washed the blood out of the loafers and sports jacket and had been wearing them. I bet the watch and keys belonged to a dead person, too. Sal was doing one of three things if he knew you existed; trying to get something from you, trying to get you to do something, or planning to eliminate you.

Maggie texted and said she and Marco were safe and settled into a beautiful little house on Clover Lake. Maggie said the place was down a private drive and had a dock. She said she had her iPad and some pre-rolls. My aunt found birdseed in the shed and filled the feeders to the brim. I pictured Maggie playing solitaire on her iPad while smoking a joint and watching birds circle the feeders. I laid in bed staring at the ceiling and thought about Maggie, Marco, and Salvatore Moretti. I was curious what kind of man Seppi thought I deserved. I wondered if things would change if Sal was out of the picture, maybe life in Bunman would be normal if he was gone. If something didn't happen soon, maybe I'd kill him myself.

CHAPTER 15
A COMEDY OF ERRORS

I THINK EVERYONE can kill under the right circumstances. People rarely stop to think about mob families, and the dynamics that exist within the hierarchy. I think most of the time, the people doing the killing are just cleaners or goons working for the boss. They are pawns and front liners who carry the risk while the boss reaps the reward. The Salvatore Moretti situation had been taking up a lot of mental space for all of us who knew that his time was running out. The man who spent all his energy threatening people into getting what he wanted, was possibly about to meet his maker. I was hoping Sal would die in his sleep, but we all know people like that live forever, unless you beat them over the head with a shovel or toss them in a mulcher. If you're not already on Team

Seppi, I found out Sal would beat Mary whenever he had a bad day. He also maintained control of their finances so Mary couldn't leave. On the occasions she can't hide her bruises, Seppi has a hard time not killing him...slowly, and while savoring every second of his father's demise.

I was sure Seppi wasn't going to do it himself, unless pushed. I wondered about the circle of men working for the family and I wondered if any of those men hated Sal enough to do the job from the inside. It seemed like a comedy of errors that Marco and Maggie were still alive, and it seemed like there were at least a couple associates who'd be willing to look the other way. I bet most of the men who worked for Sal would be happy if he cashed in his chips and did the eternal back stroke in Clover Lake.

Marco hid my aunt instead of killing her, put his life at risk to talk to me, made love to me in the most tender and loving way possible, and tried to protect me that night behind the garage. I didn't think Marco was part of the problem. Sal's right-hand man, Franco, let Marco get away instead of killing him. Mary had lived in hell since she married him. His oldest son wanted him dead. For all I knew, Vincenzo hated him too. It seemed like the layers of the pastry were crumbling for dear old Sal, even if he didn't know it yet. But I think Salvatore Moretti sensed he was losing his grip on the marionettes. I'm pretty sure there were plenty of people who'd be willing to meet Sal at the gym and spot him while he pushed up daisies.

I went for a walk with Opal, and we nonchalantly strolled past the garage. On that particular evening, the space appeared empty, but I had been fooled before. We didn't try to get inside, but walked a loop that went back by the garage, we wanted a look from the other direction. Everything appeared secure, and there were no big black sedans in the driveway, no gunshots, no one getting their bottom lip busted up by the back of my head. We stopped for ice cream and ate it in the park as the sun set, like when we were little girls. We sat in two of the Adirondack chairs surrounding the fire pit, Kane brought us a charcuterie board with cheese, crackers, strawberries and nuts. He came back with two wine glasses and a bottle of chilled Barefoot Moscato. Opal and I sipped wine while sharing a joint by the fire. Kane brought Lola out to me, she curled up by the fire and fell asleep. I glanced over at Opal, and I think that was the first time I wondered what it was like to date Giuseppi Moretti.

I wasn't sure at that point if I was experiencing hero worship or something more, but somewhere deep inside, it hurt my heart a little that she was with him. Really though, I knew I was just a broken little girl, and she was a beautiful, sophisticated woman. My sister was sexy, mysterious, magnetic, and I was none of those things. I was, and still am, just about the most transparent person you'll ever meet, what you see is what you get. There's no secret dark side, or at least there wasn't at that point in the story.

At any rate, I knew I'd never end up with someone like him and I kind of wanted to live vicariously. It's that thing of wondering what it would feel like to be with someone like that. Someone who makes you feel protected, someone who could snuff you out if he wanted to, and no one would ever know. I let the weed set in and sipped my wine. I was about to ask Opal how things were going with Seppi when she dropped a bomb,

"I'm in love with him."

That's all she said. Now, even though this would have been a big deal under any circumstance, let me tell you something about my sister. The only other person my sister had been in love with was her high school sweetheart. Other than that, she hadn't loved, or been in love with anyone. She had a handful of boyfriends, but it was never more than casual coupling with no expectations. Her last breakup was freeing and motivated her to take the trip cross-country. Now that Opal was in Bunman, she said that maybe she'd stop running for a while, she said it felt safe there. Even though I was currently battling my feelings for two men, and my aunt was in hiding, I understood exactly what she was saying. There was something about Bunman that felt right.

Back to the love business. For Opal to say she was in love with someone, there had to be something under the surface, something growing deep inside of her that no one else knew about, something no one else could see. She was one of those mysterious women who had deep thoughts and feelings about things but never said any of it out loud. But I knew Opal had been homesick, and I knew there was something telling her heart to stay for a while. Even if she didn't set down roots in Bunman, Vermont, at least there would be this window of time we had together. I wondered if Opal was in love with him, or with the idea of someone like him, someone who'd take care of everything if you let him.

I was anxious that if Opal really was in love with Seppi, that she was in love with someone who had himself wrapped up in all kinds of shady shit, even if it was only to appease Salvatore Moretti. I didn't tell her that I was pretty sure Seppi was planning to kill his father. And since I was having that entire conversation in my head, I neglected to reply, which sent Opal into a swirl of emotions, I reassured her,

"I'm happy for you, sis!"

I got up and hugged my sister, and we were still standing there hugging when Kane came out to the fire, holding a glass with a double shot of tequila on the rocks. He lit a joint, inhaled, and blew the smoke out in a stream before passing it around, I took a drag, but Opal was savoring the sweet spot from the last one,

"What did I miss?"

I turned my head, and the side of my cheek touched the cool, damp wood of the chair,

"Opal's in love!"

I didn't bother to ask if she was sure, because I knew she was. I also knew from my conversation with Seppi, that he was thinking about his future. Once Sal was out of the picture, maybe we'd all become a cozy little family. I leaned forward,

"How did you know?"

She looked at me with dreamy eyes, or maybe she was just high,

"He worries about me, keeps me safe, and he's gentle with me. I know by the way he looks at me that he cares about me. You know how many losers I've been with, and this guy is the real deal. Maybe I'm ready to let someone take care of me. He comes across as a bad boy, but I promise you, he's nothing but a gentleman, and he wants nothing more than to just live his life."

She continued,

"I've stayed over a couple times, and it's not about the bedroom, I think he just wants to spend time with someone who doesn't want something from him. We cook together and just hang out; he asked me to teach him how to crochet a scarf. I fell asleep on the couch, and he covered me up before he went to bed. He's just easy to be around. He's just a regular guy."

Well, I didn't agree with that one, Giuseppi Moretti was most definitely not just a normal guy. Kane was late to the game,

"Who are we talking about?"

I moved my eyes to his and raised my eyebrow, "Giuseppi Moretti."

Kane made a strained face at me and took another pull on his joint, eyes wide as he blew out a stream of smoke,

"That's great, Opal."

There was a period of silence as the three of us sat around the fire sipping our drinks, contemplating what it meant that my sister was with Seppi, the man who was second in charge of the Moretti mob family. I didn't know about everyone else, but I was wondering how we were going to get Sal out of the picture. As long as Seppi was under his father's thumb, he wasn't going to be able to settle down with my sister. It would be too bad if Sal decided to use a hairdryer in the shower or went skydiving without a parachute. As much as I wanted to turn the other way and ignore the situation, I knew something was going to happen, I just didn't know when.

Would there ever be a time when there wasn't a layer of darkness hovering over Bunman? A time when we could disagree with our neighbor and not feel like our life was in danger. As someone who is compassionate and giving to a fault, it's hard for me to wrap my head around people who are the complete opposite. The people with no empathy and a burning self-importance. The people who think that if they say something, it must be fact. They want you to trust every word they say, while lying to your face. I know

I'm beating a dead horse here, but there was nothing good about Salvatore Moretti, no redeeming quality. He didn't add anything positive to the world, and he'd step on absolutely anyone if it suited him. Salvatore Moretti was a narcissistic tick filled with venom. Rest assured, if Salvatore Moretti spoke to you, there was something to be gained.

If you're wondering why I have a seething disdain for narcissists, let me tell you a little more about myself. When it comes to narcissists, I have a fire burning inside of me. Narcissists are worthless. They contribute nothing but lies, manipulation, and retaliation. In the relationship before the one with the whore and the love child, I was the verbal punching bag for a narcissist. The deception and constant physical and verbal threats wore me down and just when I could have allowed Richard Kline to destroy me, I rose from the ashes.

I understood that once I cut ties with him, the punishments would start, and I was right about that. But here I am, I survived. I'm smart enough to know that people like that never change, and in the end, they never win. They will never feel remorse. People like that leave a trail of damaged exes, and children who either hate them or constantly seek their approval, or both. They swoop in like Prince Charming, work their magic, destroy marriages, and leave one after another woman chewed up and spit out after she realizes she's in a losing battle with the devil.

I was peripherally aware that Kane and Opal were having a conversation, I came back from my mental trip to my drudged-up past. The three of us were thinking about ordering pizza when I received a text from Maggie, it said, 'Hel.'

I figured it was a typo because she was texting on a burner with an archaic number pad. I replied, 'Hello to you too, how's it going?'

No reply. And then a lightning bolt of adrenaline jolted through my body, I sat up,

"Something is wrong!"

Opal and Kane looked at me. All I could say was,

"We need to go!"

I jogged toward the restaurant, I yelled back at Opal,

"Is he there?"

She shook her head,

"No, he had a family thing earlier, he's home."

I stopped in my tracks and ran back to the fire,

"We need to go wherever Maggie is, something's wrong!"

I grabbed Opal's arms,

"I don't know where she is, you need to call Giuseppi!"

Opal immediately called Seppi, and his voice was uneasy, angry, and loud enough that I could hear him on the other end of the phone,

"I'm coming."

Kane looked at me with question marks over

his head. I explained the text from Maggie and that something didn't feel right. I also reminded him I had no idea where Marco took her. I had deleted his number when I thought he blew me off after we screwed.

"Wait, I have Marco's business card on my fridge!"

I ran upstairs, grabbed the card off the fridge, and called the number. No answer. I texted him, 'Are you OK?'

There was a long pause, and my heart did a somersault when I received, 'No.'

I stood in my kitchen and sobbed, and then another tiny little switch flipped inside of me. I marched myself to the backyard and paced. Seppi pulled up in the Escalade, and for some reason, I climbed in the front seat. I was seething, if that piece of shit had done something to my aunt, I would kill him myself. I stared at the road through tears, my hands balled into fists, my jaw clenched. There was a gun in the cup holder between the seats and I didn't even care. No one said a word. We passed The Lakeside General Store and hung a right onto Lake Road. I took a deep breath and realized I could be racing to my death and reminded myself that the person next to me was close to the top of the food chain around there.

Seppi cut the lights and pulled into the driveway of a vacant house. Adrenaline was burning my stomach, and I could hear my heart beating in my ears. I had a death-grip on the back of Seppi's shirt as we moved up the private drive leading to the house. Kane's hand was gripping the back of my waistband. Opal brought up the caboose but didn't bother hanging on to anyone, she wasn't cut out for this shit and didn't want to participate.

We moved along the tree line, Seppi focused on each window, looking for movement and listening for the slightest sound. He swept the ground with his light and shined it on the flat-bottom boat that was rhythmically bumping the dock, there was a growl somewhere low in Seppi's throat. We made it to the porch facing the water and Seppi told us to stay put. The back door opened into a kitchen, and we held our breath as Seppi made his way across the threshold. Once he was out of sight, we most certainly did not stay put. Well, Opal did, but me and Kane crept over the threshold on our hands and knees and huddled in the dark under the kitchen table. We heard a familiar voice saying ominous things like,

"If I can't find you, I'll have to take it up with your stupid niece."

Seppi recognized the boat, but we all recognized the voice. There was a single gunshot and a yelp. The two of us jumped so high that our heads hit the underside of the table. We scurried out the door and into the small garage, through a side door. We tucked ourselves in with the lawnmower, a gas can, and a sporty BMW, Opal was in there too. As soon as we were hidden, we heard footsteps on the porch.

The footsteps were not rhythmic, they sounded like whoever it was had a limp. The boat started up and grew distant as it moved across the water. We needed to figure out who'd been shot. My heart was pounding in my ears, Opal was sobbing and hyperventilating, and Kane was silent, but he had 'what the fuck' written on his face. I froze for what seemed like forever before gaining composure and creeping back to the house.

Seppi was the first one I saw, he was unscathed. Opal ran up to him and threw her arms around his neck. He hugged her briefly but kept walking and told her we needed to find Maggie and Marco. Seppi flipped the lights on, and we split up, looking in every nook and cranny, there was no one there. I could see my aunt's iPad and a barely steaming cup of tea that had sloshed on the table when we hit our heads. I knew Maggie had been there. I texted her, 'Safe now, come out.'

Nothing. Kane paced,

"Where is she!?"

Seppi went back outside, sweeping the yard and dark water with his flashlight, He moved to a tiny shed and then the garage. I yelled out,

"MAGGIE!"

We heard a tiny noise and listened.

"MAGGIE!"

Something moved in the garage. Seppi pulled the gun again and held the flashlight, so it was lighting the way. He advanced into the spot where I had just been hiding. He maneuvered around the mower, the gas can and the BMW. I had tears in my voice,

"Maggie!?"

Seppi dropped the gun and put his hand out. Maggie's hand poked out from under a pile of tarps and he grabbed her by the wrist, pulling her out of the corner.

"Oh, thank God!"

I ran around the car and plowed through Seppi to get to Maggie, shoving him out of the way. He lost his balance and slammed against the garage wall with his shoulder,

"Jesus, Amelia! What's the matter with you!?"

I ignored Seppi and hugged Maggie. Opal worked her way through the obstacle course and wrapped her arms around both of us. I gave her a once-over, she was covered with blood splatter and was in shock. Kane wrapped Maggie in his sweatshirt and walked her to the porch steps.

I got in Seppi's face and didn't care about his gun or his reputation, or the fact that he was a Moretti. I shoved him with both hands,

"If your father hurt my aunt, I'm going to fucking kill him myself. I'm done with this bullshit!"

I paused and then put my finger in Seppi's face. He reached out for me, and I smacked him away,

"Go to hell!"

I plopped next to Maggie on the steps and rubbed her back. Seppi helped Marco out of the pile of tarps and gave him a once-over. He had been grazed with a bullet on the left thigh, and although it was not serious, it was bleeding like crazy. Seppi directed Kane to pour Marco a double shot of whatever he could find in the liquor cabinet. Seppi retrieved a medical kit from his car and closed the wound with steri-strips and a dressing. We all knew who had been there, and if Sal didn't die of his gunshot wound before he reached the other side of the lake, he'd be back with reinforcements.

My biggest question was, why had Sal come to take care of things himself? I think he was getting desperate. Seppi figured his father used the boat to get to the lake house undetected, and as an easy way to move the bodies out. The bodies. I cringed. The seasonal houses were packed with vacationers during the late summer, and if that house hadn't been down a private drive, that event would have been some peeping Tom's wet dream. I had no idea how Sal figured out Maggie was there, but I was impressed.

Once Seppi got Marco patched up, we loaded up in the Escalade and headed for home. Seppi pulled into the attached garage and had us sit in a room without windows. He came back with leftover food and a pitcher of ice water. I paced. He told Maggie and Marco that they were going to stay in a room in the back of his restaurant. I'm pretty sure Seppi was keeping himself busy to avoid thinking about what he'd just done. He had just shot his father, and I was pretty sure his father knew it. I was also pretty sure we were all fucked. On the other hand, that little fire inside of me was growing, and I was about fed up with this crap. For fuck's sake, was it too much to ask to have a normal day around here?

When Opal and I were back at my apartment, I paced around with a pit in my gut. I was on the verge of crying or throwing up. I was startled by my phone vibrating, my sister closing the bathroom door, a fly farting. I hadn't seen anything on Facebook. No one heard from anyone that Sal died, so I was confident it was just a flesh wound. The thing that was going to be interesting was if Sal knew who shot him. What would happen then, an epic boss battle? This was a mafia family, and if Salvatore Moretti knew his son shot him, it seemed unlikely Seppi would be consuming oxygen for long. I didn't share my catastrophic thoughts with Opal, who had just walked out of the bathroom with a positive pregnancy test. Crap.

The next morning, I was standing at my front window sipping a latte when I saw Sal limp from his stupid black Lincoln to the front door of The Meat Boss. Well, well, well. If I wasn't already certain it was Sal at that lake house last night, I was pretty sure I was looking at evidence that Sal was sporting a nice little flesh wound under those elastic waist old fart pants of his. In a way, a tiny bit of justice had been served, knowing that Salvatore Moretti wasn't invincible. He was made of flesh and bone and wasn't immortal, maybe he could even be killed.

It was getting harder and harder to go about business as usual without having frequent panic attacks and unprovoked adrenaline rushes. My fight or flight was on overdrive, I woke out of a dead sleep when Opal flushed the toilet all the way across the apartment. I thought I might be getting an ulcer but what do I know about anything. I busied myself with the store, and with all that was going on, I managed to distract myself a bit. I did, however, check my phone compulsively to make sure Opal hadn't messaged me that Seppi was dead.

To be honest, I lost track of all the crap that was going on around me. There were a lot of layers to that little onion, and I was hoping to eventually find out what was on the inside. Maybe I'd get to find out what it was like to live in Bunman without the upheaval. Let's not forget that Maggie and Marco were hiding out in a room in the back of Giuseppi's Italian Ristorante, as in, they lived there. The two of them had everything they needed, but I was anxious about how long it would last.

You can't just have a twenty-six-year-old mobster goon and a perimenopausal fifty-year-old woman, living together in a room with no windows, they'd end up killing each other. I thought about asking Kane if he was on board with moving them into our apartments, we would just need to do it in the middle of the night when there was a new moon, no big deal. While I was thinking about it, I realized

I'd slept with both of them, and probably didn't want them exchanging notes.

I knew things were going to become clear soon, but right then, there were too many unknowns. It seemed like whenever I thought I'd patched together a logical theory, another monkey wrench came flying out of nowhere. If Seppi could arrange hits for his father, Seppi could probably also find someone to kill his father. I know I keep saying it, but I wish Sal had just died in his sleep. The delicate part of this was going to be finding out who had an allegiance to him, and who did not. From what I'd heard, at that point, the scales had tipped in favor of Team Seppi. As long as he could find the right person to do it, I was confident everything would work out. If I were in a life-or-death situation, I would kill him myself. You think I'm kidding, that's cute.

I had been more scared since I got to Bunman than I had been in my entire life. We aren't talking about the 'I saw a spider in the shower' fear, I'm talking about, the 'holy crap, I might die' fear. It was supposed to be my fresh start, my new leaf, my refuge from the stressful shit. If my life is threatened, I'll fight back with all my might. Case in point, I shin-scraped Marco with a Doc Marten, and smashed the back of my head into his mouth, I'm not afraid to defend myself. Even back then, I was kind of a bad-ass.

If I'm in a position where it's them or me, I'll choose me. I was learning how to use a gun, and someday I'd feel confident being armed. But, when I think about people who just go around killing other people because someone told them to, I don't understand it. While killing someone you don't know is probably easier on the soul, it seems like there wouldn't be enough passion or anger to make it happen. I guess most hit-men use guns, because you can be far away and all you have to do is pull a trigger. It isn't as intimate, and you can probably detach enough to get it done.

CHAPTER 16
SAFE PASSAGE

LATE MORNING, I made coffee and a tray of assorted scones, muffins and tea cookies for Maggie and Marco. Was I stealthy about it? Nope. I waltzed right through the front door of Giuseppi's Italian Ristorante and headed straight for the makeshift apartment. When the staff and kitchen crew saw me coming with coffee and pastries, their eyes lit up. Sorry folks, no scones for you. I put the tray on the tacky fucking coffee table in the crude living space and decided I'd scrape up some miscellaneous things at my apartment to make the place feel cozier. I retrieved a couple of quilts and my bedroom TV so they could watch shows or movies. I carried that shit right through the front door of the restaurant too. I checked on Marco's wound and changed his dressing.

As I knelt on the floor in front of his bare leg, tending to his thigh wound, he flicked his eyebrows at me and my cheeks got hot.

Oddly, all of this nonsense had become normal, Maggie and Marco living in the back of the restaurant. It's like anything I guess, you get used to it after a while. I felt like I was getting a grip and it had been a couple days since I had a full-on panic attack. My aunt with one leg flung over the end of the arm of armchair, nose-deep in a mystery novel, a joint in the hand that wasn't holding the book. It was like some alternate reality, some portal I passed through when I went in there. When I came back through Seppi's office, he put his hand up to stop me. I followed him with my eyes as he closed the office door. He looked serious and I wondered if Opal had told him she was pregnant. She had only been in Bunman a month, they must have gotten right to it, gross. I stared up at him with question marks over my head. Pervert. He leaned forward,

"Do not bring things through the restaurant, it will make it obvious someone is back there."

He shook his head and continued,

"I want to show you something."

Seppi grabbed my wrist and pulled me to the basement. He unlocked the door, and we moved through a passageway under the alley, to a door on the other side. We entered a dark room that smelled like coffee beans and sugar. I could hear jazz. Seppi used the light from his phone to maneuver across the floor and flip a light switch. We were standing in the dry storage room below Muddy Waters. Why were all these basements connected? I was convinced there had been some sketchy shit going on down there at some point. I followed Seppi back to his office, his voice was deep and angry,

"If you're going to bring them food, or if you get the bright idea to sneak your aunt over to your place in the middle of the night, I insist you do it this way, and not through the front door of my goddamn restaurant! Capiche!?"

I stood wide-eyed and realized I might have blown their cover. I felt like a little kid who just got in trouble for doing something stupid. I was a disappointment, I wasn't built for this shit, I was just some broken little girl. I stared at him, shaking with nerves, and didn't move. I started crying and my voice was squeaky, I was crumbling,

"I'm sorry, I didn't know. I've never done this before."

He hugged me, and I buried my face in his chest. Giuseppi Moretti felt warm and smelled like Cuban cigars and Tobacco Vanille, I could see why Opal liked him. She was right, he was protective and made me feel safe. Yes, he was the same person who pinned me against the brick wall in the basement, by my throat, but even then, something about his eyes told me he would never hurt me. He reassured, his voice vibrating under my ear as he spoke,

"It's OK, just load up another tray of pastries and bring it to the staff, tell them the coffee slopped on the muffins, so you decided to start from scratch. They won't care once they have caffeine and pastries in their faces, trust me."

Seppi pulled a black tri-fold wallet out of his back pocket and handed me a crisp hundred-dollar bill,

"Use this."

I stared at the paper in my hand, I had just been given money by someone in the mob and I wondered what he did to get it, he winked,

"Use the change to get yourself a pair of those overalls you like so much, you deserve a pair without holes in them."

I nodded and changed the subject because I was uncomfortable with the situation,

"What about the TV and stuff?"

"I'll tell them you brought that stuff over for a needy family I told you about."

Seppi gestured, and it sounded just like you think it did, when he said,

"Forget about it."

I wondered how I had been there that many months without knowing the cafe's basement was connected to Seppi's. I had been in the café's storage area a million times and never even noticed the connecting door, I guess I'm not very perceptive. I changed the subject again,

"I saw the 'Meat Boss' limping into the deli this morning."

Seppi seemed giddy. That was the first time I'd seen him with a twinkle in his eye, and I wondered if maybe Giuseppi Moretti would be the one to kill his father after all. The more I watched him, the more I saw his wheels turning. Things were about to escalate, and the man who just knocked up my sister was going to be the one escalating it. I wondered if Opal had told him yet, and somewhere deep inside I kind of liked the guy and hoped the baby wasn't his.

After decades of abuse and watching his mother sport bruises that were covered up when she left the house, Seppi was ready to call the shots. He was ready to get revenge for all the pain his father inflicted on his family, and every other poor soul he killed or hurt in one way or another. I wondered how many decades I would be able to put up with that kind of shit, and then realized my mother was a watered-down version of Salvatore Moretti. I understood the dysfunction and rage.

The next couple weeks went in slow motion. I got into a routine of bringing clean laundry and food through the passageway and held Opal's hair while she threw up. I spent time with Sunny, but she was focusing a lot of her energy on whatever was going on in her relationship with Vinny. I realized what a small world it was that Opal was with Seppi, and my childhood best friend was with Seppi's little brother. I was on edge and kept one eye on Salvatore Moretti, whenever I could. It felt as if things were normal, even though that's insane considering the perpetual dysfunction. So, you know, things were as normal as possible considering I kept learning that everything I thought was true, was a lie.

My new normal was an aunt who was living in a windowless hidey-hole behind an Italian restaurant owned by a member of the mob, who just got my sister pregnant, and shot his mob boss father in the leg. Let's not forget that I was currently changing the thigh bandage of someone I'd slept with before and wouldn't mind sleeping with again. My sort of sometimes budding relationship with Kane was being put on hold quite frequently by needy little Alex. Kane and I went through the motions sometimes, but I thought maybe that ship had sailed. When Maggie told me Bunman would be the perfect change of scenery, the whole shit show I just described to you, was not what I had pictured.

I noticed Seppi was quiet, and Opal said he'd been doing a lot of soul-searching lately. She had told him she was pregnant, and he picked her right up off the floor. After that moment, he was different. He was deeper and darker and less patient with his father. I think he wanted the deed done before the baby arrived. I took advantage of Seppi's current energy, his darkness, and his growing hatred for horrible people, even if maybe he was one of them. I went into the restaurant to order lunch and chatted with Opal, she seemed tired or something. Not just because she was growing a human, I mean like something else was going on in there and the energy made me nervous. My stomach had a knot in it and I knew someday she would leave but maybe this baby changed her plans. She went to answer the phone and I made my way to Seppi's office, I had something on my mind. I tapped on the door casing and he gestured me in,

"We need to talk."

He probably thought it was about the baby, or my growing anxiety about Maggie, but that's not why I was there. Seppi sat forward, clearly interested in what I had to say, or maybe in the mood to be entertained by one of his marionettes. I pushed the door closed and stood across the desk from him,

"Buckle up."

He squinted,

"What?"

I leaned on his desk with my palms and looked him in the eye,

"You might want to buckle up."

Seppi swirled the remnants of whiskey around with half-melted ice cubes, maintaining eye contact. He was amused, his eyes smiling,

"For?"

I put my hands on my hips and very matter of factly,

"Your brother needs to go."

Besides the laugh lines and eye-twinkles I saw when I told him his father was limping, that was the most amused I think I'd ever seen him. He leaned back in his chair, drained the rest of his whiskey, and patiently waited for me to continue. I was gesturing and being dramatic,

"Listen, I know you're a good guy that gets a bad rap for being in this family, but your brother really is all those things. Are you aware that he lies to Sunny, and cheats on her, and does nothing but treat her like dog shit!?"

Seppi shook his head and shrugged, dismissively,

"You don't need to tell me what kind of a turd my brother is, I'm aware."

I wondered what their life was like, growing up with Sal. I wondered if there was ever a happy moment or if either of them had fond memories of their father. I know first-hand the damage a narcissistic parent can do and I wondered if either of the Moretti boys would be anything like their father when they had kids. I thought about men who beat their wives and men who break their hearts. Tears were creeping in, I shoved them out,

"I grew up with a little girl who watched her alcoholic father beat her mother almost every night, and sometimes worse. Sometimes he would beat Sunny too. She walked on eggshells around that man and I have my own load of childhood struggles, but we found comfort in each other. We ran away and hid in the forest, pretending to be fairies."

I was derailing, this had nothing to do with fairies, I tried to keep my voice steady,

"I hadn't seen her in almost twelve years, and in my mind, things were fine. In my mind, that little girl was happy, and all that shit from her childhood had faded into the background."

I leaned on his desk again,

"Here's the thing, she's still dealing with the fear and the head games just like she did when she was a little girl. Do you want to know why?"

Seppi leaned forward in anticipation, I'd hooked him and now I was going to reel him in,

"Why? Tell me."

"She's with your brother."

Seppi sat back in his chair like I'd taken the wind out of his sails, and I could tell a lifetime of memories were flooding in.

"Whenever she tries to leave, he makes it impossible. He doesn't want her; he just wants her to want him. He comes and goes as he pleases, screws other women as he pleases, tears her down as he pleases, and rides back in like Prince Charming, as he pleases."

I made eye contact with Seppi and could see he was feeling his feelings deep down inside, I kicked him while he was down,

"Remember when you told me I deserve better?"

He nodded,

"You do."

"So does she."

Then I pulled out the big gun, no pun intended. I looked him straight in the face, I meant business,

"If she was your daughter, you'd do something about this! You wouldn't want some guy scaring your 'baby,' or screwing around behind her back, would you? Nope, you'd make it very clear that *your* little girl is to be treated with respect, that no means no, and that there will be hell to pay if she gets hurt. There won't be any gaslighting or manipulating going on with any daughter of Giuseppi Moretti."

I stopped talking and stared at him with my arms crossed. My words punched him in the dick as he realized he could soon be the father of a little girl. I leaned on his desk again, my palms leaving sweat prints on the shellacked wood surface,

"Well, aren't you going to say something!?"

But he didn't say anything, he just stood up and left his office. I threw my hands up, what the hell was going on around here? Whatever. I slipped through the door to see Maggie and Marco before I left. Marco's wound was almost healed, but he seemed to enjoy it when I changed his dressing. I was willing to help get rid of Sal. That guy Franco was willing to assist. According to Marco, Seppi was very subtly trying to figure out who liked his father and who wanted him dead. Seppi did not involve his mother, although she'd hated his father even longer than he had.

There was a part of me that wanted to be a good little girl, and most likely helping kill an old narcissistic mob boss was not ladylike. I would be more of a poison-in-the-tea kind of a gal and not a bullet-between-the-eyes kind of gal. I'd be more of a cleaner than an actual killer. I know adrenaline would kick in, but I'm sure I would probably end up passing out and then throwing up all over the place. That would then snowball into a massive case of bubble-gut and the shits, which wouldn't be conducive to a tidy crime scene or getaway. Not that anyone had mentioned I should be part of the plan if, and when, something went down, but I'd feel left out if I wasn't involved.

Mostly, I felt like I was watching from the other side of the glass as the people close to me planned the actual murder of an actual mob boss. It was like I was in a limbo of some sort, a purgatory or figurative fence I was sitting on. I tend to sense the energy in the people around me and I could tell Marco was getting antsy, and Seppi had been spending time with several people I had never seen before. They were people like him, good-looking Italian guys dressed like rich businessmen. Opal told me the men would come for dinner, and then go in the back with Seppi and Marco. Maggie would get high, snack on leftover bread sticks, and watch her show. Opal told me she'd heard a lot of talk about the garage.

I was sure those men were talking about *the* garage, the garage I couldn't get into. Opal checked the book, and as luck would have it, the men had a reservation later that night. I planned to use that window of time to get into the garage all by myself. The men would be drinking expensive liquor and stuffing their faces full of pasta and Mama Moretti's marinara. Once those fat-cats had their bellies filled with alcohol and carbohydrates, they wouldn't be chomping at the bit to do nefarious shit at a vacant service center. When the cats were deep in the inner sanctum, smoking Cubans with Giuseppi Moretti, this little mouse would be breaking into her aunt's goddamn garage.

CHAPTER 17
WHEN THE CAT'S AWAY

I BINGE-WATCHED videos on picking locks and being stealthy. I dressed in black and took a handful of black rubber gloves from Muddy Waters. I snuck over to Kane's while he was walking Lola and looked for a utility knife or something stabby. I came away with a solid-looking flathead screwdriver he wouldn't miss. I ran through scenarios in my head and figured I'd listened to enough crime podcasts that I should be able to break into a garage without leaving a trace. I ate something that wouldn't give me stomach issues, ain't no one got time for the gravy-shits whilst executing a meticulous plan.

I made sure my phone was on silent, and I peed right before I left. I made sure Kane thought I was having a self-care night while my sister was at work.

I told him I planned on a bubble bath, face mask, and deep conditioning treatment, none of which Kane cared to be a part of. I paced around my apartment and then around the store.

Opal texted me at exactly eight o'clock, the men had arrived, and would be meeting with Seppi after they ate. I asked her to give me a heads up when they were getting ready to leave, that way I could put things back the way I found them and get out of the garage. Ten minutes later I went out the back door, creeped along behind The Meat Boss and the food co-op, and cut up a narrow alley to the sidewalk. I wore a black baseball hat and had rubber gloves and my pen light in a fanny pack. To anyone watching, I was just some chick who liked wearing black, out taking a walk.

It was almost Labor Day, but it was muggy, and sweat was dripping into my crack before I even reached the garage. I noticed how quiet Bunman was at night and wondered what went on behind closed doors. I wondered if siblings watched cartoons and ate cereal on the couch every Saturday morning, or if school aged boys on bikes delivered papers to the residential neighborhoods before dawn. I wondered if fathers drank a cold beer on a hot day after mowing the lawn or if old ladies sat on their porches petting their cats.

My phone lit up inside the fanny pack and I unzipped it just enough to read the text without pulling it out. I didn't want to draw attention to myself.

I realize it was probably dumber looking reading a phone that was in a fanny pack, I never claimed to be smart. It was Kane, 'Cover your unmentionables, I'm bringing you some ice cream.'

Crap. I would never turn down ice cream and Kane knew it. I rolled my eyes, pulled the phone out, and replied, 'I'll be out of the tub soon and when I'm all lotioned up and in my jammies, I'll come over for some ice cream.'

I zipped my phone in the fanny pack, and focused. I was standing across the street from the garage when I decided I should have asked Kane to come with me, but at that point, I was committed. I looped around the building and through the woods to the low wall. I climbed over the wall and went from tree to tree, pausing each time I stopped. It was quiet besides an occasional bark a half mile away, and the hum of traffic on the interstate. It was eerily calm. I moved closer to the driveway and then to the back door. It was hard in the dark, but I didn't want to risk using the penlight until I was inside. I tried every key I had in my possession and just like the last time, none of them worked on the back door.

I moved along the side of the building facing the tree line and ran my hand along the wall, searching for the window. Bingo. I had plenty of practice opening windows in high school when I'd break out at night, I'd close everything up completely once I was on the roof. I felt the cold metal of the window frame.

Locked. I pulled the screwdriver out of my fanny pack and popped the window open. I slid the glass aside on its track and it hardly made a sound. There was a soft motor of some sort running inside, I peered into the screen but couldn't see anything. I used the screwdriver to pop the screen out and leaned it up against the exterior wall and dragged a log over.

I stepped on the log and found that I was at the perfect height to hoist myself through the window. I was able to get my abdomen balanced on the window frame but groped around below me and realized there was nothing for me to land on. I needed light so I could see what the hell I was doing. I hopped down, snagged the penlight out of the fanny pack, and put it between my teeth. I climbed on the log, hoisted myself up, and balanced my abdomen on the window frame again. I turned on the penlight and almost shit my pants when I shined the narrow beam into the face of Vincenzo Moretti. You're probably wondering what he did to me when he saw me breaking into the garage. He didn't do a damned thing, because he was tied to a chair with a rag in his mouth.

The purple penlight fell to the floor when I screamed, it was laying askew, pointing at the dust bunnies under the fridge. Maybe Vincenzo hadn't seen me. My heart was pounding, and I was almost hyperventilating, if I didn't calm the hell down, I was going to pass out. I took inventory, I was in one piece, Vincenzo probably didn't even know who opened the window, everything was fine. And just when I thought I probably maybe got away with it, someone whispered,

"What are you doing?"

I screamed and jumped out of my skin. Here's the thing, I wasn't worried I was going to die, or that the person who found me was going to chop me up into little bits or throw me into the basement with the shoe box full of eyeballs. I didn't fear any of those things because the person standing five feet from my legs was none other than Kane Buchanan. Goddammit.

I worked my way out of the window with Kane grabbing my midsection, guiding my way, even though I could have done it myself. I looked up at him and didn't know what to say, I had lied about self-care night, and he knew it. I tried to be casual, giving him a finger-wave,

"Oh, hey, how's it going?"

Kane leaned closer and whispered frantically, palms up,

"What the hell are you doing!? This is extremely dangerous! Why didn't you tell me you were coming here!?"

"No, it's OK, the people are with Seppi."

"The people? Do you mean the people who are going to help him knock off his pops? Yeah, they left already, and I think Seppi went with them."

Kane pushed me behind the garage and through the woods to the low wall. I ran back so I could pop the screen in and slide the window shut. I chucked the log into the woods. Headlights were moving in our direction, so I got low and speed-walked to the woods and then broke into a run, jumping over the wall like the Dukes of Hazzard. The second I hit the ground on the other side of the wall, headlights swung into the driveway and hooked around the back of the building. Holy crap.

Five men climbed out of the Escalade and went in the back door, I couldn't tell who any of them were. I assumed it was Seppi and his associates, and that they were meeting at the garage instead of in his office. Maybe it was going to happen soon. Kane grabbed my hand and as soon as we stood up, we heard a single gunshot. I made an involuntary squeak and tried to pull Kane through the woods, he pulled me down,

"Amelia, shh!"

I sat down, and as quietly as possible, threw up hot bile that steamed in the cool of the night. Classy. A while after the gunshot, we made our way back home and I didn't say a word about seeing Vincenzo. Kane wasn't freaking out about the gunshot we heard, and didn't seem particularly angry with me, maybe he was high.

"I knew there was something up when you didn't want me to bring you ice cream. I know you well enough to know you're not above eating Phish Food in a bubble bath. I went over and sure enough, the tub had no bubbles, and no Amelia."

"I can explain."

But I couldn't. I had lied to Kane. I had also done something stupid, really stupid. Let's say Vincenzo wasn't in there, and I had been in the garage snooping around. Chances are, I would have had no idea anyone was there until it was too late. I wanted to find out what was going on, but I needed to be more careful about it or I'd end up dead. Kane asked,

"Why did you think that was a good idea?"

I shrugged,

"Opal told me those guys have been going for dinner next door and then meeting with Seppi, I figure they're planning something. They were at the restaurant tonight, so Opal texted me once they arrived, and I left for the garage. I guess they didn't stay."

Kane shook his head. I stared at my feet,

"There's something else."

He closed his eyes and massaged his temples,

"OK, what is it?"

"You might want to sit down."

Kane retrieved two shot glasses and a bottle of tequila. He put his hand up, poured a shot and threw it back. He topped off both glasses and slid one in my direction.

"OK, I'm ready."

"Earlier today, I spoke to Seppi about Sunny. I told him how she grew up watching her mother get beaten and that she got smacked around too. I told Seppi how the two of us struggled as little girls and how we helped each other survive. I told him I saw how Vincenzo treats her. Sunny has told me how he speaks to her, and lies to her, and cheats on her, and threatens her when she tries to break it off."

Kane looked interested but wasn't sure where I was going with it. I paced around enough that Lola started pacing. Kane threw his hands up and shook his head,

"OK, so what did he say? Is Seppi going to talk some sense into Vincenzo?"

I started hyperventilating. And that's when Opal knocked frantically on Kane's door, she sounded nervous,

"Have you seen my sister? I can't find her anywhere and she's not responding to my texts."

He opened the door and pointed in my direction. Opal hurried over,

"Oh my God, I am so sorry! I got busy in the back and when I came out, the table was empty. I thought they were in Seppi's office, but I tapped on the door and when I tried the knob, it was locked, and the lights were off. I don't understand what happened. Are you OK?"

To say I was OK would be a lie. At that point, I was sitting on the kitchen floor with my back against the cabinets, chasing my tequila with an edible and some bubbly water, trying to control my breathing. Lola was laying in front of me with her ears perked up. I can handle a lot of things, but shit was escalating, and I couldn't handle it. The two of them leaned on the counter and waited. I caught Opal up on the parts I had already told Kane. This time *she* asked,

"Well, what did he say?"

"He didn't."

Now Opal was mad,

"What do you mean he didn't say anything!? You told him his brother is acting like that, and he didn't say anything!? Are you fucking kidding me!?"

And now we were all worked up. Awesome.

"Well, he just stood up and walked out."

Opal leaned forward,

"AND!?"

There was no delicate way for me to put this,

"And I think he killed Vincenzo."

My sister seemed happier with that answer than when she thought Seppi did nothing. What the hell was happening? She kissed me on the forehead, and I patted her tiny baby bump before she went back to my apartment for the night. I didn't like that my sister was involved in this, by association or impregnation. I showered and Kane retrieved the Phish Food he had been talking about. That's when I broke down, again. I put on my favorite episode of Psych and laid in Kane's arms until I was out of tears and ice cream. I decided I needed to think about all that shit another day. I proceeded to pack it away in one of the filing cabinets in the back of my mind where I compartmentalize stuff like that. I slept like a baby.

I woke up with the feeling that I was going to get in trouble, like I had done something wrong. I backtracked in my mind. I replayed my walk to the garage, my path through the woods and over the low wall. I closed my eyes and rewound the night, my attempts to unlock the doors, popping the window open, climbing on the log, seeing Vincenzo tied to the chair, Kane catching me, seeing the headlights, running into the woods, hearing the gunshot. I sat straight up in bed as a rush of adrenaline fired off in my belly, had I dropped the screwdriver? Would it connect Kane to the garage? Shit. I swung the blanket back and frantically looked for the fanny pack. Where the hell was it? Oh, God. I was opening drawers and looking on hooks when Kane came out of the bathroom toweling off his hair,

"How did you sleep?"

I pawed through a drawer full of loose change and random junk, looking for my fanny pack. I threw my hand up dismissively,

"Fine."

I opened another drawer and pawed through that. He stepped into the kitchen,

"Can I help you find something?"

I was starting to get bubble-gut and felt a full-on panic attack creeping in,

"Have you seen my fanny pack?"

"What!?"

"The thing I had around my waist last night, my

fanny pack. I need my lip balm...it has sentimental value."

Kane looked at me like I was nuts,

"You're frantically pawing through my kitchen drawers looking for the sentimental value lip balm that's in your fanny pack?"

I nodded. Kane gestured toward his room casually,

"I have lip balms Amelia, a whole bunch of them, look in my nightstand."

Kane returned to the bathroom, and I went into his bedroom. I rolled my eyes and opened the nightstand to look for lip balm when I really wanted my fanny pack. I grabbed a peppermint lip balm before pushing the drawer shut. As I was walking away, it registered that a waft of perfume had come out of the drawer when I shut it. I turned around, and pulled the drawer open again. There was something else in there besides condoms and a selection of peppermint lip balms. I reached in and pulled out a travel bottle of perfume and a black hair tie with long blonde hairs on it. I was staring at the hair tie when Kane came into his room. My back was turned, and my eyes were brimming with big fat tears. He asked,

"Did you find one?"

My voice cracked,

"Yes, thank you."

I cleared my throat and pushed the drawer shut. I wanted to scream and cry but I held it in. Once Kane was busy in his closet, I turned around with my eyes pointed at the floor and sulked out of his apartment. I lifted the corner of the braided welcome mat and retrieved the spare key from its hiding spot. As soon as I was inside, I stood with my back against the door and fell apart. He hadn't said one way or another if he had slept with Alex. That hair tie wrapped with blonde hairs and that travel bottle of perfume were a reminder that there was another woman. And whether they slept together or not, she spent the night. She probably fell asleep in his arms. He probably made her a latte in the morning and tucked hair behind her ear. I don't want to be the kind of woman who hates another woman for coming along first, but that's exactly what I was doing.

I took the cap off the perfume and smelled it. I imagined him responding to it, wanting her, finding it attractive. It was different from the perfumes I wore, which were gourmands like Alien Elixir and Black Opium. Her perfume was brighter, sweeter, and I could see how it fit her vibe. She was nothing like me, she was my complete opposite, the figurative yin to my yang. I wondered if she made him feel good the way I did, I wondered if she knew something that drove him wild. She was light and sweet, and I was dark and fucked up and bitter. So I let my mind wander a little about how they were together and how he was with me. Did she leave the bathroom door open when she peed or did she close it like a lady. I wasn't a lady.

I wondered if he ever bought her tampons or if she sat on the lid of the toilet and watched him shave. I created this entire scenario, this entire romance novel out of their relationship. I didn't entertain the reality that they had problems and that's why they kept breaking up. My mind couldn't fathom that sometimes other people have fucked up relationships and sometimes they like it that way. But the two of them kept coming back to each other, there had to be something between them, something neither of them could live without. Did he kiss that perfume off her chest? Did he get it for her? Did I tell him I found her things in his nightstand? Nope.

But I stood there smelling the perfume for way too long, something about it was hypnotic, a spiral of something sweet like marshmallows, with a whisper of something mature and sexy. Maybe I was judging a book by it's cover, maybe she was a hell-cat in his bed, maybe she did things I had never even learned about, maybe she did something for him that I couldn't. I wondered if the 'whore' was like that for my ex, something more alluring, something more experienced in that way. And I wondered about the one before that, the one who was horrible to me in so many ways but was good to me in that one. My chest felt tight and I eyed the basket of pill bottles on top of the microwave. I slid a joint from my thrifted flip top tin and turned to head for the sun porch. When my puffy eyes moved passed the coat rack next to the door, my fanny pack was hanging there. Thank God, Opal must have taken it with her when she left Kane's the night before. I scrambled across the room and grabbed the strap of the fanny pack, yanked, and pulled over the entire coat rack. Even though Kane probably banged that blonde, I was relieved to see the flathead screwdriver in there. I zipped the fanny pack and tossed it on top of the pile of things that had fallen to the floor. Just a haphazard collection of miscellanies, and I could relate.

CHAPTER 18
YOU'VE GOT A FRIEND IN ME

WHEN I WENT NEXT DOOR to get my lunch, Seppi leaned out of his office and snapped his fingers, "Dimples."

I was standing there picking at the skin next to my thumbnail and when I looked up, he was motioning me to his office, again. I signaled to the woman behind the counter that I'd be right back and rolled my eyes as I went down the hall. It felt like I was doing the walk of shame but didn't know why. I plopped in the chair across the desk from Seppi's and crossed my arms. I narrowed my eyes at him, I was so sick of the constant drama, like a temperamental child,

"What do you want this time!?"

I dropped my eyes to avoid looking at him. He didn't reprimand my bad attitude, but I knew he was assessing my current mental state,

"Are you OK, Dimples? You look like shit."

I moved my eyes from my lap to his face, gave Seppi a dramatic thumbs up, and in a sing-songy voice,

"Gee, thanks mister!"

I leaned forward with my elbows on my knees and glared at him,

"Is that why you called me in here? To tell me I look like shit!?"

He slid something across the desk,

"I think this belongs to you."

Without looking up, I swiped the top of the desk and came back with my purple penlight. Jesus Christ. And because I'd gone off the rails when I got a label maker, the penlight had my fucking name on it. I laid my head back, closed my eyes, and pinched the bridge of my nose as I let out a full-body sigh. Goddammit. My eyes brimmed with tears, but I pushed them down deep inside and swallowed my feelings. When I glanced up at Seppi, he was eyeballing me in the most unamused way one person can possibly eyeball another. My face flushed with heat, and I felt like I was being scolded by my mother, only Giuseppi Moretti could do far more to me than just hurl soul-crushing criticisms and ground me for the weekend.

I clenched my jaw and stared at my lap as my heart pounded in my ears. I felt like I was going to shit my ratty vintage overalls in Seppi's fancy leather chair. Fuck. I wondered if I was going to end up at the bottom of Clover Lake with a bullet in my forehead. Whatever. Seppi retrieved two rocks glasses and poured expensive whiskey over perfectly square ice cubes, he slid one of them across the desk to me. I wrapped both hands around the glass and broke down, again. But this time, I had taken off all my armor, and I was sobbing in Giuseppi Moretti's office while my lunch was cooking. His eyes soften and he put his hand out,

"Come with me."

Seppi led me to the garage and I climbed in the passenger seat of his Escalade. As he drove out of town, I kicked my shoes to the floor and hugged my knees to my chest as I cried. We got on the highway and made the drive to the southernmost point of Lake Elysian. I dug the thrifted flip-top tin out of my bag and retrieved a joint before plucking my rocks glass out of the cup holder. I swallowed fire and I got high. Seppi stopped at a deli along the way and came out with turkey, bacon & Swiss paninis, kettle chips, and fresh squeezed lemonade. We parked and ate at a picnic table on the edge of the lake. I stared across the water and felt some of the tension leave my body. In that moment, I wasn't sure if it was the water that was calming me, or the person I was with. That was the first time I looked at Seppi in that way, and it made my insides do things. I felt like I didn't need to hide my wounds from him, and his mere presence made me feel less broken.

I guess that's when I started to realize we had a connection. Not because we were in this pocket of time where he was with my sister, but because the two of us had our own connection. A connection that didn't have anything to do with the bullshit swirling around us, something that had nothing to do with the mob. But at that point, I would still put my guard up with him at times. That day though, Giuseppi Moretti turned the tables a little, he leveled the playing field, or at least he tried. But back then, I was still battling with so many demons that my first instinct was to be an asshole.

Seppi let me sit in silence while I ate my sandwich, tears rolling down my cheeks as I focused my thousand-yard stare on the water, I wanted to go home. I'm not talking about going back to my apartment or back to where I came from, I'm talking about, home. I wanted to be done with the bullshit, I wanted to find somewhere safe. I wasn't currently dealing with my mother or running into my ex, his whore, and their love child, but I was starting to realize I was involved in something exponentially worse. He put his hand on mine briefly, it was warm and covered mine completely. His voice had something different in it that time, a quality that conveyed an interest in holding my broken pieces together,

"Are you OK, Dimples?"

I shrugged because I didn't know the answer. There's something about a powerful man wanting to take care of a woman's feelings, something that melts most of us into a puddle, in more ways than one. No pun intended.

"No."

Seppi knew I'd shut down if he spooked me, so he didn't come across as he was hurt or angry,

"Opal told me."

Great.

"I just wanted to know what was going on in there."

It sounded whiny when I replied. I could see hurt in Seppi's eyes, and I realized he cared what I thought of him,

"You think I killed my brother?"

I reassured him,

"No."

 But that was a lie.

 Seppi retrieved his hand and I felt a wave of rejection, he searched for his words,

"Listen,"

Seppi leaned forward and laced his fingers together on the picnic table, I listened,

"I'm not mad, but I need you to stop poking around in matters that don't pertain to you. I'm doing my best to keep you out of trouble, but you have got to stop digging around. You're going to get yourself killed."

I had a million questions spinning around in my mind. Where did Seppi go after I told him about

Vinny? Why was Vinny tied to a chair in the garage with a rag in his mouth? Why had Kane and I heard a gunshot? What would happen if I kept poking around? Would I get killed? Was Seppi only watching out for me because of Opal? Was Vinny a bad guy, or was he acting like this because of his father? Did I just get my period?

"I want to know what's going on in there."

He made eye contact,

"No, you don't."

I leaned forward and narrowed my swollen eyes at him,

"Yes, I do."

We would have gone back and forth for all eternity if he had decided to play along, but he didn't,

"Do you trust me?"

I shrugged, even though the answer was yes,

"I guess."

He shifted,

"I didn't kill my brother, but he's in deep shit. Vinny is involved with a woman who's married to a very powerful man."

I felt bad for Sunny, knowing she was involved with someone who was involved with someone else, even if they weren't exclusive at the time,

"Did the woman's husband find out about it or something?"

"He's got his share of mistresses, so it isn't even about that. They have an agreement in that respect, but Vinny managed to get the woman pregnant and that poses a problem."

"Why? Can't she just play it off like it's her husband's kid?"

"No. The husband was sick when he was little, and his swimmers don't swim, if you know what I mean. There is no way it's his baby, and everyone will know it. There's something else."

Seppi pulled his phone out and showed me a picture of the woman, who was fair-skinned and naturally very blonde with blue eyes. He searched for another picture and turned the phone around to a pale skinned light-haired man with deep blue eyes. I nodded as I pictured the baby coming out with a dark pompadour, Italian eyebrows, and a glass of expensive whiskey over perfectly square ice cubes,

"What does that have to do with where you went the other day, and why Vinny was tied to a chair in the garage? And what about the gunshot?"

He fidgeted a little, and that man doesn't fidget,

"There's a lot going on right now and I needed to clear my head. When you said I'd fix it if my own daughter was being mistreated, I couldn't even stand the thought of it, it made me sick."

That was the first time I saw Giuseppi Moretti as a man who put his pants on one leg at a time like everyone else. He looked down at his hands,

"My life is in shambles right now."

I laughed awkwardly because sometimes

feelings make me uncomfortable. Seppi's eyes filled with tears, but he tried to blink them away,

"I have a baby on the way...a baby. Do you realize what that means?"

I was too intimidated by his vulnerability to offer up anything meaningful,

"Yeah, it means you're going to have a baby."

Seppi flicked his eyes at me, shook his head, and sighed,

"No, I mean, do you realize what it means that I'm having a baby?"

I took a deep breath and got off my high horse,

"What does it mean?"

The tears in his eyes teetered at the edge,

"It means I have a chance to be what my father wasn't. It means I have a chance to be a good dad, to read bedtime stories, and give baths, and stay up until midnight wrapping presents on Christmas Eve. It means I can go to ballet recitals, baseball games, band concerts, or whatever this kid likes to do. It means I have a chance to do better than my father."

At that point, I was even more uncomfortable with his tears than I was with his feelings, so I acted accordingly,

"So, what you're telling me is that you have Daddy issues?"

Seppi glanced up from the table and I could see he was trying to show me some of his broken pieces,

"I'm trying to be real with you here, Amelia, and I don't make it a habit to show people my vulnerabilities."

Well, wasn't that a kick in the teeth. Why was I like this? I stared at the table, my face flushing again, a sick feeling settling in my stomach. I was needlessly acting like an asshole to the one person in my life who was being straightforward with me. I put my hand on his,

"I'm sorry, Seppi.

I teared up but pushed it away so I could be strong for a member of the mob,

"I'm here, I'm listening, and I appreciate that you trust me with this. I know you drew the short straw when it came to fathers, but you're not going to be anything like that."

Seppi stared across the water and tried to change the subject, he needed to come up for air before diving back into his feelings,

"Have you been to Lake Elysian before this?"

I shook my head,

"No, but it's really pretty here, I like it a lot."

His eyes followed some birds across the sky,

"If you ever get the chance, you should visit the village, the downtown is like a Norman Rockwell painting. It's a little slice of heaven and there's a café you'd like."

I knew Seppi was trying to change the subject, but he was being sucked back into his head like a tornado and couldn't put the armor back up fast enough. In that pocket of time, I felt something about the fact that Seppi knew I'd like that café he was talking about, maybe it meant he thought of me sometimes. He bit his bottom lip and when he blinked, one tear fell. It startled me when I realized he was letting his guard down. But when that tear fell in my presence, it caused an adrenaline rush because I knew not many people had ever seen him that way. I wondered if my sister had seen him that way. It felt like a big responsibility, and I knew Seppi's vulnerability with me meant something regarding our relationship and connection. I was starting to realize that we were a lot alike, and maybe he needed me just as much as I needed him. Just this broken little girl with so much darkness deep inside, and when it came right down to it, he was just a broken little boy,

"Amelia, I'm having a baby."

I went to the other side of the table and slid in next to him. I put my arm around his back and leaned my head against his left shoulder, I was trying not to fuck it up or scare him back inside of his shell,

"I know, and you're going to be a great dad, you want to know why? You already care more about this kid than your father ever cared about you."

I just sat there with my arm around him, his body shook as he cried, and it brought tears to my eyes that he was in pain. Seppi leaned over and kissed the top of my head, letting out a sigh of tension. He paused with his lips against my crazy curls,

"Thank you, Dimples. Please don't tell anyone I'm weak."

I glanced up at him,

"You're not weak, you're the strongest person I've ever met. Strong people still have feelings, you know."

He didn't say anything, so I continued,

"I wonder if people listen to you or if they just pretend because of who you are."

I paused,

"But I'm not putting on some act, I don't care who you are to everyone else, you're just Seppi."

I met his eyes,

"I listen because I want to, not because I'm getting anything out of it. I've spent most of my life being disregarded so I know what it's like. You're just someone I care about; I'm not looking for anything in return."

I felt some of the tension leave his body and it was an important moment in our story. I was reciprocating, for once, and knew Seppi wasn't a man who let his guard down very often, but he felt safe enough to do it with me. You probably already know this, but I feel like I need to make sure you understand that I wasn't doing any of it on purpose. My connection with him was something I didn't ask for or expect, but I had stopped hiding my broken pieces from him, and maybe that made him feel safe doing the same with me.

From that moment on, I never doubted that Giuseppi Moretti was one of the good ones. I was safe when I was with him, and he was safe with me. Eventually, I broke the silence,

"What about your brother, why was he tied to a chair with a rag in his mouth?"

Seppi scanned the small group of people walking their dogs before determining no one was within earshot,

"The husband, Connor, is a high-profile lawyer, we have a mutual agreement with him. We keep him on retainer for legal issues, and he uses us to threaten or eliminate people who cause him trouble."

I choked on the last sip of my lemonade and screeched as quietly as I could,

"Eliminate!?"

He glanced over, his voice low and matter of fact,

"I'm in the mob, Dimples."

I scrunched up my nose and pretended to gag. Seppi's eyes smiled, and he continued,

"Connor encouraged his wife's relationship with Vinny. My brother comes off as young, dumb, and full of cum, so Connor figured there wasn't any risk. Vinny's nothing more than a plaything when the cat's away bopping his secretary. That woman would never leave Connor for my brother; it would completely upend the lifestyle she's accustomed to. The trips and fancy cars, the vacation houses in exotic places, the yacht and the jewelry, the designer clothes and Botox, the fake tits. Vinny lives in an apartment above the hardware store in town. His assets include a PlayStation, a crotch rocket, and a four-foot bong. My brother isn't a guy who's taking anyone on a cruise or popping in with something special from Cartier."

I moved back to the other side of the table and nestled my chin in my hands,

"Go on..."

Seppi's eyes smiled again,

"Vinny managed to get her pregnant, and now she has decided she wants to be a mom."

"Oh."

"Yeah, oh. Connor is feeling threatened because, in his eyes, even with all his money and power and material possessions, my brother gave her something he can't. And even though the couple has an agreement about extra-marital relations, the one deal-breaker is that those activities cannot affect the facade they display for the rest of the world."

I played it back,

"OK, so she can sleep with Vinny, and Connor can sleep with his secretary. Then the two of them go home at night to their beautiful home in some fancy gated community, and pretend they're a happy couple."

"Right."

"And now that she's preggers with Vinny's kid, it not only poses a threat to Connor's masculinity, but it poses a threat to the facade they've created, a facade that doesn't include children."

Seppi sat back and let me continue,

"She wants to have the baby, which is going to disrupt their lives, and Connor would have to go along with it. He'd have to watch his illegitimate son play t-ball or his illegitimate daughter dress up as a fairy for Halloween. He'd have to buy the kid a car and pay for college. And heaven forbid Vinny wants to be involved in his kid's life, that would cause another set of problems entirely."

And then it hit me. Oh. I realized that Vincenzo and Giuseppi Moretti grew up in the same house, and probably had the same daddy issues. I'd just listened to Seppi confide that he wanted to be a better father than his father. Like a lightning bolt, I realized Vinny was probably feeling the same thing. Maybe the stress of having to deal with his own father made Vinny feel out of control. And suddenly, I realized that even though he wasn't faithful to Sunny, maybe Vinny wasn't such a piece of shit after all.

"My brother leaves something to be desired in the Prince Charming department, but if he has a chance to do better than our father, he's going to take it."

Both Moretti boys were about to become dads. I wondered if those two babies would be mobsters like Seppi and Vinny someday. We picked up our wrappers, and cups, and made our way to the car parking lot. When we were in the Escalade, I could feel that Seppi's energy had shifted, a weight had been lifted, and his calm spread over me like a blanket. He drove a little further north, into the little village of Elysian and pulled into a space in front of a diner style café. As he was cutting the engine,

"You're going to love this place."

I met Seppi on the sidewalk and it felt like we were in a different world when we were there. If my sister decided to stick around, I would need to do something with the feelings I was starting to have for him. Even though, at that point, it was innocent, and it was more like the promise of freedom within my own soul. I don't even know if I can explain this in a way that will mean anything to anyone. It's a long story but I had not really felt safe inside my own mind since I had been hurt as a little girl, I guess. I mean, there were moments when I felt safe, but not in a way that really mattered to me. I'm not talking about being protected from the Boogie Man or the Grim Reaper, I'm talking like that man made me feel safe from my own demons. In that odd, unlikely calm within the storm, I had never known anyone like that before and he felt the same way about me. And maybe everything would be fine, maybe we would be life-long friends or in-laws.

Seppi held the door of Elysian Eats and we crossed the threshold. A wiry man with blonde dreads and a mustache with curlicues buzzed around making lattes, and the aroma of bacon and fresh bread danced with the espresso and steamed milk. His hand rested on my lower back for a split second before he pulled it back and leaned down to me instead,

"What do you suggest?"

A wave of panic crashed over me when I realized Giuseppi Moretti was asking me to make a recommendation. If he didn't like it, would I end up at the bottom of Lake Elysian?

"I usually get a maple oat latte and a warm scone."

The barista asked if we were ready to order. Seppi pointed to the sign above the man's head, and then to the case,

"We'll have two of the maple oat lattes, and a couple of those scones, warmed if you could."

I stood there biting my bottom lip, my face muscles sore from smiling. I could feel the heat coming from his skin. I was in the moment, really in the moment, and I wanted that day to last forever.

"For here or to go?"

I opened my mouth to tell the guy we'd take everything to go but Seppi beat me to it,

"Here, please."

He paid with a fifty-dollar bill, and when the barista turned around to make our lattes, he slid the twenty-seven dollars change into the ceramic tip jar next to the register. We took the booth in the corner and as we sat across from each other, I knew it was the beginning of something. That day was some sort of cosmic intervention, it had to be, there's no other explanation. Seppi was in the mob, and I was just some crazy girl with her dysfunction on display. He was this powerful man with the weight of the world on his shoulders, and I was just this broken little girl who needed to feel whole. As we sat there, I watched as he got lost in his thoughts, staring across the street at the park. While I had him cornered,

"Can I ask you something?"

Seppi moved his eyes to mine,

"Anything."

I knew he meant it.

"Is Marco a good person?"

Without hesitation,

"Yes, Marco's a good guy."

I smiled to myself, Seppi continued,

"But he's not one to make a commitment."

Seppi glanced out the window again,

"Use caution when giving that man your body or your soul, I don't want to see you get hurt."

I knew he meant it, and it made me feel things that he said something about giving my body to someone. I listened to what he said, but I kept his words on the periphery, people change, maybe Marco was ready to be in a relationship. And maybe I didn't care either way, maybe my feelings for Marco were sparked by the situation, and my need to be distracted. Maybe in any other situation, we wouldn't have been together in the first place, but it didn't really matter at that point,

"Can I ask you something else?"

Seppi flicked his brows at me,

"Shoot."

I made a face at him, and he smiled,

"What were the clothes and stuff I found in the freezer?"

I already knew the answer to the question, but I wanted to hear it from him. Seppi worked his jaw, and I felt like I had to convince him I could handle it,

"Stop protecting me."

He scanned the room and shifted in his seat, deciding whether to tell me the truth or some fluffy variation. He leaned closer, elbows on the table,

"All you need to know is that those things belonged to people who were eliminated in one way or another by my father."

He gestured toward my left wrist,

"Ditch the watch, it was custom-made, and if the wrong person sees you wearing it, you'll end up dead."

I nodded, satisfied with myself for not going all sparkly when I realized I'd been wearing a murdered man's one-of-a-kind wristwatch. Something was happening between us, but I didn't have any idea what it was, or how deeply it would eventually affect my life. Maybe we just happened to be broken in the same places or something.

The guy behind the counter waved as we made our way to the door, and we took a lap around the park. I gave Seppi my phone so he could take a picture of me in a gazebo that was bigger and nicer than the one in Bunman. I used that picture as my wallpaper for a long time and had no idea that life would bring me back to that town someday. Before we went home, Seppi drove to a secluded gravel pull off at the edge of Lake Elysian. He put his hand out, so I brought my open palm down on his in a horizontal high five of some sort,

"What?"

He moved his eyes to my wrist,

"The watch."

I rolled my eyes and undid the clasp and placed the watch in Seppi's hand. He slid from the driver's seat, pitching it in a high arc across the water. I watched the classiest thing I ever owned, as it did somersaults through the air on its way to the bottom of the lake. He looped around and nosed the Escalade toward home, I sat there pouting over the watch,

"I'll buy you a new one, Dimples. Forget about it."

Fine.

I finished the watered-down whiskey in the fancy rocks glass I'd left in the cup holder and sat cross-legged instead of hugging my knees. There was a level of comfort with him, and I was grateful we'd had that time together. Even if there was never another day like that, I would hold onto that one until the end. Being close to him made me feel safe, and maybe I had made the right decision coming back to Vermont. That was the first time I felt what it's like to be loved. I'm not talking about 'that way,' I mean, loved. Seppi made me feel accepted, cared for, and protected. He let me try a puff of his cigar and I didn't like it, at all. Just, why? I moved my eyes to his hand as it rested on the steering wheel. In that little pocket of time, he was lost in his head, and I was lost in mine. He seemed tired and hadn't shaved that morning, he looked somewhat disheveled even if it did something for me,

"Are you OK?"

He glanced over but didn't say anything.

"I mean, like, are you OK?"

He nodded and searched for his words,

"I carry a lot of weight on my shoulders and I'm not about to burden you with any of it, but I appreciate you asking."

We sat quiet for another ten miles before he circled back to our previous conversation,

"Connor contacted someone to put a scare into Vinny, but it turns out, he called a friend of my family. I told my friend, go ahead and get Vin, bring him to the garage and give him a scare, then he needs to go somewhere else until the dust settles with Connor."

"So, he's alive?"

Seppi nodded,

"He's safe."

We were on the final stretch of highway, so I only had twenty minutes until Seppi would be able to avoid my questions if he wanted to,

"What's going to happen with your father?"

I watched him work his jaw some more and his knuckles turned white on the steering wheel,

"He's got to go, but I'm still working on how it's going to happen, his boss is Silvio Genovese."

That didn't mean anything to me, I shook my head and went palms up. Seppi continued,

"The Morettis have history with the Genovese family."

He paused and then pivoted slightly,

"It needs to look like an accident, otherwise we're going to be looking over our shoulders everywhere we go. If Silvio even suspects I had anything to do with my father's death, my life, and the lives of those I love, will be in danger."

Seppi's cheeks were flushed, and I could see tension around his eyes as he clenched his jaw,

"It needs to look like an accident, so it's complicated, requires planning, and must be meticulous. There cannot be any mistakes, do you understand!? There cannot be any mistakes!"

Seppi was yelling and crying, and spit was flying as he spoke. I was crying right along with him. I reached over and touched his arm, his muscle rigid with anger, my voice trembled on his behalf,

"I'm sorry, Seppi."

We didn't talk after that, I just tried to give him space as he cried. Getting to know Seppi was an adventure. When Kane told me about the Morettis, I never thought I would become so closely entwined with them. Besides the fact that he was with my sister, and they were expecting a baby. Seppi exhibited the highest level of control, and I was just a frantic loose cannon, but we had become friends. It's bizarre how life works, how paths cross and worlds collide. Never in a million years did I think my orbit would line up with someone like Giuseppi Moretti. It seemed unlikely that the eldest son of a mob family, and a fucked-up twenty-something trying to find herself would have anything in common, but there we were. It was a real head-scratcher. Wait until you hear what happened next.

CHAPTER 19
HEAD GAMES

NOW THAT SEPPI was going to be a dad, it was like a timebomb was ticking. In a way, Opal was the time bomb, and he needed to get his father out of the picture before she exploded. Seppi refused to involve his future children in the family's mob associations. He did not want to show up to baseball games or ballet recitals with someone else's literal, or figurative, blood on his hands. Seppi did not want to sit in the bleachers in a long 'douche bag' duster, perpetually preoccupied with coordinating orders to closers and cleaners. He wanted distance from his family's ties to crime, and drugs, and murder, he just wanted to live his life. And that was all true before he found out he was going to be a dad, but having the incentive and a timeframe pushed things a long a little bit.

But then that decision created a dilemma because the person Seppi needed to eliminate was higher up on the food chain than he was. Seppi needed to figure out how to make his father go away while making it look like an accident, that wasn't going to be easy. Sal's death had to be a well-choreographed dance. Silvio Genovese would notice Sal was gone, and all hell would break loose if there was even a suspicion he was whacked. As Seppi said, anyone involved would be looking over their shoulder for the sliver of time before they faced a slow and painful death.

Besides the fact that Seppi was starting a family, he had emotional baggage when it came to his father. To understand the deep hatred Seppi had for his father, you need to understand what it's like to be under the thumb of a narcissist. At that point, I'd spent a fair amount of time with Seppi, and I'd listened to countless stories about the abuse he faced as a child. His father was one of those people who should never have had children, because all he did was try to destroy them from the moment they popped out of the womb. I won't give you all the details, but you'll know enough that you won't blame anyone for wanting him dead.

When Seppi was little, he witnessed his father verbally abuse his mother, daily. Nothing Mary did was good enough. She would clean and cook and make sure she looked pretty when Sal came home from work. Seppi would sit at the dinner table crying to himself about how his father treated her, and then he'd hear the head of the bed rhythmically hitting the wall in their room. Seppi knew his mom was crying as Sal got his rocks off. Sal paid for Mary to have her hair and nails done regularly at a salon, paid for a boob job and liposuction. It was Mary's job to tend to Sal in every way, regardless of how he treated her, and she needed to look good while she was doing it. Afterall, Sal reminded her every day that he could have any woman he wanted, and usually did. Personally, I thought Salvatore Moretti was delusional, but whatever, no one asked me. I doubted he was 'The Meat Boss' in the bedroom, and even if he was packing a huge salami in his pants, I wouldn't touch that thing with a shovel.

Seppi's mother would try to 'find herself,' spend time with friends, or express interest in learning something new. Sal would remind Mary she was a housewife; she didn't need to waste time taking painting or pottery classes with her bitchy friends. Sal told her she wasn't worth the money for college classes. He would then tell Mary he only respected the 'educated people,' but wouldn't allow her to get an education. Mary became depressed and withdrawn, which meant Sal had to focus his venom on his children. A person like Sal cannot get their narcissistic supply from someone who doesn't care anymore. I'm not sure what he expected, you treat someone like shit for long enough, they stop liking you. As a child, Seppi needed to be fed, clothed, and sleep under a roof at night, so he tried his best to stay in line while watching a horrible man do horrible things.

Seppi's birthday parties were elaborate and orchestrated to reflect positively on his father's ability to spend, even if that had nothing to do with his ability to parent. Sal would have miniature pony rides on the back lawn and hire superheroes to jump from the roof. None of Seppi's friends seemed to give a shit about any of that, Seppi's friends had their birthday parties at McDonalds, Pizza Hut, or the bowling alley.

Sal never asked Seppi what he wanted for his birthday, it was understood that what mattered was that people come to see the 'mob house,' ride the ponies, see the fireworks, and laugh at the clown. Most of the gifts Seppi received were impersonal and served as tokens of his father's money or power. Lessons Seppi didn't want, or trips to places he didn't want to go. Once, Seppi received expensive equipment for ski lessons. If there was one thing that was very clear to Giuseppi Moretti as a child, it was that he had no interest in skiing, learning how to ski, or even riding a ski lift. I don't think Seppi would get on a ski lift if you had a gun against his head. Seppi has a handful of fears, and one of them is heights.

As Seppi got older, he was expected to reflect his father's exemplary parenting. Parenting that brought long days at work, business trips out of town with mistresses, bottles of bourbon, and bruises on the inside and out. There were countless nights Seppi heard his mother crying alone in bed and would crawl in next to her. Salvatore didn't try to hide the fact that he had women throwing themselves at him because of his money and power and position in the mob. One woman even paraded around town in the same exact Tiffany necklace and bracelet set Sal had given to Mary for their anniversary. After all, like a complete douche bag, he had Tiffany & Co. on speed dial, as his way of smoothing ruffled feathers and hurt feelings. Apparently, some women forgive their husbands for fucking someone else if they get a new pair of diamond earrings out of the deal.

As a teenager, Seppi learned that nothing he did was good enough. Around the dining room table with family or friends, Sal would sing his son's praises and boast about Seppi's accomplishments, as if that somehow meant Sal was a loving and supportive father. But when it was just the two of them, Sal told Seppi that the only reason he was worth anything was because he was made from Sal's 'boys.' Sorry dude, you don't have superior sperm, you narcissistic fuck. Whenever Seppi had friends over, Sal's 'little man, big keychain' switch would flip.

Sal would pull an antique ice cream machine out of storage or set up a full-sized arcade version of Pac-Man. Sal would make Seppi and his friends go for rides in his Ferarri. Seppi's buddies would ask him who his father was trying to impress, their fathers drove beat up pickup trucks and Chevy Cavaliers, they didn't care about the Ferarri. Seppi remembered telling his friends that Sal had daddy issues. He would stand at the grill with big rings on all his fingers like a complete tool, boasting endlessly about how his burgers were the best burgers. Sal would mix maple syrup in with the ground beef when he made the patties, and most of the time, the burgers were disgustingly sweet and undercooked. All the 'very best burgers' ever did was give people diabetes and the shits.

Academically, Salvatore chased his own father's praise, and collected about half a dozen bachelor's and master's degrees. Professionally, he'd find a job, do a piss poor job of making any amount of effort, spend the entire time talking about himself, and then retaliate against the higher-ups when he earned a piss-poor performance review. After burning every professional bridge possible, Sal 'decided' to run the deli with Mary. Sal was a man who thought his shit didn't stink, a man who believed that if one of his children was good at something, it was because of his superior sperm. A man who had no sense of reality, no empathy for others, and was on a constant desperate journey to get positive praise from his own father.

As a child, Seppi knew he didn't want to be anything like his father. He hated Sal and was one of those kids who was counting the days until he turned eighteen. And then Seppi was expected to go to the university his father attended, several states away, even though there wasn't a single major there that interested him. Going anywhere else was not an option. Following his heart was not an option. Seppi was to follow in his father and grandfather's footsteps at Crocker University and that was the end of the conversation. He managed his way through the first two years of college with a seething hatred for school, and an even deeper hatred for his father.

Seppi met the woman who became his first wife, and immediately he tried to be better than his own father. Things were fine in the beginning, but it was a slippery slope. Seppi told her he would make all her dreams come true. They were young and stupid, she struggled with bi-polar, and a little too much cocaine. He struggled with daddy issues, ego, and a little too much whiskey. They grew apart and Seppi ended up cheating on her. He made up for his infidelity with jewelry and lies because it worked for his father. His wife left him six years later. The difference is, Seppi is good deep down in his soul, but was parented by a narcissist who treated everyone like shit and expected people to kiss his ass. Newsflash, asshole, that's not how things work. You catch more flies with a spoonful of high-quality local honey than with a bucket of bullshit stories about your self-importance. Idiot.

When Salvatore's mistresses would inevitably cut ties with him because of the psychological abuse and compulsive lies, he would retaliate against them without batting an eyelash. One of the women was a teacher. As she grew sick of his bullshit and he felt she was going to leave him, he worked his way onto the local school board and told the woman he could 'get people fired.' While that was complete bullshit, the threat kept the woman complacent for a while. But in true narcissist form, once she finally cut ties with him, he attempted to get her fired from her job. It goes without saying but Sal failed miserably, it doesn't take a rocket scientist to spot a liar who's out to sabotage their ex. Oh, that's the other thing, narcissists think that they are smart, and you are stupid, even though it's usually the other way around. If someone said no to Sal, they'd get punished, right out in the open. Even so, some piece of shit trying to mess up your career is a better option than having to be in a relationship with them.

And then there's the gaslighting. If there's one thing Salvatore Moretti was good at, it's gaslighting. For anyone who hasn't had the pleasure of experiencing such a thing, it's a skill in every narcissist's toolbox. Buckle up, it's a good one. A narcissist will lie to your face, that's a given. They will also usually cheat on you. But if you catch a narcissist red-handed, and have the balls to confront them on it, evidence in hand, they will make you out to be a crazy liar. They'll look you in the eye and tell you it's in your imagination or that you're making shit up to make them look bad...as if you're the stupid one. Cringe-worthy, I know. Dude, you're a fucking idiot, you don't need any help looking bad, and if you've forgotten, you're also a douche bag. It's the same thing that happens when you go to a cocky doctor, tell them something you've been experiencing, and they tell you, you're wrong, and it's in your head. No, you're being gaslit by a doctor, who is also probably a narcissist. Again, little man, big keychain energy. Limp dick, big talk energy. Broken little boy in grown man's clothing energy. Wolf in sheep's clothing energy.

After two years at Crocker to appease his father, Seppi transferred to a culinary school in New England to pursue his dream of becoming a chef. His father refused to pay for culinary school and stopped contributing financially to Seppi's education...unless he changed his mind and transferred back to Crocker. Seppi stuck with it anyway and had the student loans to prove it. Back then, Sal was the one who owned most of the commercial property in Bunman, and that included Giuseppi's Italian Ristorante. He gave Seppi a 'rent-free lease' for the space after he graduated from culinary school and Seppi thought his father was proud of him for once. Wrong again folks, Sal just wanted to steal Seppi's thunder, and boasted to the world that he 'gave' his son a restaurant.

Sal also enjoyed taking credit for the success of the place after Seppi spent years building it up from nothing. His father would bring groups of associates in for lunch, boast about 'his' restaurant, and expect Seppi to comp a bottle of fifty-five Mouton Rothschild Cabernet Sauvignon, to the tune of two-thousand dollars a bottle, effectively sucking Seppi's profits down the drain. And let's not forget that along with Sal's presence came the dark mafia energy that remains to this day.

Salvatore made it no secret that he could pull the restaurant out from under Seppi if he wanted to. When the properties were sold to Maggie's husband, Sal included a stipulation that he would maintain control of one of the properties, and who rented it. The legally binding contingency specifically regarded whether Seppi could continue occupying the commercial space that housed his ristorante. Sal would also maintain access to the basement under, what turned into, Whimsy. I'm not sure what hold Salvatore had over my aunt's husband, but he agreed to the arrangement. I'm sure there was blackmail involved somehow, but we'll probably never know.

Seppi had admittedly jumped through his father's hoops, threatening people, participating in drug smuggling, and laundering money. When Seppi was my age, he was pressured into performing hits for Silvio Genovese, an arrangement that wiped away one of Salvatore's debts to them. That was all while trying to keep his nose clean, his attempt to distance himself from the mafia ties, and establish himself as a legitimate gourmet chef and business owner in Bunman. Fast forward to the present, Seppi was ready to leave all that behind, once and for all, he wanted to focus on running the ristorante and being a good dad. I can tell you, without a shadow of a doubt, that Seppi did the best he could while dancing like a marionette for his father. Between Sal's mistresses, his wife, 'business' associates, law enforcement, and his children, Salvatore Moretti was a regular old master of puppets. Yes, that's a Metallica reference.

At the time, I assumed mobsters had tommy guns and hit men, so if someone's in the mob, you'd think it wouldn't be that hard to whack someone or have them whacked. Who knows, if killing Salvatore Moretti would mean that my sister would have a better life, maybe I could do it myself. Passion gives people the override they need to make bad decisions.

When your mother throws you to the wolves to be groomed and abused by the neighbor boy and his relative from out of state, it's bad enough. But when your mother finds out about it and sweeps it under the carpet instead of handling it, you die a little inside. It adds insult to injury when the kid's mother doesn't give a shit either, I guess it's better to protect the perpetrator than it is to rescue the victim. It makes you realize as a little girl that you were brought into the world by a coward who was more worried about keeping up appearances than dealing with confrontation or making sure their daughter was OK. You could say I had a vested interest in the situation with Salvatore because I understood it deeply and on a cellular level. I had enough anger deep down inside of me that if I ever snapped, someone would probably go into the ground. I had a pilot light flickering inside of me and knew that if that part of me was ever ignited, something really bad was going to happen.

It messed with my head that someone strong and threatening like Giuseppi Moretti was dealing with fear and vulnerability. It felt good to know he was a regular guy, but it was unsettling, nonetheless. If Seppi was just a regular guy, that means 'bad guys' are just regular guys who've been broken. Do you realize how profound that is? Do people with two supportive parents and emotional security end up becoming hit-men? Do people with a secure and loving upbringing have the capacity to destroy the lives of others? Can people be fixed once they're broken? I'm broken, can I be fixed?

While we're at it, it's a good time to discuss my mental health, which wasn't great. I got sick of swallowing a handful of pills for my depression, ADHD, and the OCD I cultivated to comfort myself as a child. Nothing makes you feel more broken than needing pills to help you function without completely losing your mind. Besides, the meds had made me gain twenty pounds, so I woke up one morning and decided to stop taking them. The collection of pill bottles lived in a basket on top of my microwave, but I pretended I didn't need them.

At that point in the story, I think I'd been off my meds for a week or two. I had already lost a couple pounds, but I was starting to feel a little more unhinged than usual. It's fine though, I was managing the situation with bad decisions, sex, and copious amounts of weed. I needed therapy, especially after the shit show with my last therapist. Here's the thing, I had a deep fear that the bad stuff I experienced wasn't 'that bad' compared to what might have happened to someone else.

Maybe my mental health issues were because I was a spoiled brat who didn't feel like I got enough hugs when I was little. Maybe I was making a mountain out of a molehill. Maybe getting sexually abused at the neighbor's wasn't that bad compared to other things. Maybe turning to food and writing and obsessive-compulsive disorder to pacify my feelings as a child wasn't that bad, maybe that's how people dealt with their feelings. Maybe feeling like I didn't want to be inside my own head anymore wasn't that bad, maybe that's what self-medicating was for.

I thought I would feel a sense of relief when I moved away from my mother, or because I managed to get away before my ex and his whore had their love child. I thought reuniting with my aunt and childhood best friend, or falling for the cute barista, would give me the warm-fuzzies. I thought the idea of becoming an aunt would spark some joy. For the record, I wasn't feeling relief, the warm fuzzies, or joy. I was angry, unstable, and unsuccessfully grappling with my demons, I was desperate to feel whole.

I thought living in Roundelay was causing my misery, but it turned out that I was miserable in

Bunman too. When you're a broken little bitch like me, it doesn't matter where you go, you're damaged goods until someone fixes you or puts you out of your misery. I'm not trying to come off as flippant, or melodramatic about what was going on in my head. It's just that, eventually you learn to deal with things in your own way. At the foundation of it all was the fact that I desperately wanted to be loved by someone. I wanted to be accepted, even with all my broken pieces, the ones on the inside and out. The whiskey and weed numbed the pain and made it easier to make bad decisions, but the feelings would come back in the morning.

CHAPTER 20
HAUTE & COLD

I HADN'T TOLD Kane about the hair tie or the perfume. He was convinced I was depressed and needed to see a therapist, astute observation, Merlin. I'd been down a couple times to sit around the fire pit with Kane and Connie but hadn't bothered with anything else. My aunt was getting restless, the honeymoon period ended a long time ago. She was staying in my apartment, and she was driving me fucking nuts. We're too much alike to live together, and most days I felt like I didn't have anywhere to go.

Some nights, after she fell asleep, I'd sneak over to the back room of Giuseppi's and watch movies with Marco. I'd sit with my knees tucked up, hugging my legs for comfort. He would put his arms around me and pull me close during the scary parts. Sometimes we would get high and dance to Bob Marley. A couple times, we made popcorn in the commercial microwave and snuck into the walk-in to steal meatballs and tiramisu. We would sit, holding hands while we read, or kiss, or a little bit more. After a couple weeks, the backroom rendezvous felt normal. I should have known then that the feelings I had for Marco, stemmed from the fucked-up situation. Looking back at the whole thing, it seems obvious, but I try not to judge myself too harshly, it was a strange time in my life.

Things were different between me and Seppi after our drive to Lake Elysian. I stopped pushing or giving him attitude for a little while and knew he would tell me what I needed to know about the situation with his father. Opal seemed content at times, even though I could see that she was restless under the surface, or that something was wrong. She was good at wearing masks too, but I was hoping that wasn't the case and maybe she just needed time to adjust. I'd see her buzzing around the ristorante, smiling, and I'd convince myself she was happy. If I hadn't come back to Bunman, Opal wouldn't have met Seppi, even though I was kind of starting to wish that hadn't happened. So, if nothing else, maybe Bunman would give her the fresh start she needed, even if it hadn't really worked out for me.

Sofia had her baby and wouldn't be back for a while, if at all. Sunny worked at Whimsy more often once Sofia was gone, I managed the other stuff and took care of 'the books.' Some days, I'd help at the cafe if they needed me. I could be around Kane most of the time without any drama, hyperventilating, or crying fits in the corner. I knew this thing we were doing was probably never going to amount to anything, and even though I could see myself with him, I knew I'd get bored. I mean seriously, my life would revolve around coffee beans, watching a man play his acoustic guitar, and falling asleep in his arms. It would mean drinking maple oat lattes and feeling the buzz of electricity it creates when he tucks loose curls behind my ear. Thinking about it made my heart hurt,

"Amelia!"

I jumped.

"What are you doing!? I've been standing here forever!"

I scratched my forehead, blinked, and tugged at my apron,

"I was...thinking."

It took everything I had not to cry.

"I need you to make the sandwiches for the big pick-up order?"

Kane threw the bar rag over his shoulder nonchalantly, like we hadn't seen each other naked before and because he was all business, I started to cry. I tried to hold it together, but the whole time I was making paninis and wraps, tears were rolling onto my apron. I brought the paper-wrapped bundles to the counter and was vaguely aware of someone picking them up. I mindlessly put things away and sanitized the counter. Lost in my head again, trying to ignore the battle taking place in my heart. I backed up and bumped into the only other person there, I squeaked out,

"Sorry."

I turned around to see Kane in front of me. I looked up at him, almost a foot taller than me. He tucked a loose curl behind my ear, and at that moment, it was more than I could handle. The closeness and physical touch, the intimacy of it all, and the jealousy I felt toward Alex. I closed my eyes, took a deep breath. and tried, but another tear fell, and I blurted out,

"Don't!"

I grabbed another pick-up slip and cried while I made more sandwiches. He started to say something, but the phone rang, he walked away to answer it and never came back. Why was I like this? I would go weeks without wanting him, and then he'd look at me a certain way. He would be concerned about me, or tuck a curl behind my ear, and I'd fall for him all over again. But I couldn't let him hurt me again, and I couldn't compete with Alex. Where was Alex? Maybe I had made something out of nothing. Maybe I was just lonely.

Marlaina came in to help at the tail end of the lunch rush and covered the counter while I cleaned up. Besides afternoon refuellers, it was going to be quiet until closing. I was incapable of dealing with people at that point and needed to flee before I fell apart. I hung my apron up and speed-walked toward the stairs, eyes pointed at the floor. Kane strolled out of his office, and I slammed into his chest, I didn't look up,

"Sorry."

I weaved around him,

"Amelia."

I turned to him with my puffy eyes and barked,

"What!?"

I could tell he didn't know whether to reach out for me or keep his hands to himself. Neither of us had any idea what our relationship was or what it would be, he sounded genuine when he asked,

"Are you ok?"

It would have been so easy to fall back into bed with him, but instead, I took a deep breath and looked up at him again, my eyes brimming with tears,

"I'm fine."

I turned around and went up to my apartment where I laid, face-down, on my bed and screamed into my pillow. Maggie heard me from the other room,

"You, ok?"

I rolled my puffy eyes,

"Yup."

A little after four, there was a tap on the door. Maggie hid in the bathroom, and I opened the door to Kane,

"Would you like some lemonade?"

I stared at him like he had three heads,

"What!?"

Kane all but rocked back on his heels with his thumbs in his pockets, like an awkward schoolboy,

"I was just wondering if you would like to come over for some lemonade...or hard cider, or something."

I narrowed my eyes at him and put both hands on my hips,

"Why!?"

"Amelia, please. What happened? Do you think I'm mad at you for going to the garage? I'm not, I swear, I was just worried about you."

I locked eyes with him and replied, flatly,

"Don't worry about me."

I pushed the door shut but Kane stuck his hand out to stop it,

"Please talk to me. What happened? Why did you leave?"

I rolled my eyes,

"Really!?"

Kane looked confused,

"Yes, really, what happened? You were fine and then you weren't."

I was jealous and felt rejected, I longed to feel less broken and unhinged,

"Really!? That's strange, I was fine and then I wasn't. I wonder why that is."

"Did I do something?"

I shrugged and went palms up,

"You tell me."

Kane shook his head and ran a hand through his hair,

"You need to be more specific."

We locked eyes again and I flicked my eyebrows at him,

"Do I!?"

I put my finger up and went to my nightstand to retrieve the hair tie and perfume. I returned to the door and gestured for Kane to put his hand out. When I placed the items in his palm, his face dropped,

"Where did you get these!?"

I crossed my arms,

"You told me to get lip balm out of your nightstand."

He stood there staring at the things in his hand and all he had was,

"I."

I closed the door and locked it, yelled to Maggie that it was safe to come out and was just about to plop down on the futon when there was another tap at the door. Maggie turned around and went back in the bathroom, I turned around and went back to the door. I swung it open and barked again,

"What!?"

Kane tried again,

"Would you like some lemonade?"

What the hell was happening? Was this Groundhog Day? It was clear I wasn't going to get rid of him until I agreed to talk,

"Whatever."

I hollered to Maggie that the coast was clear and closed the door behind me. As soon as I was in Kane's apartment, Lola barreled out of the bedroom and whacked me with her wrecking ball tail. I played with her ear as Kane poured tequila instead of lemonade or hard cider. We sat on the couch in silence. I threw my hands in the air and shook my head,

"What the hell is happening!?"

He looked like a deer in the headlights,

"I love you, Amelia."

And that was it, I snapped,

"What the fuck are you talking about!?"

"I love you."

I stood,

"Wow, you're a real asshole, you know that!?"

His voice trembled, confused by my response,

"What!?"

I swallowed the fire and slammed the glass on the coffee table before moving toward the door. Kane rose from the couch and stepped in my way,

"Wait."

I stiff-armed him,

"Move."

But he didn't move, he just stood there. My face felt hot, and I clenched my jaw. I shoved Kane out of my way with both hands, I was frantic and needed to get the hell out of there,

"MOVE!"

He stepped to the side and went to the door but when I tried to open it, he pushed it shut and the knob slipped out of my hand. I spun around and looked up at him,

"What are you doing!?"

My back against the door, his right hand over my head holding the door shut, that was the most he had ever tried to dominate me. I swallowed the tears in my throat, but I wasn't scared of someone like him, I could have kneed him in the balls if I needed to. We made eye contact and were both breathing heavily, my hands flat against the door and he tucked a loose curl behind my ear. He put his nose to mine, breaking the barrier between us, and you know what my body did. Our mouths hovered, almost touching. I grabbed the back of his head and kissed him like we were racing somewhere. I heard him whimper and that's when I realized if I went any further, I'd be signing myself up for a cruise to the Bermuda Love Triangle. I froze and he looked down at me,

"What's wrong?"

I stared across the room and wanted another shot of whiskey or an edible or a TV Guide to flip through, anything,

"I can't do this."

He took a step back and held both of my hands, his voice softer,

"Did I do something?"

I could have answered that in a couple different

ways. I knew Alex was the big reason I couldn't move forward with him. I felt like she had dibs, as stupid as that sounds. I knew that if it were me, I would want to see how things played out, without some frantic chick with overalls and glorious dimples, twat-blocking me. Honestly, things weren't the same as when I met him, back when I thought Kane was a blank slate. I know that makes me a hypocrite since I was dragging along an entire set of my own emotional baggage, but that didn't mean I wanted to unpack someone else's.

"Amelia?"

"You didn't do anything wrong; I just can't do this."

I was upfront with him,

"Things haven't been the same since I saw you with Alex. Before all that, I thought we had something. And I'm sorry I blew up at you, and slapped you, and gave you the cold shoulder. I take responsibility for that; it was childish and fueled by past relationship trauma. But when I saw you with her, it did something to me. I'm fucked up and compartmentalize the things I don't want to face. I was able to pretend you weren't sharing your bed with Alex, until I found her things in your nightstand."

Kane took my hands again,

"I know, and I should have told you about her, but it never felt like the right time. I guess I should figure things out before I move forward with our relationship."

"I have to tell you something."

I was anxious but I knew I was going to tell him anyway,

"I've been spending time with Marco, and I want to see where that goes."

Kane and I lived across the hall and worked together, so there had to be a level of professionalism in the intermission, or ending, or whatever this was. Maybe we would get another chance someday, but right then, I was too broken to be in a situation where I felt threatened by another woman. And it wasn't fair for Kane to use me as a distraction. I found the right words to say,

"I care about you very much and I'm grateful for our time together."

Kane seemed to understand, he hugged me and kissed the top of my head, winking,

"You can still come over for a couch cuddle when you're feeling sad or scared, and I'll check out any random guys who come in and offer to do free handyman work."

I knew he cared about me, and I knew I cared about him. But maybe sometimes things aren't meant to be. Sometimes, your time with someone helps you realize the things you really need; sometimes relationships are just a pit stop on the way to where you're meant to be. Before I left, we kissed on the lips again, but it wasn't a means to an end. Being with him felt safe, until it didn't. Kane Buchanan wasn't in the mafia and didn't have a laundry list of people he'd whacked but he had managed to leave me hanging by a thread, until I was ready to cut it.

I got in bed and stared at the ceiling, trying to figure out if I had made a mistake. I liked them both, in different ways. With Kane, I felt comfortable and safe, like he was a big brother who watched out for me. With Marco, there was chemistry, and our jagged parts didn't frighten each other away. But even then, I wondered if it was just lust. Who knows, but I listened to my gut and had my answer. When I was with Marco, I didn't feel like I was cheating on Kane, but when I was with Kane, I felt like I was cheating on Marco. When Maggie settled in for the night, I padded through the passageway and curled up with Marco, we watched Halloween.

I felt like this was a turning point in my relationship with him, if that's what you want to call the thing we were doing. And as Marco blinked at a scary part, I straddled him and kissed his neck. He pulled my shirt over my head, wrapped his arms around me, and kissed my chest. I ran my fingers through his hair and rubbed myself against him. We were hungry for each other and made love while Michael Myers killed the guy with the glasses. I'm not sure whose moans were louder.

CHAPTER 21
HERE'S YOUR IPAD

A WEEK LATER, I was eating lunch with Maggie, you know, filling her in on my love life drama. But instead of participating, or giving me any kind of response, she told me she needed her iPad. OK, great. I'd go through the passageway, get her iPad from the hidey-hole in the back storeroom of Giuseppi's Italian Ristorante, and be back in five minutes. I went into the hall, and bounced down the first couple stairs, Maggie hollering after me,

"Where are you going!?"

I hollered back,

"I thought you wanted your iPad!"

She came into the hallway and looked down the stairs at me,

"Yeah, but where are you going?"

I motioned for her to get back in my apartment and shut the fuck up already. I jogged back up the stairs, what kind of question was that?

"I'm going over to the restaurant to get your iPad."

There was a pause. Oh, for fuck's sake, I wasn't in the mood. But maybe if I retrieved her iPad, she would listen to my story,

"OK, where is it? At your house?"

And then I remembered where I saw her iPad. It was on the table at that lake house. Crap. I sat down at the table and continued to eat my lunch, maybe I could get her a new one. I was casually chewing a bite of my sandwich when she moved her eyes to mine and I was mentally pinching the bridge of my nose before she even opened her mouth,

"Well, can you get it? I need it to pay bills, and everything is on there. I also want to monitor the cameras at my house and see if the bird feeders need to be filled."

I was pissed. First, she disappeared, and then I was afraid she was dead. Then she was holed up in her bunker, and then a lake house, and then a storeroom, and now my apartment. The last time we were at that lake house was one of the most traumatic nights of my life, and I was being asked, nonchalantly I might add, to go back. I couldn't tell Kane, Marco, or Seppi, and I couldn't take Opal since she was working at the restaurant.

I was sure Sunny would come with me; she had been asking if we could hang out, but I had been so preoccupied with things that it hadn't happened. I was pacing around in front of the row of windows when Salvatore Moretti exited The Meat Boss and slid behind the wheel of his black Lincoln. I watched as Sal drove away, and then immediately went down to the cafe, got a lavender rose latte, and speed-walked to the deli. I could tell Mary had been crying, busying herself so I wouldn't notice. I slid the paper cup across the counter while she fiddled with papers, her back turned.

That woman spent decades under the control of that horrible man. She was never allowed to take classes or spend time with friends, unless she did it in secret. I doubted she had many friends left at that point; what kind of life was that? The emotional toll it must take to cater to someone your entire life and get nothing in return. I asked where her sidekick was, and Mary said he was making a trip to Boston but would be back late that night. Once I had the information I was looking for, I wrapped up the conversation and told Mary I'd see her Sunday. She came around the counter, hugged me, and kissed me on both cheeks before thanking me for the latte.

Don't judge me too harshly when I tell you I exited the deli, sprinted to my car, and drove straight to Sunny's. She swung the door open as I approached,

"What's up, fucker?"

I crossed the threshold and followed her to the kitchen where she returned to a cigarette and a cup of tea. As Sunny blew cigarette smoke into the fan over the stove, I asked if she wanted to come with me to get the iPad. I didn't want to go alone, and maybe it would be fun. Sunny flicked the butt into the garbage disposal and dumped the rest of her tea on top of it. Five minutes later, she was bouncing along next to me in a blue elbow-sleeve gingham dress and sandals, a woven bag slung over her shoulder, a spritz of Light Blue on her pulse points. Her yellow sunglasses were nestled on the top of her head, strawberry blond braids resting on her shoulders, loose curls framing her face. I tried to keep my cool, this was no big deal, we'd be back in two hours, and it would have been even quicker, but Sunny wanted to dangle her feet in the lake. I was a little anxious we'd be sitting ducks and had I known that my phone was on my kitchen table, I would have realized I'd made a huge mistake.

I felt guilty for involving Sunny. I told her I was grabbing my aunt's tablet from a lake house, but not about the situation with Sal, or that Maggie was holed up in my apartment until further notice. I spotted a pull off for the Long Trail about a quarter mile from the lake house. I nosed my car into a spot, amongst a couple of other rusted-out Subarus that looked about like mine, probably hikers. Sunny and I meandered along the gravel road, picking up pretty stones along the way. She told me she was being ghosted by Vinny and I had to bite my tongue. She took a selfie in front of an almost naked maple tree, while sitting on the remnants of an old wooden rope swing.

We moved cautiously down the secluded driveway; the coast was clear and when we got to the house, it appeared vacant. I bet no one had been there since the night we rescued Maggie and Marco. I wondered where the owners were, and why the house was always empty. The two of us meandered across the grass to the back porch and when I turned the doorknob, the door didn't open. Maggie's iPad was on the table, I could see it from where I was standing, and knew there was probably a window open somewhere. We cautiously walked the perimeter, inspecting things, trying the front door and the windows, but everything was locked up tight.

I peeked under the doormats and above the door frame, investigated the flower bed for a hide-a-key that looked like a rock or pile of dog shit. Bingo. A minute later, I was standing in the kitchen looking at the iPad and the mug of tea that still sat on the table. I shoved the tablet in my bag and snooped around the kitchen. Because I'm nosey, I looked at the stuff on the fridge, and there were pictures of a couple at formal events. The woman was middle-aged and athletic. She wore a silver sparkly gown in one picture and a black gown in another. In both pictures, the man next to her wore a black tuxedo with long tails, a bow tie, and a unique enamel maple leaf pin on his lapel. I stole two sodas from the fridge before locking up and returning the key to the fake piece of dog shit where I found it.

It was quiet. We sat on the dock and dangled our feet in the chilly water. We drank the sodas while we watched boats pulling the season's last water skiers, and people on jet skis as they made circles on the lake. I rooted around my bag for my phone and realized I didn't have it. That would have been fine if Sunny's phone wasn't about to die. No big deal, we were two adults taking a little visit to the lake. I had retrieved my aunt's iPad, we had a car, and we were only twenty minutes from town. There was a time, not too long ago, when people drove cross-country with nothing more than a TripTik and a sandwich bag of dimes for the pay phone. Most likely, two fully grown women could go to the lake and back and nothing horrible would happen just because we didn't have a phone.

I sprawled out on the dock with my toes in the cool water, it was hot for late September, but I knew soon enough, it would be sweatshirt weather. That was the most peaceful my mind had been in a long time, besides that day I spent with Seppi in Elysian. Maybe things were going to be normal soon. If nothing else, Sal's grasp was loosening, and the people who worked for him were starting to switch teams. Seppi was building a solid foundation of men he trusted. Sooner or later, the deed would be done, and none of us would have to worry about Salvatore Moretti again.

Sunny plucked one of her organic hand-rolled

cigarettes out of a monogrammed silver case, no doubt a gift from Vinny. I slid a joint from my thrifted flip-top tin. Sunny smoked her cigarette and then we shared the joint. We sat there swinging our legs from the dock Sal used to tie up his boat when he stopped by to kill my aunt. Still, for some reason, all of that had faded into the dark recesses of my mind, and it was almost like it hadn't happened. The lake was a place of beauty for fuck's sake, not a place of fear, gunshot wounds, and bullshit narcissistic mob bosses. I closed my eyes and basked in the moment.

Sunny had fallen asleep next to me, and I could hear her gently snoring. I realized that just like me, she had grown up on the outside. Still, the little girl I knew long ago was somewhere on the inside and I knew it. It's like that with all of us, I grew up on the outside too, even though there's still a broken little girl inside. Sunny was one of those bubbly types that had a dark side, a perpetually manic lightning bug with a little fire inside, it was nice to see her recharging her flame. Sunny's strawberry blonde braid was shining in the sun, the hem of her gingham dress dancing in the breeze. Before the sun started to set, we made our way toward the car.

When my twenty-six-year-old piece of Swiss cheese came into view, I could see a rusty silver minivan on the driver's side, and a black Lincoln Continental parked behind it. As in, the black Lincoln was blocking my car from backing out of the space. I pulled Sunny into the brush on the side of the road, someone hadn't gone to Boston after all. Sunny got all excited, looking all around, eyes wide,

"Why are we stopping? Did you see someone naked through their bedroom window or something!?"

Far from the reality of the situation,

"No."

I shook my head. Sunny asked again, jumping up and down, anticipating something fantastic, she clapped her hands together,

"What!?"

But really, I didn't even know where to start, I felt bad for inadvertently involving Sunny in the situation, even though I knew exactly what I was doing when I invited her,

"It's a long story, but the short story is that we can't leave."

I pointed,

"See the black Lincoln blocking my car?"

Sunny nodded,

"Are there people fucking in the back seat?"

I shook my head, and she could see that whatever it was, was serious,

"I'm pretty sure that car belongs to Salvatore Moretti."

She stood up and screeched,

"WHAT!?"

I pulled her back into the brush and motioned for her to be quiet,

"Shh!"

I didn't know what to tell her. Sunny was aware that Vinny's father was the reason for most of his bad behavior, and here was his big-shot mob boss father blocking us from leaving. I was afraid she would march right over there and confront Sal for being a shitty father. I started to panic and tried to distract her, talking about stupid shit that didn't have anything to do with anything. I checked my bag for the tenth time and still didn't have my phone. I had my wallet, my keys and my hand sanitizer. I had a maxi pad, some of Maggie's chocolates, and a collection of crumpled receipts. I also didn't have a good answer for Sunny about what was going on, why Sal was blocking my car, and why we couldn't leave. Maybe we couldn't run to the lake and back without trouble after all.

I started crying on the inside but tried with all my might to hold it together. Action is a distraction, so I grabbed Sunny's hand, and we moved along in the brush. I made a mental note to check for ticks when we got home. We were deep enough in the overgrowth that no one would see us. I knew if we waited long enough, that old fuck would need to go take a leak, or it would be time for his blood pressure pill, stool softener, or cod liver oil. Whatever, I don't know what old people do.

Sunny and I moved closer to the parking lot and hid fifty feet from the car, camouflaged in the ferns and brush. We sat against a tree and waited. We pissed in the woods and then shared the last of a piss-warm bottle of water. I felt I owed Sunny an explanation, so I told her the watered-down version of the situation with Sal. She had spent enough time with Vinny that she knew about Sal's power, his reach, and his influence and none of that was very reassuring.

When it was almost dusk, a teenage couple stumbled out of the woods, tangled together with their gangly arms and legs. They got into the rusty minivan and headed toward town. The black sedan hadn't budged. It had been hours since we got to the lake. If anyone was looking for me, they wouldn't have any idea where to find me, unless they asked my aunt. Even then, I didn't know if she'd tell anyone the truth, I'm pretty sure she knew this was a bad idea.

At dusk, we backtracked through the woods and once we were shielded by a small bend in the road, we scurried to the other side and jogged up the driveway to the lake house. We could sit on the porch and at the very least, I could get us in the house if we needed a place to sleep. And then a light bulb went off. I picked up my purse and stared at the maple leaf pin, I was pretty sure it was identical to the one in the photo I saw on the fridge. I started putting the pieces together and pawed frantically through my bag for the Bulgari key ring. I pushed the lock button on the BMW fob. Chirp. I screeched,

"Oh, my God!"

Sunny jumped up and looked around,

"What's that!? Who's here!?"

"Come on!"

I grabbed Sunny's arm and pulled her toward the same garage I hid in the night Seppi shot Sal. As I was pushing the door open, headlights swung into the driveway. We only had a few seconds before the headlights would illuminate us, so we dove behind the car and held our breath. Once the Lincoln came to a stop next to the house, Sal stepped out and circled the perimeter checking to make sure everything was locked up tight. When he was on the other side, I gripped the bumper and said,

"Please don't ask me why, but I have the keys to this car, come on."

Then I halted,

"We need to be careful getting in, I don't want him to see me. Hopefully, he'll just think it's the people who own the house."

Deep down, I knew the people who owned the house were long dead, but in the moment, I was incapable of facing reality. Adrenaline was humming in my ears, and I felt like an elephant was sitting on my chest. I'd had a pipe dream that I could return the keys if I ever found the car, and instead I was stealing it to get away from a sociopath. I would be careful and planned to return the car without a scratch. I'd even fill the tank with gas in case the people weren't dead. I'd write a note explaining what happened, even if it made me look like a criminal, I was sure they would understand this was an emergency and I didn't have a choice. My good old-fashioned fight or flight kicked in, and I was choosing flight.

Sal returned to his car and slid behind the driver's seat but didn't start it. The sporty BMW we were in was backed into the garage, so it would be an easy escape once we got in the car. I motioned to Sunny, and on the count of three, we crawled inside. The dome light illuminated the passenger cabin, and the door of the Lincoln swung open. Oh, God. I jammed the key into the ignition, put my foot on the brake, and turned the key. Shit. I realized it was a manual transmission so as Sal was exiting the Lincoln, in the way every old fuck exits a Lincoln, I slammed my foot on the clutch, turned the key, and the car started up. The headlights came on and I shoved the car in first gear. I tried to speed out of the garage and past Sal, but the emergency brake was on. Shit. He was charging in our direction and he was pissed.

I released the emergency brake and peeled out of the garage with a chirp, driving on the lawn to get around the Lincoln. Sunny's middle finger obscured my view but I saw him jogging back to his car as we were speeding away, we were golden. I drove faster than usual around the winding gravel road toward The Lakeside General Store. If we could make it there, everything would be alright, we would be alright. People would be there, and we could get help or hide or call the police. In the moment, I thought everything was going to be alright, we had dodged a bullet, no pun intended. Sunny screeched,

"Holy shit, go!"

She was enjoying the thrill but had no idea what was happening, or why. Just then, lights came through the trees, and the Lincoln bared down on us. We were in a car, we were safe, we would get to the store and get help, we would be okay. That old fuck could follow us all he wanted. And then the headlights grew closer. I sped up and the back end of the car swung out on a corner, but I regained control. The Lincoln swung out behind me and regained control. My heart was pounding in my ears. I sped up. The Lincoln approached again, and this time, it rammed the back of the BMW. We skidded almost sideways on the gravel road, and I knew we would be dead if he trapped us in a ditch. I lifted my foot from the gas, downshifted, regained control of the car, and sped up again. Gentle with the gas pedal, Amelia, gentle.

I glanced in the rear-view mirror and saw Sal's left hand out the window, was he flipping us off? What a fucking idiot. And then a bullet zinged through the back window, through the passenger cabin, and through the windshield. We shrieked in unison, and I went a little faster. Sunny dug around in her bag and then leaned out the window, pop-pop-pop. My eyes were bugging out of my head when I looked over to see Sunny shooting a cute little handgun out the window at Salvatore Moretti. I screeched at her,

"Are you fucking crazy!? You're going to get us killed!"

Bullets were pinging against the back of the car, we were almost to the store, one more mile. I floored it, the Lincoln matched my pace and then some. The headlights grew closer, but Sal must have emptied his clip. I entered a sharp corner and lost control again. We were rapidly approaching a row of two-hundred-year-old maple trees, Sunny and I screaming so loud that I hurt it my eardrums. Somehow, I regained control, glanced in the rear-view mirror again and saw the headlights of the Lincoln swing out in a skid. Sal over-corrected and went off the road before he saved it and returned to his pursuit. Shit.

A half-mile before we reached the store, Sal started shooting again. I sped up on a straightaway and as I approached the final corner, a bullet bit into my right shoulder and exited the windshield. Sunny screeched again, flailing her hands around, panicking,

"Oh my God, oh my God, oh my God!"

A fresh shot of adrenaline coursed through my veins as I maneuvered the last turn. I went into another skid but corrected it and made it to the last straight away before the store. Sal lost control, got cocky and over-corrected, went into another skid, over-corrected again, and slammed the side of the Lincoln into a row of towering trees.

We made it to the store, skidding into the lot behind the building, and I cut the lights. We sat there hyperventilating and holding our breath all at the same time. Sunny's eyes wide, frantically digging around in her bag,

"Jesus, Amelia, are you OK!? What the fuck was that!?"

Sunny clamped a wad of purse-napkins over my shoulder, which I had completely forgotten about, thank you adrenaline. The gunshot wound was more of a graze, but I had never been shot before and it was starting to burn. I took a couple deep breaths so I wouldn't pass out. We waited in the dark, watching for headlights, but there were none. Sunny gave me the sweater she had in her bag, and I threw it over my shoulders. She licked her finger and scrubbed the dots of blood off my neck and cheek. We casually went in the store and I asked to use the phone. I called Giuseppi's Italian Ristorante since I didn't know anyone's number off the top of my head.

"Thank you for calling Giuseppi's Italian Ristorante, this is Opal, how may I help you?"

When I heard her voice, my adrenaline crashed, and emotions flooded in. I squeaked and Opal said,

"Amelia!?"

I tried to regain some composure so I wouldn't panic her but when my voice came out, it went an octave higher than usual and there were tears on the periphery,

"Hi, is Seppi there?"

"Yes, why?"

My voice cracked,

"Could I speak with him, please?"

My sister threw the phone down and I heard her frantically calling to Seppi. Hurried leather-soled footsteps grew closer, and then a worried voice, deep and low,

"Dimples!?"

I tried to hold it together, but hot tears rolled down my cheeks and the woman behind the counter looked at me like I was crazy. I took a deep breath, cupping the mouthpiece,

"I kind of did something stupid."

Seppi's voice grew deeper and lower, gritting his teeth since he was sick of my bullshit,

"Where are you?"

I squeaked out,

"The Lakeside General Store."

There was a pause, and I could hear Seppi breathing, I imagined he was pinching the bridge of his nose. He sighed,

"I'm on my way."

The call ended.

We thanked the woman, went back to the car, and locked ourselves in, watching for headlights on the lake road. It didn't feel real, none of it did, how was that my reality? I'm not saying I was quite as naive as when I rolled into town, but I think there was a part of me that was still refusing to believe any of it. Maybe all of this was just some psilocybin trip, maybe Opal took me on some fantastic adventure, maybe this was all in my imagination. Because that makes a hell of a lot more sense than admitting I was waiting for Giuseppi Moretti to rescue me. I made no sense. We shared a mediocre turkey sandwich and half a bag of cheese puffs and as we waited, my fingers dressed in dried blood and orange dust. I almost sucked my fingers but thought better of it. We were finishing our fancy dinner when Seppi skidded to a stop with the Escalade, I watched as he scanning the parking lot for the idiot he had taken under his wing. We poured out of the BMW and waved our arms in the air, Seppi skidded to a halt in front of us. We climbed in the backseat, and he was kicking up gravel before our asses hit the seats. He glanced over his shoulder,

"Seatbelts."

That's all he said. I could tell he was angry by the way he breathed, but he stayed quiet on the ride back to town. He pulled into the secured garage, the door closing on its own once we were inside. Seppi herded us into his office and retrieved a pitcher of ice water. He closed the office door, and we sat there crying big fat tears on his fancy leather sofa. My mind was spiraling. Minutes later, Seppi returned with Opal, opened the storage room to collect Marco, and marched through the passageway to fetch Maggie from my apartment. She hugged me to her chest, and I could tell by the look on her face that she had been shitting her pants with worry. She pulled away and gave me a once over, her eyes bugging out when she saw blood working its way through Sunny's sweater,

"Did you get shot!?"

You could hear a pin drop, and everyone was staring at my shoulder. Seppi shook his head and ran a hand through his hair,

"What the fuck happened to you!?"

Maggie looked like she was about to get in trouble. I rooted around my bag, met her eyes, and said,

"Here's your iPad."

CHAPTER 22
COLLECTING CASTAWAYS

SEPPI STOOD THERE staring at us like he was evaluating his life choices. Maggie and Marco had been holed up in the storage room of his restaurant. I just got into a car chase and gunfight with his father, and I was sporting a decent gunshot graze to my right shoulder. Everyone in Seppi's immediate circle was in his backroom, like a pack of stray dogs waiting for scraps or a safe place to sleep. He paced and Opal retrieved an etched rocks glass with ice and a bottle of Johnny Walker Blue. Seppi slammed back a double shot and poured another before tending to my wound. I snagged the bottle of expensive whiskey from the coffee table and lifted it to my lips, Seppi slammed his hand down and barked,

"For Christ's sake, use a goddamn glass! I don't

need your tears and backwash in my liquor!"

I made a face at him, and he flicked his eyebrows at me like I was writing a check my ass couldn't cash. Opal scurried to the bar and slid two glasses in front of me. Sunny slammed hers down and poured another before lighting a hand-rolled cigarette. Seppi knelt in front of me and pulled on black rubber gloves as he examined my shoulder, moving his eyes to the glass in my shaky hands,

"You might want to toss that down the hatch, this is going to hurt."

I did as I was told and Seppi picked pieces of fabric out of the gelatinous scab before cleaning it and closing the wound with butterfly stitches. His hands were gentle, even though he was angry. I could smell the whiskey on his breath, a hint of stress sweat on his shirt, and Tobacco Vanille on his skin. Opal delivered salads, a pan of lasagna, and garlic bread even though food was the last thing on my mind. Seppi let us say goodbye and then took Opal out and locked us in his office with our food. When he returned, he had determined Sunny was not in danger. The two of us hugged and she kissed me on the cheek,

"I love you, fucker, be safe."

I sort of smiled up at her, despite the situation,

"I love you too, Seppi will keep me safe."

When I flicked my eyes in his direction, I could see that it meant something to him that I thought that. At that point, I knew he was capable of certain things and it suited him in some way, that he had a dark side, because I was starting to know the other one. I watched as he worked things out in his own head, the wheels turning, the problem solving itself or presenting an answer. He made a couple phone calls and the dinner dishes were taken away. Seppi locked the door again and stood over us as we huddled on the couch like three pathetic dogs. I mean seriously, what the hell was all this? My shoulder was throbbing pretty good by then and I just wanted to go home and get high, maybe eat a couple Pop Tarts over the sink. I sat there with Maggie and Marco, just staring up at him, waiting to hear our fate.

Seppi wasn't pleased with any of us. I knew he was mad but I could tell he was under control, there was something sexy about it. Knowing him well enough to know I could trust him. Not just some puppet who jumped through hoops or kissed his ass as a means to an end. I didn't have an angle, I didn't want anything from the man, and I think that intrigued him for a change. I thought maybe he was a man who was so used to people bowing down to him that he didn't know what to do with me. Eventually, Seppi escorted me and Maggie through the passageway to my apartment and sat on the futon while we packed. I couldn't believe that man was in my apartment and I wondered if he could smell stale weed. Whatever, who gives a shit, who am I trying to impress? I focused and remembered pads so I wouldn't have to cob-job something out of toilet paper again. I was sure he was putting us up somewhere fancy, like a climate-controlled storage unit on the other side of town. We returned to the restaurant through the passageway and Marco had gathered his things while we were gone. I sat on the couch, listened to my guts gurgle, and hoped I wasn't going to shit my pants.

At one in the morning, a black Lincoln Navigator pulled into the garage and the three of us got into it. Franco was driving, and now that I had a good look at him, he seemed like a big teddy bear. He was well over six feet tall and about 300 pounds, jacked versus doughy. He backed out of the garage, and we made our way into the night, en route to an undisclosed location. Two hours later, we stopped at a rest stop in New Hampshire and Franco gave me a Red Sox cap to pull down low when I went inside to use the bathroom. I was escorted into the liquor outlet by a bodyguard type who was armed to the teeth, and I came out with a bag of various ninety-nine-cent shooters. Once I was in the car, I tossed back an edible and washed it down with a shooter of raspberry vodka.

We hopped back on the highway and continued to the other side of New Hampshire. We went over the Piscataqua Bridge into Maine, and twenty minutes later, the Navigator was exiting toward Kimbrook Beach. It was four forty-five in the morning when we pulled into the garage of an impressive home overlooking the ocean, the door closed behind us and an alarm activated. The three of us followed Franco up the stairs with our things like orphans. We dropped our bags in the kitchen and ate the pizza Seppi sent along. After that, Franco brought us up another set of stairs and showed us to our rooms. To recap, shit escalated quickly.

When I woke up, I started to panic for the first time since the most recent episode of the shit show started. I watched the waves crash and leaned off the bed to open the sliding door to the balcony. Things with Sal were coming to a head, so I strapped on a waist holster and pulled the handgun out of my bag. I'm not confident shooting it yet, but I'd been working on grip and response time. I stood in front of the mirror doing drills. I'd hang my hands casually at my sides, and time how long it took me to lift my shirt, remove the gun from its holster, and aim it at my imaginary assailant. There was a tap on the bedroom door frame. Marco was standing there in pajama pants and no shirt, holding two mugs, unfazed by the gun,

"You should see the setup in the kitchen down there, it's legit. There's a fancy espresso machine, but I didn't know how to use it."

Marco handed me one of the mugs and kissed me on the cheek,

"I made a pot of coffee, but I'm warning you that the filter folded in on itself."

He shrugged and smiled at me with his eyes. We sat on the balcony watching seagulls and listening to the waves crash. I put my feet on his lap, closed my eyes, and breathed in the ocean air. It felt like we were the only people on earth, we just sat together sipping coffee as we looked at the ocean. Marco rubbed my foot with his thumb and it felt like we had done this before, and in all this chaos, being with him made it feel like things would be okay.

Looking back, I think the situation with Sal had sparked some sort of misdirected hero worship for Marco. I'd come to terms with the fact that Kane had too much baggage for our relationship to turn into anything. My heart was pulling me toward Marco, and right then, I thought I could trust myself. I had never been through anything like that before, it was easy to confuse some things and misinterpret other things. When I got to the bottom of my coffee, I chewed on some grounds and smiled at Marco.

"What?"

I tipped my mug so he could see the bottom. He nodded and his eyes smiled at me as he slurped the grounds out of his own mug,

"Told you the filter caved in on itself. I'm glad I don't work at Muddy Waters, I would never be able to cut it as a barista, I can't even use a fancy Mr. Coffee."

Before Marco left with our empty mugs, I rested my face on his chest and closed my eyes, listening to his heartbeat. I ran my hands down his back and squeezed his ass. Marco kissed me before he left, and I felt it everywhere. Eventually I went down to the kitchen and was standing at the fridge when Marco sauntered in. He wrapped his arms around my waist, and I tilted my head back so he could kiss my neck. I turned around to face him, and he kissed my forehead softly, I was starting to be a little less interested in breakfast, and a little more interested in dragging his sweet ass right back up the stairs. He wasn't quite on the same wavelength and fidgeted with his hands,

"I just want to make sure I'm not getting involved in a love triangle or anything. I like you."

He caught me off guard, but I had been thinking about the same thing,

"I've decided I don't want to be in a relationship with Kane, there's too much drama with him."

His face lit up,

"Really?"

"Really."

The fact that I was entertaining romance at a time like that says a lot about what 'normal' and 'safe' felt like at that point. I was sporting a bullet wound from a car chase with a mob boss, and now I was hours away from home, squirreled away in a fancy beach house. Right then, it was all about staying distracted and not freaking out. That was the part where something was going to happen soon, something had to happen soon. The three of us were being hidden by Giuseppi Moretti, and that wasn't a long-term solution. I was pretty sure Seppi was going to expedite the plan and eliminate the problem. Maggie entered the spacious kitchen in a fancy floral bathrobe. Marco poured her a cup of coffee with some grounds at the bottom of the mug and I made pancakes. He glanced over,

"I like pancakes."

He took a sip of his second cup of coffee and flicked his eyebrows at me. It was as if 'pancakes' was code for 'doing it.' My aunt looked at Marco, and then at me, and then at Marco,

"Are you two sleeping together?"

I barked, and Marco spit out his coffee. We were still laughing when another set of footsteps came down the stairs, probably Franco. I glanced up expectantly and was surprised to see Vincenzo Moretti stroll through the kitchen. Was Franco even there anymore? Vinny waved at us casually with puffy eyes, a cigarette hanging out of his mouth,

"Morning."

He stretched, grabbed a handmade mug out of the cabinet, and made himself a latte on the fancy espresso machine. I just stood there staring at him like a nut-job. Vinny was good-looking like Seppi, and they shared a lot of the same features. I wondered if that's what Seppi looked like almost a decade and a half ago when he was my age. He always smelled good, and he seemed softer than I remembered. The twenty-something mobster seemed less intimidating in a vintage Giuseppi's Italian Ristorante T-shirt, Sponge Bob pajama pants, and crocheted slipper socks his mommy probably made for him last Christmas.

He carried his latte to the couch, opened one of the sliding glass doors with his foot, and lit a big fat joint. Blowing out a stream of smoke, and as if we were on vacation, he asked,

"Does anyone want to go out on the houseboat later?"

I didn't want to start right off arguing with the guy but,

"Aren't we supposed to be laying low?"

Vinny waved his hand dismissively and blew out another stream of smoke, his face saying, 'big whoop,'

"Whatever, it's the ocean."

I went palms up and shook my head. He moved his eyes to mine and leaned forward, looking at me like I was stupid,

"In case you've never been to the ocean before, it's pretty big. I think we'll be OK, you need to take a chill pill, lady."

A chill pill? Well, what the fuck was his problem? He just sat there running his mouth like a macho man who was really just a spoiled rich kid in a grown man's body. Some cocky fuck who was dating my best-friend, just some know-nothing who knocked up some prominent guy's wife, he was nothing special. I finished making the pancakes as Vinny flicked the butt of his joint through the door into the sand. He stood, stretched again, and sauntered into the kitchen like he owned the place, leaving the sliding glass door askew. He grabbed the top four pancakes with his bare hand, carried the stack across the kitchen, and tossed them on a plate. No fork, no syrup, just walked off with four pancakes. I hollered after him,

"Enjoy."

Vinny threw his hand up in a half-assed wave and disappeared up the stairs with half a rolled-up pancake hanging out of his mouth. I gave the remaining pancakes to Maggie and scanned the kitchen for something else to eat. Marco held out a plate with half a pancake drenched in maple syrup, I waved it away,

"You eat it, I'll find something else."

Well, wasn't that some bullshit. I flipped open the cardboard box on the counter and snagged the last piece of pepperoni pizza. I made a latte and plopped on the couch in front of the big windows with my feet crossed on the coffee table, listening to the ocean while I ate. It wasn't lost on me that I was just casually sitting on Giuseppi Moretti's couch, no big deal. When everyone was finished eating, and I had done the dishes, I went back to my room and Marco followed behind me. I closed the door and leaned in,

"Do you have any idea what the plan is?"

He tried to appease me,

"Things are moving."

That wasn't going to cut it and what the fuck did that even mean?

"OK, great, because from what I can see, all he's doing is moving everyone here and who's going to manage my aunt's store?"

Marco tried to reassure me,

"It's going to happen soon."

I put my hands on my hips,

"If one more person shows up here, I'm going to lose my shit."

He rubbed his forehead and moved from foot to foot,

"I know. Do you realize how long I've been in hiding? Months, Amelia, months. I think you can handle it for a couple days before going feral on me."

He gestured toward the beach,

"There's worse things than being holed up at the ocean."

He had a point. But I shrugged, retrieved my phone from the front pocket of my hoodie, and called Giuseppi Moretti. He answered after two rings,

"Amelia?"

"Hey."

Seppi's voice was concerned but gentle and reassuring,

"Is everything alright?"

"Yeah, we're fine. So, what's the plan here? Are we trapped in the house indefinitely or...what's the deal?"

Marco's eyes bugged out of his head, and he mouthed 'Is that Seppi!?,' I waved him away dismissively, apparently Marco wasn't on the same level with him as I was.

"As long as I know where my father is, you can leave the house for a little while, but stay close. My mother will let me know if he takes off, and I'll give you a heads up. He can't be in two places at once, and at this point, he's running low on people who are willing to do his bidding. Right now, you're safe."

"Thanks, Sep."

Marco appeared mortified and mouthed,

'Sep!?'

"My room is at the end of the hall. There's cash in my dresser, take as much as you need. And there's a white Benz in the garage with Florida plates, if you need to relocate, you'll use that, there's a tracker on it."

The silence stretched on too long and made me feel things. Seppi finally broke the silence with a sigh,

"Be safe."

The call ended and I couldn't imagine what it was like to be Giuseppi Moretti, the weight of the world on his shoulders.

"We can leave if we stay close."

I found Seppi's room with Marco and his wide eyes trailing behind me. I went for the drawer I would have used if I had to hide money in my dresser, and under some socks and underwear I found stacks of banded hundred-dollar bills. I picked up the cash and glanced at Marco, that time I was the one with the wide eyes,

"Umm!?"

I stared at the stack with my mouth hanging open as I flipped through the bills like you see people do on movies,

"I bet there are thousands of dollars here!"

Marco gave the stack a once-over, and did some mental math,

"Ten grand if I had to guess."

"Holy shit!"

He laughed and I asked,

"Where does he get it all?"

Marco shook his head and went palms up,

"I'm not privy to that kind of information but this is only the tip of the iceberg. People need to reach a certain level of wealth before they casually leave ten thousand dollars banging around with their Fruit of the Looms."

I corrected,

"Balenciagas."

Marco nodded,

"Like I said."

He stood there while I googled how much one pair of Balenciaga boxer briefs cost. If you're wondering, it's one-hundred and seventy-five dollars, and there was a drawer full of them. Marco got sick of standing there,

"We can take a walk to the store or something later, I'm gonna go work out."

He kissed the top of my head and disappeared down the hall. I stood there in Seppi's bedroom holding a fat stack of cash. I snooped around without touching anything and followed my nose to the bottle of Tobacco Vanille on his vanity. As I was pressure washing dog shit off cement floors and sipping Sanka, with adorable old men in the 'Day Room,' not one shred of my being imagined this in my wildest dreams. There wasn't a pressure washer strong enough to take care of shit this deep, for that job, I'd need a shovel.

CHAPTER 23
UP IN FLAMES

EXACTLY ONE WEEK after we arrived in Maine, I was ready to go home. Don't get me wrong, I'm all for having access to fat stacks of cash and the ocean but, come on. I'm a simple girl with simple needs, and none of those needs revolve around being holed up in a mobster's beach house three and a half hours from home with a spoiled brat, my crazy aunt, and my maybe boyfriend. I was bored out of my mind, spending way too much time getting high, and obsessively contemplating how they were going to kill Sal.

I imagined things like that usually went down in some sort of catastrophic gunfight like you see in movies. And even though it was imperative that the killing was stealthy and undetectable, part of me hoped I was there to see it go down. To see *him* go down. I was aware of how much danger I was in, and how much more danger I'd be in, if I knew anything about the murder of Salvatore Moretti. I also knew that as soon as that guy was dead and buried, we'd be able to move on with our lives.

Vincenzo was on the houseboat and the three of us sat on a balcony overlooking the beach, with drinks and joints and a fancy charcuterie board. We were on an island of sorts, even though there were still plenty of people in Kimbrook. Although most of the beach houses were closed-up for the season, there were several resorts along the way that would be busy until it got really cold. The public lot for the beach was less than half a mile from the house so we could watch people stake their claim on a section of sand for the day before packing up and going home. I wanted to go home.

I sent Opal a couple texts that day, but she was working the lunch rush and probably didn't have her phone. I'm the type of person who's resentful if you expect an immediate reply from me, but then assumes you've died in a catastrophic accident if I don't receive an immediate reply from you. Depending on my mental state at the time, I just assume you've decided not to bother with me anymore. She would FaceTime me to say goodnight, but mostly I think she just wanted to see for herself that I was still in one piece. I could handle the calls until it was time to say goodbye, something about that part made me feel like I was on a different planet.

Even though Seppi had far more important things to do, he took the time to reassure me that everything would be OK, soon. Things were happening, even if it didn't seem like it, and soon enough, we'd be sharing lunch again. He told me where he kept his guns, even though he knew I wouldn't touch any of them. It made me feel things every time he called me Dimples. It wasn't lost on me how odd our friendship was, even though it was more like a trauma bond. The person everyone warned me about was becoming my protector, and it was starting to feel like he was a little bit more than that.

Sometime during that day, the vibe changed, and the energy shifted. It felt eerily quiet, like the calm before a storm, and I guess I'd expected things to be more chaotic. But I needed something interesting to happen or I was going to lose my ever-loving mind. I was at the ocean which you'd think would be a delight, but it wasn't. There was this undertone of impending doom, and I was a little sick of being around Maggie and Marco. I get it, I was looking at the world through piss-tinted glasses, but I couldn't help it, and I was going crazy.

I was running low on weed and was pissed off that I couldn't do what I wanted. I was annoyed that I was wrapped up in whatever the fuck was going on. We could leave the house for an hour at a time but had to be tied to our phones, in case Seppi sent us the ominous text that his father had taken off. What was the point? We'd gone out a couple times, but stayed close, and the low-level dread wasn't worth the feeling of being vulnerable. Maggie never left the house, but Vincenzo was gone most of the time, doing who knows what with who knows who, and he was planning to stay on the houseboat because the three of us were, 'cramping his style.'

I took stock of the weapons at my disposal, I mean besides Seppi's actual arsenal. The tool shed offered up a beautiful trowel and an expensive-looking shovel with the tags still on it. There were some other miscellaneous yard tools but nothing useful for defending myself. I had my Sig Sauer, and a holster. Even though I had been doing drills, at that point, I didn't feel confident enough to carry, and I was woefully unprepared to use it in a gunfight with an actual mob boss. Most of the time, I didn't even want to pick it up. I knew it was pointless for me to collect trowels and shovels and handguns because there was no way anyone would suggest I be involved in any of what was going to happen. Either way, I felt a little better after I put the shovel next to my bed.

It kept me distracted and I felt like I was doing something productive if I was planning, or gathering tools to defend myself if the boss battle took place in Kimbrook. I was on edge that, at any minute, Seppi would tell us his father left Bunman. I checked and rechecked the location of the keys to the Benz, in case we needed to make a hasty getaway. And as much as I didn't want Sal to come to Kimbrook, I also didn't want things to go down in Bunman while I was hours away. I wanted to enjoy all the explosions and bullets and flames and whatever else was involved in whatever they were planning. But maybe they would do something that made it look like Sal had a heart attack. Maybe someone would make him a coffee with arsenic in it and end this bullshit once and for all.

Maggie was in her room, and I was lying on the couch reading a book next to Marco when the garage door opened. What the hell!? I froze and moved my eyes to his. He shrugged and we didn't know whether to hide or grab a butcher knife and charge down the stairs into the garage. There were voices but I couldn't figure out what they were saying. We did circles in the kitchen, trying to figure out where to go and ended up in the pantry with the louvered doors closed all the way. We stood with our backs against the shelves in the dark. If we didn't move, we would be OK, no one would look in there. I grabbed Marco's hand and both of us had sweaty palms. The garage was under us, and we could hear car doors closing. I dropped and put my ear to the floor,

"What the hell!?"

I hopped up and slid the door open, stepping into the kitchen. Marco whispered and swiped at my arm,

"Get in here!"

He gestured frantically for me to get back in the pantry and I waved him away,

"It's my freaking sister, what the hell is she doing here!?"

Marco scrunched his face,

"Are you sure?"

I swung the door open as Opal made her way up the stairs with a Louis Vuitton duffel and a bag from McDonald's. She had been crying, her mascara was running, and she looked exhausted. I did a double take because her face was smudged with something black. She dropped the duffel on the kitchen floor and sat on a stool eating the rest of her french fries, staring at nothing, lost inside her own mind. What the hell was happening? I went to the top of the stairs as Seppi was coming up, he had smudges on his face too. What the fuck was going on? Opal looked overwhelmed, but she was pregnant and had been sucked into the middle of whatever the hell you'd call all of this. I gazed at the microwave; it was eleven fifty-three.

Seppi didn't say anything, he just took their bags up the stairs to the master bedroom and got in the shower. When Opal was done eating, she went upstairs, and I followed. She went in my room and got in that shower. Had they done it? Was Sal dead? Why weren't they saying anything? They just came in, put their shit down, and took showers. We had no idea they were coming, no idea why they were there, and no idea what was going on. It was a Friday night, so maybe they'd decided to come for the weekend. But something was wrong, and what the hell was all over their faces? Dirt? Soot? I brushed my teeth while Opal showered. I pretended I wasn't fishing for information,

"How are you feeling?"

"Fine, not as sick anymore. I've missed having you hold my hair when I throw up though."

Her clothes smelled like a bonfire, had they killed Sal and burnt up his body? Holy shit, had she helped!? I pushed the irrational thoughts out of my head and changed the subject. Even though it sounded ridiculous that they would come to the hole-up house on a vacation,

"Are you two on a little weekend getaway?"
Silence.

I caught a glimpse of Seppi as he passed my room on his way to the stairs. I aborted the fact-finding mission in the bathroom and jogged down the hall to catch up with him. It was after midnight, but Seppi had dressed again, in pants and a button up shirt instead of his pajamas, there was a holstered handgun at his hip. My body filled with emotion and adrenaline, I grabbed his wrist,

"What's going on!?"

Seppi was expressionless. He looked numb and stared at the intricate pattern on the fancy wallpaper in the hall. I tried again,

"What's going on? Did you, do it? Is he dead?"

Nothing. What the hell was happening? I smacked his arm to snap him out of it,

"Giuseppi!"

I grabbed his hand and yelled at him, I couldn't stand the silence, my eyes were brimming with tears for some reason. His energy crashed down over me like a ton of bricks,

"Did something happen!?"

His bottom lip quivered. Shit, something had happened. I put my hand on his back and my voice did something that made me wonder what my heart was doing,

"Hey, are you OK?"

I waited, rubbing his back as a single tear rolled down his cheek. There was deep sadness in his eyes, swirled together with immense anger and hatred and fire. I hugged him because I felt like he needed it. He stood there with his hands balled into fists at his sides, staring at the wallpaper some more. And finally, he put his arms around me and let himself fall apart. I glanced up to see Marco, he paused and retreated down the stairs. As Seppi cried quietly, hot tears ran down the back of my neck. Something started to shift right then, even though neither of us knew it yet.

Opal stepped into the hall in one of the plush bathrobes, toweling off her long, dark ringlets,

"Did you tell her?"

Seppi shook his head so slightly that it was almost imperceptible. I moved my eyes to his, and then to my sister's, and back to his, the energy in the air was making me sick to my stomach and I was panicking. Why wasn't anyone saying anything?

"Tell me what!? Did something bad happen!? Is he dead!?"

Opal threw the towel over her shoulder, walked over to Seppi and pulled him from my arms, into hers,

"It's going to be OK, Seppi."

She rubbed his back, and I leaned against the wall with my arms crossed, waiting. I knew someone would say something eventually. I thought Seppi would deescalate in her arms like he had in mine, but he didn't. He seemed to tense up again and I asked one more time, trying to keep my voice calm but it wasn't,

"Did something happen!?"

Maggie heard the commotion and wandered into the hall, drunk, and high as a kite,

"Hey guys, what's a...what's going on?"

Me, my sister, and my aunt followed Seppi into an office with dark wallpaper, hardwood bookshelves, and a gorgeous desk. There was a bar cart against the wall, he poured a double shot of whiskey into an etched-glass snifter and threw it down the hatch. He refilled the snifter and paced, sat at his desk, lit a cigar. Maggie helped herself to some vodka. I sat in the leather chair across the desk from his and waited. Seppi stared into his glass and then moved his eyes to mine,

"He burnt my restaurant to the ground."

I gasped and my jaw dropped, I glanced at Opal

with wide eyes. She nodded and moved her eyes back to Seppi. He looked numb and unhinged all at the same time, sitting there with a glass of whiskey and a thousand-yard stare. I stood,

"Oh my God, are you guys OK!?

Opal came to me so I could give her a once over, and she placed my hand on her little belly. I didn't know whether to stay or give them privacy. Marco stuck his head in the door,

"Is everything OK?"

I shook my head and excused myself, pulling him into the room across the hall,

"Sal burnt the restaurant to the ground."

Marco's eyes bugged out of his head,

"Holy shit, are they OK!?

"They weren't hurt, but Seppi is short circuiting or something, I think that was the last straw. I wouldn't be surprised if shit hits the fan."

Seppi gestured for the two of us to come back to his office. We watched as he gathered his thoughts and searched for his words. He rubbed the etched surface of the snifter with his thumb and shook his head as he stared at the desk, I could see him bubbling up inside and wanted to save him. Seppi threw the snifter against the wall, it shattered into a million pieces as if it had exploded. Tiny fragments of glass ricocheted to the floor while what was left of the whiskey ran down the fancy wallpaper. The four of us held our breath for a beat before Marco broke the silence,

"I'm really sorry about your restaurant, man, that sucks."

Yeah, that sucks. Do you know what else sucks? I'm pretty sure the seconds were counting down on the ticking time bomb sitting across from us and I was pretty sure it was time to duck and cover. Seppi glanced at his watch, action was a distraction.

"Where's my brother?"

I shrugged and then said,

"He might be on the boat, he told us we were cramping his style."

Seppi clenched his jaw and called Vinny,

"Where are you?"

There was a pause,

"Yeah, well you need to come back to the house."

And then,

"He's not far behind me."

My eyes bugged out of my head. Seppi hung up and we followed him down the hall to his room. We went into a closet that was bigger than my bedroom. Behind a rack of dark button-up shirts was an almost undetectable door in the wall that led to a panic room. Seppi gestured to me, Maggie, and Opal,

"Get in."

I squinted at Seppi like he was crazy, I wasn't getting into that thing, I'd go crazy in there. Maggie and Opal stepped inside, and he moved his eyes to me,

"Get in, Amelia, I don't have time for your shit."

I bristled and threw my hands up, pleading,

"I'll go crazy in there!"

Seppi was losing patience with me and appeared to be sick of my bullshit. He was possibly less amused with me than anyone had ever been, he sighed,

"I'm not playing games, Amelia, get in."

I crossed my arms and looked him in the eye,

"No!"

Seppi shoved me and I shoved him back, and then we did that a couple more times before he threw his hands up in frustration. He didn't have the energy to argue with me. Seppi closed his eyes and pinched the bridge of his nose before shaking his head, he muttered

"Mi arrendo."

OK, whatever that meant. Opal and Maggie were in the panic room, getting a lay of the land. There was a small TV, a mini fridge and shelves, the space was fully stocked with water, yogurt, peanut butter crackers, and bubbly water. There was even a tiny bathroom in there. Opal and I made eye contact, and I could see that something had changed. It had all happened so quickly, and I should have known then that she wouldn't stay. She was trying not to cry, but I could see in her eyes that she wondered if she would ever see me again. She tried to keep her voice steady, but it trembled anyway,

"Be safe until I see you again."

I think that's when I realized I might not make it

home in one piece. I blinked away my own panic, and nodded, but couldn't say anything. I hoped her eyes were wrong and I hoped I'd get to see her again. As Seppi closed the door, he reminded Maggie she wasn't allowed to smoke weed in the panic room and she was rolling her eyes at him as the door clicked shut.

Marco and I followed Seppi downstairs and closed the drapes on all the beach-facing sliding-glass doors and windows. A few minutes later, one of the sliding-glass doors slid open. We held our breath and Seppi pulled his gun. Vinny pushed the curtain to the side and stepped into the living room, making eye contact with the business end of his brother's gun,

"Jesus, Vin!"

Seppi holstered the gun.

"Bro, calm down, what the hell!?"

"He burnt the restaurant to the ground, Vin, just like he always said he would."

Vincenzo shed his tough guy facade and hugged his big brother,

"I'm sorry bro, what do you need?"

"Do you have a gun?"

Vincenzo seemed to like that question,

"Are we finally going to put an end to this bullshit?"

Seppi glanced at us as if he was apologizing for his family dysfunction, I waved dismissively. He had enough to worry about without stressing about the fact that we were getting a front-row seat to his defective family. Vincenzo jogged upstairs and came back with his gun. Marco retrieved the big handgun Seppi had given him the day we rescued Maggie. I retrieved the shovel from next to my bed, and when I returned, I stood in the middle of the living room, eyes wide, gripping it proudly. The three of them stood there with their loaded handguns and looked at me like I was nuts. I was curious if the restaurant fire had changed the whole thing from a 'we need to make it look like an accident' kind of situation, to a 'no holds barred' type of thing.

CHAPTER 24
SETTLING THE SCORE

THAT WAS one of those times when time stood still but it also went in fast-forward. The energy in that room was disgusting in so many ways, I can't even explain it. I've been in situations like that too many times to count, but that was numero uno and I was crapping my pants. The three men were just pacing around and breathing heavy, it made my hands sweat. It was like the pin really had been pulled from the grenade, and it was like something really bad was going to happen. Looking back, that was the last night before I was broken on a different level. Before that, I was a damaged little girl, just this woman who felt like a child. I glanced around the room and had both a feeling of unrelenting hero worship and absolute terror. One day I'd be standing instead of kneeling on the couch peering through the drapes. One day, I would be a help and not a hindrance, but right then things were spiraling and I was terrified. Then a car approached slowly and cut its lights. That wasn't good.

"Hey, someone cut their headlights a little way up the street."

Seppi, Vincenzo, and Marco stood, and I followed suit. No one was saying anything, and I couldn't stand the silence, or the fact that I had no idea what was going to happen next,

"Is there a plan, or are we just winging it?"

In retrospect, I realize I was the only one who didn't know the plan, and it was presumptuous of me to think I'd be included. The only reason I was down there with them was because I refused to get into the panic room, it wasn't like I had been invited, and I knew I was more of a hindrance than a help. I wrapped my fingers around the smooth wooden handle of the expensive shovel, and the three of them rolled their eyes at me in unison, as if they had rehearsed it. I was highly offended by their behavior. Sure, I was a girl with zero experience defending myself against a mob boss, but that didn't justify locking me in a panic room or leaving me at home. I waited, but no one said anything. The three men were at the counter, loading extra clips for their guns, an intense energy swirled around me as I watched. Thirty-seconds later, I couldn't stand it anymore,

"Shouldn't we try to lure him away from Opal

and Maggie, they're sitting ducks!"

Seppi's face grew more tense, if that's possible and he worked his jaw. He didn't look at me, but I knew he wanted me to stay behind, even if I wasn't in the panic room. I considered hiding in the pantry again, tucked under the shelf with a bag of potatoes that were sprouting eyes. I still had time to bail if I wanted to, but when the men descended the stairs, I was close at their heels with my shovel. We piled into the white Mercedes Benz with the Florida plates and sat in silence. Seppi pulled the cameras up on his phone and looked closer, he made a growl deep in his throat. He pushed the ignition and waited, watching the mini version of reality on his screen. I leaned forward and peered over his shoulder. Salvatore Moretti was dressed in black, slinking along, with his back against the exterior wall of the garage, gun out like you see on the cop shows. As he approached, Seppi threw the Benz in reverse and slammed his foot on the accelerator, blasting through the metal security door.

We had just missed his father, and with the door blown apart, Sal had easier access to the house. I leaned back and put on my seatbelt. Sal made eye contact with Seppi, and scrambled, getting off a single shot at the back of the Benz. Seppi increased our distance from the house, luring Sal away from Opal and Maggie. He flicked his eyes to the rearview mirror repeatedly, looking for his father. We didn't have to wait long before headlights appeared behind us. I was starting to panic, if I ducked down, Sal wouldn't see my silhouette, and maybe he wouldn't know I was in the car. I played it off as leaning on Marco's shoulder, and he leaned over to kiss the top of my head. I was trying not to cry, but I wasn't cut out for this shit. I should have gotten in the panic room; this was men's work. What was I thinking? They with their guns and me with my shovel, off to save the world.

Seppi growled as Sal rammed the back of the Benz. Seppi didn't lose control like I had; he knew what to do in situations like that. I wondered what Sal was driving, since he'd slammed the passenger side of his Lincoln into a row of trees the week before. Seppi swung the car onto Harbor Lane and sped down the gravel road with dust billowing up in our wake, Sal's headlights cutting through as he approached. He rammed us again and I gripped the shovel tighter, my hands slippery with sweat. The Benz lost control on a turn, but Seppi lifted his foot from the accelerator, downshifted, and steered into the skid, regaining control. I squirmed around and my stomach started to gurgle, I was the only one on the verge of hyperventilating.

Salvatore Moretti was good at gaslighting people, being a narcissistic fuck, and ramming people with his car. I felt like this was déjà vu, as bullets pinged into the back of the Benz. A single bullet flew over my seat before burying itself in the headliner.

Jesus. If I had been sitting up, I would have been killed. A wave of nausea churned in my stomach, and I thought of my sister as adrenaline surged, I hoped I would see her again. Sal rammed us one more time and that time Seppi went halfway off the road before regaining control.

We reached a straightaway and Seppi put some separation between the Benz and whatever car Sal was driving, skidding to a stop in the parking lot of a wildlife refuge. Vinny switched the dome light so it wouldn't come on when they opened the doors. Seppi, Vinny, and Marco piled out of the car and sprinted to the tree line as Sal pulled in behind us. It didn't feel like we had the upper hand, I held my breath and locked the doors before curling into a ball on the floor behind the driver's seat. Sal cut his engine, and I heard footsteps on gravel as he approached my side of the car, my heart skipped a beat when he tried the driver side doors, he had no idea how close he was to me. Once his footsteps faded, I popped my head up and peered through the windshield at the tree line, everything was moving in slow motion. Sal was getting close to where the other three went into the woods and my heart was beating in my ears, I needed to slow my breathing, or I'd pass out.

I slowly lifted the handle, and the door popped open. I slid out quietly, holding the shovel and carefully pushed the door shut, click. Sal was driving the Lincoln, the damage on the front end and passenger side wasn't as bad as I thought it would be. I snuck behind the Benz and speed-walked the ten feet to the tree line on the side of the lot. It was almost pitch dark out there in the trees. I had no idea where I was, where everyone had gone, or what I was supposed to do next. I held my breath and moved slowly from tree to tree. I made my way toward where I saw everyone disappear, but I had no idea where they went after that and would have no idea what to do if I found them.

When I was about fifty feet into the woods, shielded by a row of trees, I heard one gunshot and then another. I dove behind an ancient oak to shield myself from the chaos. There were shouts and another gunshot. It seemed like everyone was shooting because each gun sounded a little different, bullets zinging through the branches, digging themselves into trees. After one of the gunshots, there was a loud yelp and another gunshot. I gripped my shovel and tears came, what if they all got killed out there, what would I do? I didn't even have my phone, I was panicking. By the sound of that yelp, someone had been shot and I was freaking out. There was a pocket of eerie silence, and I pictured everyone reloading their guns. Just then, I caught movement and saw the three men running toward the Benz.

One of them was limping but I couldn't tell which one. The Benz started up and the headlights came to life, the tires spitting gravel as Seppi peeled out of the parking lot onto Harbor Lane, I watched helplessly as the taillights faded. Shit. I was out there all alone with Salvatore Moretti, and no one knew it but me. I wondered how long it would take Seppi to realize I wasn't in the car. I had tried to run after them but froze about ten feet from the parking lot. I waited for what seemed like forever in the silence and wasn't thinking rationally, maybe I could use the Lincoln to get out of there. If the keys were in it, I'd be golden, if not, I'd be fucked. Even if Sal was dead in the woods, I was still stuck out there without a phone or flashlight. I had no idea how long it would take me to walk back into town.

When I was convinced, it was safe to move from my hiding spot, I saw him. Sal's back was turned, his dark shirt and hat camouflaging him in the darkness. I reasoned, maybe I could just wait for him to leave, then I could walk into town. It felt like I had an elephant on my chest as I tried to breathe. Fire burned inside my stomach as I stared at the back of Sal's head. My mind spiraled, don't be a chicken shit, Amelia, handle it. Stop running away. Stop hiding, what ails you? Stand up for yourself, you broken little bitch. I took a deep breath and held it. The fire grew until I saw red, and you might think that's when I lost my mind, but I think that's when I found it.

Maybe what I did next was unprovoked and maybe I'm trying to justify it. But I was alone in the woods, ten feet from a man who needed to die. Say what you want because I don't really care what you have to say until you've walked a mile in my dingy white Chuck Taylors. In case you haven't been damaged like me, and even if you have, I have a tidbit of wisdom for you. When all the pain you've stuffed deep inside, flies out of the box you tried to keep it in, you rage like an animal. Nothing will contain it. There were times when I wondered if things would have been different if someone had been there to stop me, but I doubt it.

I gripped the handle tight, and after one more deep breath, I silently moved forward. I could see Sal scanning the darkness, what was he looking for? And what kind of a sick fuck burns their son's restaurant to the ground, and then drives three and a half hours to kill them? What an absolute fucking psycho. And he was the grandfather of my sister's baby? Nope. And that, folks, was the last straw. My body erupted with rage for all the people he killed, all the bruises he inflicted, all the tears he caused, all the destruction he left in his wake. I had a flash of being pinned to the bathroom floor at the neighbor's house when I was six, and about my mother sweeping it under the carpet. I heard her criticisms and hypocrisy, I thought about my ex fucking that whore. I grit my teeth, held the shovel tight, and ran out of the woods, screaming bloody murder, closing the gap between myself and Salvatore Moretti.

Sal spun around and got off a single shot that tore through my left shoulder, it was time to kill or be killed. Before he had a chance to try again, I swung the shovel like a baseball bat and hit him on the left side of his head, *thunk*. Sal stumbled and tried to focus his eyes, but when he squeezed the trigger, the bullet went through his own windshield. I tightened my grip and took another step closer, swinging the shovel like my life depended on it, *thunk*. That time, I heard bone crack and wetness, a fine mist of blood rained over me.

A lightning bolt of fire shot through my right shoulder, and I had blisters from my death grip on the shovel. A car was approaching but still in the distance, if it wasn't Seppi, I was fucked and didn't care. No turning back now you broken little bitch, finish the job. Sal was swaying back and forth, frantically trying to regain his balance, flailing his arms as his gun fell to the ground at his feet. I saw the pain on his face, the confusion behind his eyes, he was no longer a threat. My gunshot wound was throbbing with my pulse, I touched it and when I pulled my hand away, it was slick with blood. A wave of nausea and darkness closed in, I wiped my hand on my pants and shook my head to clear the cobwebs.

My palms burned as I gripped the shovel, another shot of adrenaline coursing through my body to numb the pain. I filled my lungs and grit my teeth before releasing a guttural scream as I swung the shovel one last time, *thunk*. That time, a more intense spray of blood rained over me, I tasted salt and metal when I licked my lips. He weaved back and forth on his feet, moaning, disoriented. Fear enveloped me as

I realized the handle of the shovel had cracked, what if he was faking it, what if he tried again. But then, Salvatore Moretti gurgled, stumbled, and fell face-first onto the gravel as headlights illuminated the parking lot. I was a deer in the headlights, standing over a dead mob boss with a bloody shovel in my hands.

CHAPTER 25
STITCHES & EMBERS

THE BENZ skidded to a stop and Seppi ran to me. I dropped the shovel and tried not to collapse; unaware how much I was bleeding. Seppi pulled me close, his right hand cradling the side of my head, it was dark, and I was wearing black, so he hadn't noticed I'd been shot. Seppi's body heaved with each panicked breath, his deep voice trembling,

"I am so sorry, Amelia."

My legs were jelly, and I felt like I was going to pass out. Seppi lowered me to the ground, and I threw up. Sal's body was three feet from me, I kept looking over to make sure he wasn't moving. Vincenzo knelt, giving me sips of water as Seppi opened the trunk of the Lincoln and moved things around. I sat in that gravel parking lot; between my pile of acid puke and the man I had just killed with a shovel, Vincenzo yelled to Seppi,

"She's been shot, we need to get her to the hospital!"

Seppi dropped everything and ran back to me, kneeling on the gravel in his expensive tailored pants, his hand holding the left side of my face,

"Are you OK!?"

I nodded, but it was a lie, it was the adrenaline talking,

"I'll be OK, go do what you have to do."

But as the two of them lifted their dead father off the ground by his hands and feet, I felt my adrenaline recede and the pain in my shoulder sent another wave of nausea and darkness. I felt my shirt, it was warm and wet with my blood. I glanced up to see Seppi and Vinny lowering their father into the back of the Lincoln. The shovel and gun went in next; my eyes followed the lid of the trunk as it closed over him. Salvatore Moretti's body was trapped in the trunk of his own car, and I knew there wouldn't be anything left of him, long before his corpse was cold to the touch.

They tried to be patient with me, but I was losing a lot of blood, and there was a dead mob boss in the trunk. Seppi and Vinny lifted me by the armpits and loaded me in the front seat of the Benz. Vinny slid behind the wheel of his father's car and then threw the door open again, as he got out, the trunk popped open. I cringed. He reached in and dug the keys to the

Lincoln out of the pocket of Sal's elastic waist old fart pants. He spit in the trunk before slamming it shut again. He slid behind the wheel again and disappeared into the night with his father's dead body, leaving a trail of dust behind him.

As Seppi reached the end of Harbor Lane, shock set in and I was fading in and out of consciousness. I was shivering, sweating, and covered in blood that was mine and someone else's. As the adrenaline dumped some more, the pain from my wounds became unbearable, the ones on the inside and out. Seppi handed me a flask and I threw expensive whiskey down the hatch. I glanced over at him through blurry eyes, my voice full of pain,

"Where's Marco?"

He hesitated and then said,

"Right now, what's important is making sure you're OK."

I blinked at him and wiped my eyes with hands that were sticky with blood,

"Yeah, but where's Marco?"

I could tell Seppi was keeping something from me. I could tell he was trying not to upset me, but that upset me even more. Tears came again, my voice was weak and hoarse from screaming,

"Did something happen to him? Was he the one who got shot?"

Seppi sighed,

"I need to get you to the hospital; we can talk about Marco later."

I had lost a decent amount of blood, and because I wasn't built for that kind of shit, I spent some of the ride unconscious. The car skid to a stop, a wall of cold air rushing in around me when Seppi opened his door. Everything was black behind my eyelids. My door opened and I felt a hand on my right shoulder, the hand gripped hard and shook me, the person shouted,

"Amelia!"

I tried to pull myself back from the shadows. I could hear Seppi's voice, he was frantic, and I had never heard him sound that way. Maybe he was worried my sister would leave him if he didn't bring me back in one piece, but I knew she would probably leave him anyway. Seppi yelled out, but no one was there to hear it. His voice was filled with dread, despair, and powerlessness. In the darkness behind my eyelids, I wondered if Giuseppi Moretti had ever felt like that before. He touched me again, pleading,

"I don't know what to do Amelia, there's so much blood! Amelia, please! No! Wake up, please wake up!"

He was screaming then, shaking my shoulders violently, every muscle in my body screaming. I was trying to pull it together, I wanted to let him know I was in there somewhere, but I couldn't.

"WAKE UP, AMELIA!"

Seppi leaned in, and slapped my left cheek, "WAKE UP!"

I took in a sharp breath that pulled me back to the surface, I gasped for air,

"Thank God, Amelia!"

He unbuckled my seatbelt and scooped me into his arms, my body coming to rest against the warmth of his body. His adrenaline had dumped along with mine, his emotions bubbling to the surface, reality setting in a little. My legs turned to jelly, and Seppi lowered me to the ground. He sat on the curb with my battered body in his lap, sobbing. His lips rested on the top of my head, and I could feel his breath as he exhaled, hot on my scalp in the chill and the darkness. I think everything was crashing in around him, he knew there was no turning back after that. The four-ways were flashing and the next car that came by, pulled to the side of the road, a middle-aged man jogged over,

"Are you okay?"

Seppi told the man he'd found me there, bleeding on the side of the road, a gunshot wound in my shoulder. The man came to me,

"My name is Walter, I'm a paramedic."

Walter knelt next to me and Seppi slid from his spot behind me, running to the car for his phone. I heard him talking about me to the person on the other end, I blinked my eyes up at Walter, got sparkly, and went lights out.

When I came to, I was being wheeled into the emergency department. Moments later Seppi appeared and called my sister as they hooked me up to monitors and got me ready for an x-ray. I could hear Seppi trying to calm Opal, he promised he would come get her, as soon as he could. It was clear that Opal was screaming at him, enraged that he would put me in a dangerous situation, I knew she had one foot out the door. Seppi didn't tell her I had killed Sal, but he told her they could come out of the panic room. Seppi sugar-coated my bullet wound the best he could, and didn't tell her how much blood I'd lost, or that he left me at the refuge alone with his father.

When Seppi saw my gunshot wound under the harsh fluorescent lights, his face looked like pain feels. I watched as Seppi realized his father's blood had rained down on me as I killed him. Between my blood, and Sal's, my shirt and pants were ruined, not that I would have worn them again, but I would clean my dingy white Chuck Taylors. I watched Seppi's wheels turning, as he evaluated what he'd told Opal, it was obvious things were much worse than he said, and she would see that for herself when she got there.

Seppi held my sticky blood-covered hand while they checked me over. I thought the amount of blood on my hands was gross, but it didn't even phase him. He refused to leave my side until I had settled. When he finally left the room, I took the chance to use the bathroom. I stood up too fast for my jelly-legs, with my I.V. and all my wires. I got light-headed but took two steps forward instead of sitting down on the bed and went down like a rhino full of tranquilizers.

When I woke up, I was in a dimly lit private room with Opal by my side. I had a blood pressure cuff on one arm and an I.V. full of red liquid in the other. My wound had been stitched up on the inside and out, and x-rays showed that the injury was isolated to tissue. I did not need surgery, I just needed to take antibiotics twice a day, have someone tend to the dressing, and wear a sling for comfort while it healed. The only reason I was admitted was because I went unconscious multiple times, passed out and hit my face on the floor, and needed to receive a pint of blood. Thanks to my attempt to use the bathroom on my own, I was also sporting a black eye and two stitches through my right eyebrow. I was doped up on pain medicine when I asked Opal,

"What happened to Marco?

She held my hand, and it took her a long time to respond. It was almost like she couldn't look at me, like looking at me caused too much pain, or like she was disappointed in me. I started spiraling, but now I know it was something else entirely. She was somewhere else in her head, even though I didn't know it. She finally replied,

"He was shot in the leg, he's in surgery."

My eyes wide,

"What happened!?"

She looked at the ceiling and took a deep breath, she seemed anxious,

"Sal shot Marco in the femoral artery. The saving grace was that Seppi brought him to the rescue squad building two miles from the refuge. He was still alive when the ambulance got to the hospital, but he lost a lot of blood."

Even though I was laying down, the room started to spin, and I thought I was going to pass out. It felt like she was keeping something from me. I tried getting out of bed, hyperventilated, and threw up in the trash can. When the nurse came in, Opal spoke with her in the doorway, and the woman asked me if I wanted a sedative. I was starting to think the police would be coming, or that someone would whack me in the night. I accepted the sedative and drifted to sleep with Opal by my side. I woke up to see her sleeping on a fold-out couch under the window. I was trying to figure out if any of it was real, maybe I had been dreaming. Several minutes later, a dread crept in that something bad had happened, something besides my gunshot wound. My mind was garbled and foggy from the meds, but I knew I had killed Salvatore Moretti.

Opal woke when the nurse came in at the change of shift. I was being discharged later that morning, so she called Seppi, and he said he'd be there in plenty of time. She could tell by his voice that he hadn't slept. What a mess. A couple hours later, I was eating a cup of fruit cocktail and a food service muffin with fake blueberries in it, when a woman came in to ask me how I was doing. I gave her the side eye,

"I'm OK, I guess."

The woman looked at Opal and then at me,

"My name is Maria, and I'm here to make sure you're OK before you go home."

I blinked at the woman, a bloody curl glued to my cheek,

"Are you, my doctor?"

Maria shook her head and then settled into the chair next to me, she wasn't dressed like a doctor,

"You probably experienced emotional trauma during the drive-by last night, things like that can cause a lot of fear and anxiety, so I wanted to make sure you received a list of supports, just in case you need them."

I caught movement in the doorway and glanced up to see Seppi crossing the threshold with flowers and some tiramisu. His eyes brightened when he saw me. I moved my eyes back to the woman,

"Drive-by?"

Seppi made eye contact with me again and flicked one eyebrow,

"Oh, umm, yes. And I think something happened to my boyfriend."

I was still pretty doped up and only vaguely present for the conversation. No one had said the word dead. I decided that if no one said the word dead, and I hadn't seen Marco dead, then he must have made it out of surgery. I wanted to know, but I didn't want to ask. I got scared when the woman showed up and started talking to me about trauma. It didn't seem like she knew about Sal, and people had told her I'd been in a drive-by, but what was the trauma she was talking about? Had she come to tell me Marco died? The woman handed me some pamphlets and papers,

"This is a list of supports you can access if you feel like you need help."

I scanned the list of support groups and therapists, I didn't even live in that state, and the resources were for victims of violent crimes. I scrunched my eyebrows, wasn't I the one who perpetrated the violent crime? Was this some fucked up reverse psychology? Was I in trouble? Was I going to jail? Had I really murdered Salvatore Moretti with a shovel? My mind was racing, and I started to panic again.

Seppi sensed that I was freaking out, so he moved to the end of the bed, his hand on my foot. Opal sat there looking at me like I was even more broken than usual, at least she got to see me again. I could have been feeling a lot of things, but I was pissed that I was being doted over, tended to, and mollycoddled. I just wanted to go home. I was still in shock over Marco and wanted to know what was going on. No one was saying anything. I convinced myself he was dead, and no one wanted to tell me.

After the woman left, Seppi kissed me on the forehead and handed over the open clamshell container of tiramisu and a plastic fork. He seemed worried when he patted the top of my head awkwardly. I was grubby and gross, but Seppi put his hand on my head and rubbed it with his thumb,

"How are you feeling?"

I shrugged as I brought a plastic forkful of tiramisu to my lips, I paused,

"Fine. How's Marco? Please just tell me."

"He's going to make it. He lost a lot of blood and needed surgery to repair the damage in his leg. He's sleeping now."

I looked at Seppi skeptically, raising my eyebrows at him,

"He's sleeping."

"Yes, Amelia, he is sleeping."

I didn't believe him. The emotions that flooded in the night before had numbed me, and over the last twelve hours, the adrenaline and numbness had receded in waves. Until I saw Marco with my own eyes, it would feel like everyone was lying to me. And why was that woman in my room earlier, what was the trauma she was talking about? Getting shot? Marco getting shot? Beating the life out of a man with a shovel? Was I going to get in trouble? Was I going to get arrested? Was what I did to Sal considered murder? I started panicking again and Seppi stood,

"I'll be right back."

Seppi kissed me on the top of the head, and I realized I wasn't just dealing with a bloody curl stuck to my face, several of my ringlets were glued together with dried blood. Seppi kissed Opal on top of the head and walked out the door. I squirmed. Was he getting someone to give me more Valium? I wanted to rip out my I.V. and follow him down the hall in my blue grippy hospital socks,

"Where's he going?"

Opal took her place in the chair next to my bed, "He'll be right back."

I felt like no one was telling me anything, they were treating me like a child, and everything was closing in around me. I couldn't breathe and felt like I was going to pass out. Opal took the plastic fork and tried to feed me a bite of tiramisu. I stared out the window and my eyes filled with tears, the figurative tide had gone out and I was raw and broken and tired. She sat there holding my hand as I cried, the tears left stripes of clean skin as they flowed through the dirt and blood on my cheeks. I sucked ginger ale out of a foam cup filled with crushed ice.

Seppi entered the room again and handed me his phone. He had gone to Marco's room and took a picture of him sleeping and then took a picture of the heart monitor so I would believe he was alive. I wasn't going to feel better until I saw him myself and I couldn't visit until I was discharged. The rest of the morning was doctors and nurses and paperwork.

Once I was released, Seppi brought me to see Marco. He was sleeping when I went in. He woke up to me holding his hand, tears dripping into my lap. Marco's eyes opened as I was rubbing the back of his hand with my thumb. I could tell he was still out of it from the pain meds but once his lunch arrived, he perked up and came out of the fog. I fed him half of a tuna sandwich and some applesauce. We didn't say much, what was there to say? The potential for infection from the surgery, delayed reactions from the multiple blood transfusions, and other complications were making my mind swirl into catastrophic places. But I'd also realized I didn't feel the way I thought I did, and I think he realized the same thing.

Seppi and Opal left me with Marco while they picked up my antibiotics. When they returned, I said goodbye and kissed him on the forehead. Our eyes connected and maybe we had volumes to say to each other once we were home, but maybe we had said everything there was to say.

I was on an emotional roller coaster as we made our way back to Kimbrook. Seppi tried to distract me with an Oreo McFlurry and large fry. Once I was back at the house, Maggie ran down the stairs, frantically giving me a once-over, and I assured her I'd be fine. I stripped off my clothes and got in the shower, forever. There was a waterproof dressing on my shoulder, but I tried to avoid the force of the water. Same thing with my right eye, the pressure of the water made it ache. A large bruise had formed around the wound, and moving my left arm was excruciating, now that the heavy-duty pain meds had worn off. The bullet graze from a week ago was healing but still painful to the touch. I stood with my head under the hot water, sobbing. Breaking up blood-hardened curls with my fingers, and too much shampoo. I was having flashbacks of Sal, the shovel, throwing up in the parking lot, the pain, and the reality that I had killed someone. Opal sat on the lid of the toilet,

"Hey sis, are you alright?"

My mind was swimming, I was far from alright, but I lied,

"I guess."

She stayed there with me while I showered, but I was still all alone with my thoughts. I didn't bother with the curl cream, it didn't really matter anyway, I mean seriously, who gives a shit? I had killed a mob boss; I knew I was on my way to the bottom of some lake with a bullet in my forehead. I shrugged into an expensive robe and went out onto the balcony, my sister following at my heels. I stared at the waves as my mind shifted into denial mode, there was no way I had killed a man with a shovel, there was just no way. I spiraled into a panic attack. Was I going to get arrested for what I did? Was I going to jail? My brain couldn't fathom, decipher, or comprehend most of what had happened.

I sat at the foot of my bed, and that time Opal left me alone with my thoughts. A while later, Seppi came in and sat down next to me. When he finally spoke, there was pain and tenderness in his voice, the Jersey-style Italian even more so when he was emotional,

"I don't have the words I want to say to you right now, Amelia."

Seppi leaned closer and rubbed my back, which made my broken, damaged body, feel things. The feelings I had for him were swallowing me whole as I sat there, aware of all my wounds and scars, the ones on the inside and out, the ones he didn't make me hide. My brain focused on something else entirely, I swallowed the lump in my throat and glanced up at him, choking on my tears as I spoke,

"I'm sorry I broke your shovel."

My voice trembling and weak,

"I promise I will buy you a new one."

Seppi pulling me to his chest, and once I was safe in the warmth of his arms, I completely fell apart. Seppi held me like that for a long time as I sobbed, his lips on the top of my head. I could feel his body shake as he cried, I didn't mention it. Seppi spoke softly into my hair,

"I'll do whatever I can to make sure you're okay. Tell me what you need, and I will give it to you."

I wondered if my sister had threatened to leave, maybe it didn't really have anything to do with me. Seppi hooked my chin with his finger and tilted my head up to his. Our eyes met, and somewhere deep inside, I knew there was more to it than that,

"I need you to be okay."

In that moment, I didn't know what it meant, or if it was even possible for him to care about me, given what I'd just done. I looked up at him and lied, but I don't think he believed me,

"I'm fine."

I was angry I had gone along, angry Marco had almost died, and angry people like Salvatore Moretti existed in the first place. I wanted to take a long nap, but we were packing and heading back to Vermont. The security company was repairing the garage door, and there was no trace of the Lincoln or gun, the broken shovel, or the body of Salvatore Moretti. It was business as usual. Mafia families, am I right? I went to Marco's room, and tucked all his things, in his backpack. I stood at the door to the balcony of his room and wondered if I would ever be back in that house.

We left for Bunman once the garage door was repaired. I took an edible and washed it down with a shooter of blueberry vodka. We got food from a drive-thru and made the journey home. I curled up in the backseat of the Escalade with a pillow, and looked out the window as highway signs went by, reality sinking in. I was okay until we got to Bunman. I was anxious about being back home, and panicked that Marco would die, or that Mary Moretti would hate me for killing her husband. Did she know I killed her husband? Were the police waiting for me?

Seppi pulled onto Maple Street and the remains of Giuseppi's Italian Ristorante came into view. I had forgotten about the fire, and my stomach dropped when I laid eyes on the smoldering embers. I leaned forward and put my hand on Seppi's shoulder,

"I am so sorry about your restaurant."

He nodded,

"It's OK, Dimples, we'll rebuild better than ever, it's just material."

He glanced back at me,

"There is a lot to be thankful for."

Despite the recent events, I was grateful to be in Bunman, and knew I wouldn't have to go through any of it alone. Seppi nosed the Escalade into the spot next to my Subaru, one of his men had retrieve it from the parking lot near the lake. He carried my things inside and then came back out to get me. Opal was making me tea when he went to talk to his mother. Seppi was leaving my apartment as Kane was coming back from walking Lola. I could only imagine what Kane thought when he saw Giuseppi Moretti leaving my apartment. And then I heard a ruckus,

"What do you mean she was shot, where is she!?"

Opal moved over to the kitchen door and was about to open it when there was a frantic knock,

"Amelia!? Are you in there!?"

Opal opened the door and Kane rushed in with Lola at his heels. He sat on the futon and wrapped his arms around me, I winced, and he realized he was bumping my wound. He pulled back and didn't know what to do with his hands, his eyes were sad, and I knew he didn't understand any of it,

"What happened?"

Opal delivered a steaming mug of tea to me and moved her eyes to Kane's,

"Not now, she needs to rest."

He looked hurt, and I watched as he moved things around in his mind, realizing we weren't together, realizing he didn't have any idea what I'd been through. He looked at me with his dark chocolate eyes, and knew I wasn't the same person anymore. He stood up, told me to feel better, and reluctantly walked out the door with Lola following at his heels. Something had happened deep inside of me, I had changed. The rage I ignored my entire life had erupted out there in the woods. I could have done what I always did, I could have stayed quiet, I could have stayed hidden until the threat passed, but I didn't. When I saw Sal, I knew I was going to kill him. Sometimes things are a metaphor, and other times things are exactly what they seem. Every time I swung that shovel, I was killing another person who had hurt me.

Mary stopped by with a maple oat latte and some lemon poppy seed muffins. She held me close and kissed me on both cheeks. I thought about how the average widow would feel two days after their husband passed away, and that's not what I was looking at here. I was looking at a woman who was free for the first time in her life, an ornate bird who had finally escaped her cage.

Seppi would be able to rebuild his restaurant without worrying about his father destroying it. Even if I wasn't sure what their future held, Opal and Seppi would be able to have their baby without looking over their shoulders. Maggie would be able to stop hiding, and Sunny was single because Vinny decided to try like hell to be there for his baby. Marco would heal and be able to cherish more time on Earth, even if none of it included me. If you told me at the beginning of all this, that I'd be the one to kill Salvatore Moretti, I would've told you, you're out of your goddamn mind.

As you can imagine, I was a mess following the night at the wildlife refuge. I went through all the stages of grief, even though I was the one who had done the killing. I realized I could be pushed to the breaking point and that was somehow comforting. While my face healed, my mental health took a nosedive into the abyss, I sustained myself on whiskey and weed. When I was lucky, it was Seppi's whiskey, and something about the inner sanctum made me feel untouchable. That was one of those times when the scars on the inside were infinitely deeper than the ones on the surface. A couple stitches wouldn't fix the new level of fucked-up I had become.

I spent time on my sun porch watching the October birds at the feeders and decided to adopt a cat. I daydreamed about that fresh start I was looking for and did a lot of thinking about life in general, but especially about the time before I came to Bunman. I guess, before then, I had never felt like anyone cared for me. I know that sounds insane, and maybe it is. Even with the adrenaline rushes, car chases, and bullets flying, even with what happened at the wildlife refuge, I felt somehow safer than ever before. And I wondered what the broken little girl inside of me would have done differently, if she knew she was capable of murder. As far as my immediate plans? I was just hoping to find myself and adopt a cat.

THE END.

THE TWISTED TIES SOUNDTRACK

1. Aventine - Agnes Obel
2. Waiting Game - Banks
3. Black - Kari Kimmel
4. Fall For That - Suzanne Santo & Gary Clark Jr.
5. River - Bishop Briggs
6. Garden Dove - Samantha Crane
7. Raise Hell - Dorothy
8. Devil's Backbone - The Civil Wars
9. Civilian - Wye Oak
10. Hide - Little May
11. Tell That Devil - Jill Andrews
12. I Don't Give A... - Missio & Zeale
13. Bullet - Riot Child
14. I'm Not Afraid - Tommee Profit & Wondra
15. Angry Too - Lola Blanc
16. And So It Went - The Pretty Reckless
17. Devil in Disguise - Emm
18. Joke's on You - Charlotte Lawrence

ABOUT THE AUTHOR

VANESSA FELL IN LOVE with writing in elementary school and spent hours typing stories on an old Smith Corona. After pursuing degrees in Sociology, Nursing, and Education, Vanessa's heart brought her back to writing. She became obsessed with the writings of Sue Grafton and Janet Evanovich, and was inspired to create a raw and relatable female main character.

As a survivor of childhood trauma, Vanessa is no stranger to fighting her own demons. The unapologetically broken female lead in this series will feel like an old friend you'd meet for coffee, or a well-aged glass of whiskey. Vanessa's no-filer writing style cultivates an instant connection to a world filled with ruthlessness, mental demons, and self-medication.

This series is planned to have at least ten titles. Vanessa is currently writing a gritty southern novel about a female outlaw, and a YA fiction about finding connection, even when you don't fit in.

SMALL BUSINESSES MENTIONED IN THIS BOOK

TO THE BRIM is a Vermont hobby-brand owned and operated by the author. Vanessa creates one of a kind ceramics in her basement studio. You can find her creations on Etsy. You can follow her @tothebrimvt

BLUE SKY FRINGE is a Vermont business owned and operated by Mina. She makes breathtaking beaded fringe earrings. You can follow @blueskyfringe

STEVENS FARM FRUITS & MARKET is a Vermont business specializing in gourmet pastries and local produce. You can follow on Facebook @ Stevens Farm Fruits and Market

CREATIONS BY CANDRA is a Vermont business owned and operated by Candra. She creates handmade jewelry, plant stake, and sun catchers. You can follow @ creationsbycandra

FROG HOLLOW FARMSTEAD is owned and operated by the Reinke family in Hubbardton, Vermont. They also own and operate The Farmstand Cafe in Castleton, Vermont. You can follow them @thefarmstandcafe
@froghollowfarmvt

MORE SMALL BUSINESSES MENTIONED IN THIS BOOK

WITHIN APOTHECARY is a Vermont business owned and operated by Sorrelle. She creates herbal tea blends and candles with a focus on holistic practices. You can follow @withinapothecary

802 CRAFT CANNABIS is a Vermont business owned and operated by the Knapp family. They carry a wide range of CBD products. You can follow them @802cc

UPSTAIRS ALCHEMY owned and operated by Ann. She makes handmade body care products out of her home in Fair Haven, Vermont. You can follow @ upstairs_alchemy

BROWN'S FAMILY FARM is a family owned business located in Benson, Vermont. They carry a full line of maple products including syrup, maple sugar, and maple candies. You can follow @ brownsfamilyfarmsugar